Warmaster 1: Dungeon Spiteful

Melissa McShane

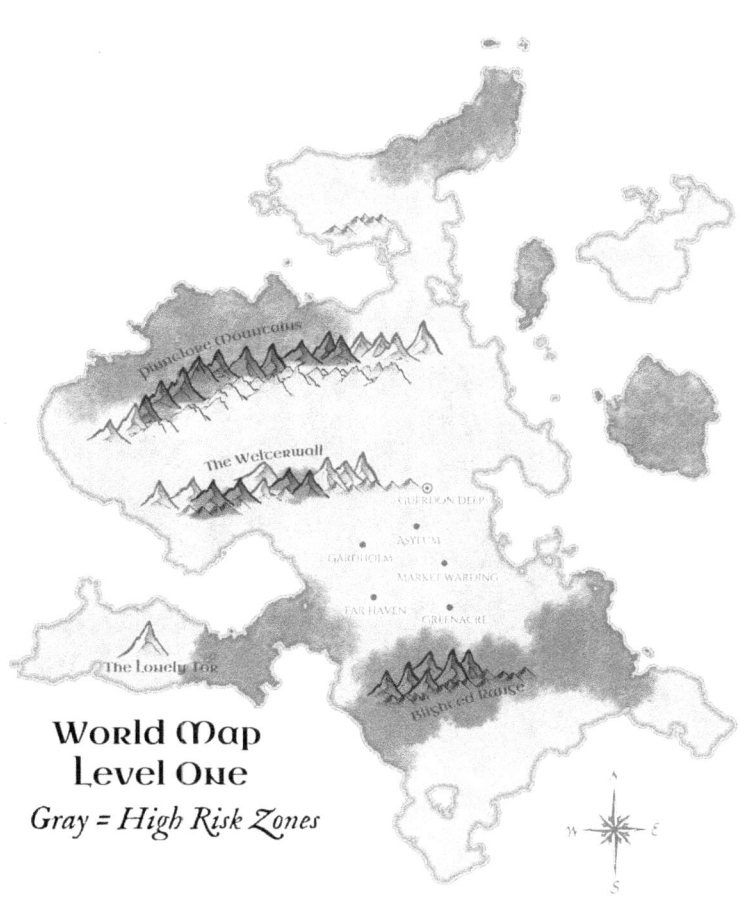

Manelong Mountains

The Welcerwall

GUERDON DEEP

ASYLUM

GARDHOLM

MARKET WARDING

FAR HAVEN   GREENACRE

The Lonely Tor

Blighted Range

World Map
Level One
Gray = High Risk Zones

CHAPTER ONE

Aderyn was scrubbing the kitchen floor when she got the Call. She was the youngest of her parents' children, the only one still living at home—the only one who hadn't received the Call—and that meant the chores piled on. At least scrubbing the floor was better than scrubbing the privy.

She didn't know what the strange tickling sensation in her right ear was. It itched deep down, farther than she could reach with her finger, so she rubbed the outside of her ear, pressing down hard. The itching just got worse. Just as she'd stopped caring about safety and was looking around for something long and thin, the itching faded, replaced by a throbbing hum like her pulse pounding in her temples. It didn't hurt, just made her feel like she'd run across town at her top speed without stopping.

Aderyn sat back on her heels on the wet floor and tilted her head one way and then the other. The throbbing hum didn't change. Then her vision blurred like she'd been crying, making her blink rapidly to clear her eyes. It didn't work. Fear filled her. Maybe she was dying. This could be a stroke like what had killed old Gammer Ilani three months back—except Aderyn was only twenty, and wasn't that too young for a stroke?

In the next moment, a crack like the snap of an invisible whip cut across the sound of Aderyn's frightened breathing. Her vision cleared until she could see better than ever before. Trails of mist that glowed silver twisted and tangled in front of her. Whatever they were, they didn't have substance, because Aderyn waved her hands at them and her fingers passed right through without disturbing the mist.

The trails came into focus. Instead of mist, they were lines of bright silver light that formed letters floating half a foot in front of Aderyn's face.

Greetings, Fledgling! You have grown to an acceptable level of development and may now choose to advance your destiny.

Accept the Call? Y / N

Aderyn's breathing sped up. She'd been waiting for this moment for five years, long before she was old enough to receive the Call.

The letters Y and N stood out from the rest of the silver words, outlined in gold that flowed like liquid metal. Without hesitating, Aderyn touched the letter Y. As she did so, she remembered that she hadn't been able to touch the letters before, but the Y felt warm and moved slightly beneath her fingers.

Instantly, the words vanished. New words blinked into existence.

Welcome to Level One

Aderyn waited impatiently for more. Most everyone believed the system chose your adventuring class based on the skills you'd learned as a young adult, but Aderyn's father Dalin said he didn't think that was true, because he'd studied books of magic when he was young and the system had made him a Swordsworn, a master of the blade, instead. Aderyn had decided not to try to guess what the system had in mind for her. She hoped it was something amazing.

After what felt like an eternity, the message vanished. A few seconds later, more words filled her vision:

Name: Aderyn

Class: Warmaster

Level: 1

<u>Skills:</u> **Bluff (1), Climb (1), Conversation (1), Intimidate (1), Sense Truth (1), Survival (1), Swim (1)**

<u>Class Skills:</u> **Assess (1), Awareness (1), Knowledge: Geography (1), Spot (1)**

It was a lot to take in, but Aderyn's attention focused on the second line. *Warmaster*. She'd never heard of that class, but it sounded important. It sounded like someone who was a powerful fighter. It might even be better than a Swordsworn, though she would never say that to her father.

She realized she was clutching the scrubbing brush so hard her hand hurt. She dropped the brush into the bucket with a splash and raced for the door, shouting, "Mother! Father! Guess what?"

She found her mother Lyzette in her workshop, carefully adding some smelly green liquid to a bottle, drop by drop. Aderyn came to a stop in the doorway as her mother raised her other hand. "Quiet, dear, this could explode if I add too much," Mother said without looking away from the bottle.

"I'll be back," Aderyn said, and backed away quietly until she couldn't see into the room anymore. Then she hurried to find her father. Both her parents ought to be there for this announcement.

Her father was in the big room at the front of the house where he taught sword mastery to other Swordsworn, as well as to eager youngsters hoping to influence the system by gaining fighting skills. He was putting wooden practice swords away in the rack and smiled when Aderyn burst through the door. "In a hurry, sweetling?"

"I got my Call," Aderyn said, too excited for anything but a straightforward announcement.

Father's eyes widened, and the last wooden sword fell from his grip. "Did you tell your mother?"

"I wanted you both to hear."

Father left the practice sword on the ground and put his arm around Aderyn's shoulders, steering her back through the house to Mother's workshop. Mother had set aside the stinky green liquid and was pouring hot wax over the bottle's cork to seal it. "Now, what are you so excited about?" she asked.

"It's my Call. I got the Call." Aderyn bounced excitedly on her toes.

"Well?" Father asked, inviting her to share the news further.

Aderyn drew in a deep breath. "I'm a Warmaster."

She waited for the excited congratulations, for hugs and encouraging words. Instead, her parents' faces stilled, going so blank it looked like their emotions had been completely wiped away. They looked at each other, not at Aderyn, and she could tell they were trying to find words. "It's good, isn't it?" Aderyn said. "I mean, Warmaster, that's... it means someone who is good at fighting, right?"

Father steered Aderyn to sit on an unoccupied stool near Mother. "Well, yes, that's what it *sounds* like," he said, and Aderyn's heart sank further. "The truth is, well..." His voice trailed off, and he looked at Mother imploringly, like he wanted her to break the bad news instead.

Mother clasped Aderyn's hand and patted it. "What your father is trying to say is that no one's ever been able to figure out what a Warmaster is good for," she said.

Aderyn's hopes surged again. "You mean it's a lost class? Something—"

"Not that," Mother said, shaking her head. "I mean that Warmasters are, well... useless. They don't have any special fighting skills, they don't know how to use magic, they don't have specialized knowledges. About all they're good for is recognizing monsters and their abilities, and every adventurer can do that."

"We had a Warmaster in our team once," Father said. "He was obnoxious. Smug and convinced he knew everyone else's abilities so well he could do their jobs for them. We didn't let him die, of course, but no one was terribly sad when a bog beast took him down."

Aderyn's eyes ached with tears she didn't want her parents to see her cry. "Useless," she whispered.

"Don't take it so hard," Mother said. "I didn't mean *you're* useless. If you were assigned this class, I'm sure it's for a purpose. Maybe you'll be the first Warmaster to... to..." Her voice trailed off as Father's had done.

Aderyn stood. "It's fine," she said. "It's not like I only have to do what Warmasters do, right? There are all those other skills I can train in."

"That's the way to look at it," Father said, but he didn't sound confident, and it was getting harder for Aderyn to hold back tears.

"I'm going for a walk," she said. "Sorry about not finishing the kitchen floor."

"Don't worry about it, sweetling," Mother said. Aderyn was already out the door.

She walked through the streets of Far Haven without seeing the many thatch-roofed houses or the people who lived in them, even when those people called greetings to her. As a sanctuary city, at the heart of a safe zone where few monsters roamed, Far Haven attracted people who'd retired early from adventuring so they could raise families, and Aderyn had grown up surrounded by friendly faces. Her parents were unusual in having reached level twenty, the highest possible level, before coming to live in Far Haven. Everyone in town knew Aderyn, which made everything so much worse.

She tried not to dwell on what a failure this made her. Her brother Nollan and her sister Pia were Swordsworn like their father; her brother Borrus was Staffsworn, but that was nearly as good. Four warriors in the family, with her mother a renowned Spiritsmith who brewed potions that could enhance the body or cure anything short of death, and now her. The useless one.

She realized she'd walked the length of the town just before she walked into the Sunwise Gate. She stopped and tilted her head back to look up where it reared high above her, blocking her view of the forests that grew beyond the protected expanse surrounding Far Haven. All she could see were the walls of gray-brown stone and the stout oak door, unmanned on this side. The guards faced outward, watching for travelers approaching. Entering Far Haven meant having someone open the door. Leaving Far Haven was a different matter.

Aderyn had never left Far Haven on her own. No one could who hadn't accepted the Call. It was a protection for those too young or unskilled to defend themselves outside the town. For years, she'd watched her parents press their palms against a spot on the right-hand stone doorpost, a spot that was dark from centuries of men and women doing exactly the same thing. When Aderyn had sneaked up to try it, nothing had ever happened, but for her parents, that spot made the heavy door swing open on noiseless hinges.

Now she approached the doorpost, hesitating in case someone might try to stop her. But no one did. This time, when she was within a few feet of the door, the dark spot flickered and glowed with pale blue light in the shape of a palm print. She hesitated a moment more, then pressed her hand flat against the glow.

The door swung silently open.

Feeling slightly more cheerful—at least she wasn't a total failure—Aderyn stepped through and looked around, though she'd been outside with her parents and knew what to expect. Untilled land covered with grasses burned golden by the summer sun surrounded Far Haven. A wide dirt road extended through the fields from the doorway, rutted from long use and dusty at this time of year. The road was completely empty of travelers and disappeared from sight as it passed under the trees of the forest to the east.

Aderyn looked over her shoulder at the guards, who stood atop the wall-walk on either side of the arch the door was set into. They didn't seem to notice her, but Aderyn knew one of them, a middle-aged man named Farren who regularly bought potions from her mother, and she was sure he was just pretending not to see her, he was that curious. She cast her gaze down the road again. She didn't actually have a purpose in going outside other than to prove she could, but she didn't want to turn around and go back like a foolish youngling.

She set off down the road. She would go as far as the forest, which would be cool and shady. The heat of the sun was already making her sweat and wish she'd worn a hat, even though hats were for old ladies. Maybe there was sense in hats, after all.

Fifteen minutes later, she reached the forest. At first, the trees were spaced widely, and there were stumps where people from Far Haven had cut down trees for lumber or firewood. Gradually, as Aderyn walked deeper into the woods, the trees grew more thickly, with wider trunks and branches that extended over the road to make a leafy emerald roof. The air that had smelled of dust and heat now smelled of damp leaves and fresh, growing plants. Aderyn inhaled deeply, and a little more of her despair fell away.

So, Warmaster was a useless class, was it? Good for bossing people around—well, Aderyn didn't believe in being bossy and arrogant. If you couldn't convince someone with reason and superior ability, there was no point in being overbearing. Besides, Aderyn had never felt the need to be a leader. She'd imagined herself as part of an adventuring team, sure, but not as the leader. It wasn't in her nature.

She breathed in again—and stopped where she was. Underneath the pleasant smells of the forest lurked something dark and bitter. She didn't recognize the scent, but she hated it. Her heart pounding, she sniffed again, turning her whole body in an effort to identify where the stink was coming from. It seemed to come from everywhere.

A jolt of fear shot through her. Maybe it was a monster. The territory around Far Haven was safe, but that was only by comparison to the Forsaken Lands, where terrible monsters thrived and even experienced adventurers sometimes met their deaths. There were still monsters near here, weaker ones suitable for beginners to fight. Except Aderyn wasn't armed, and she had no weapons skill in any case, and even a weak monster might be too much for her.

A high-pitched chittering sound reached her ears, *clickety-click*, faster than rain on a metal washtub and with an accompanying whistling sound that set Aderyn's teeth on edge. The sound stopped for a few seconds, then began again, louder this time. Aderyn took a step backward.

Something the size of a large dog, but stretched out long and thin, slid around the trunk of a nearby tree at head height. Its segmented body glistened with shivering rainbows like oil poured out on a table. Hundreds of tiny legs skittered as it swarmed up the trunk and paused there. The creature stared at her with a dozen lidless black eyes.

Aderyn's rapid breathing dizzied her. She shifted to take another step backward. Instantly the creature sped around the tree, out of sight, and for half a second Aderyn thought it had run away. Then it erupted from the bushes that grew around the base of the tree, scrambling on its horrible little legs to attack her.

Aderyn screamed and ran.

Chapter Two

Behind her, the chittering noises grew louder, and they echoed oddly. Aderyn risked a glance over her shoulder. There were *two* of them! Aderyn pushed herself harder. She didn't care if it made her look weak and stupid, she had to reach the safety of the gate and let the guards deal with the creatures. She cursed herself for being so rash as to leave Far Haven unarmed. She might not have ranks in Swordsmanship, but she still knew which end of the blade to impale the enemy with.

A shout from behind her made her stumble. "Hey! What are you —*shit!*"

That last word had sounded surprised. Aderyn, almost against her will, slowed to look behind her again.

A young man with blond hair had come up behind the slithering monsters. He held a heavy, gnarled tree branch in both hands and wielded it like a weapon. As Aderyn watched, he slammed the branch against one of the monsters, knocking it to one side. The young man immediately advanced on the second monster, which hadn't stopped coming after Aderyn. He hit it, and the thing jerked and stopped moving.

Aderyn became aware of a light blinking in the corner of her right eye, a blue light that matched the palm print on the Far Haven gate. She raised a hand and swiped at it. Immediately, silver letters rose up in front of her eyes.

Name: Giant Centipede

Type: Vermin

Power Level: 1

And, below that block of text, the single word **Assess?**

"Hey, are you all right?" the young man asked, lowering his makeshift weapon.

"No, don't!" Aderyn shouted.

In the same moment, the fallen giant centipede shook itself and swarmed in a tight circle, reversing direction and throwing itself at the young man. He brought the branch up just in time for the centipede's fanged jaw, dripping green venom, to fasten on the wood instead of the man's arm.

Again, the word **Assess?** blinked in Aderyn's vision. "Yes, yes!" she screamed, swiping at the glowing word.

In the next moment, glowing blue lines outlined the centipede, sweeping across its grotesque body like searchlights. The lines converged on a spot at the back of the monster's head.

"You have to hit the back of its head!" Aderyn exclaimed.

The young man shook the branch, dislodging the centipede, and whirled the branch around so its heavy tip, the size of a big man's fist, connected solidly with the blue spot. The centipede let out a thin, high shriek that hurt Aderyn's ears and convulsed, curling up on itself into a loose, stinking ball.

More words formed in front of her eyes.

Congratulations! You have defeated [Giant Centipede]
You have earned [5 XP].

The young man, breathing heavily, waved a hand vigorously in front of his face. Then he spun around, raising the branch, and blocked the attack of the second centipede. This one got its jaws into the wood and wouldn't let go no matter how the man shook the branch and cursed the thing. Aderyn's gaze swept the path and the woods to either side. She rushed into the undergrowth, looking for another branch, and found a sapling cracked at its base so the length of it was nearly broken off. It was thinner than the branch the man was wielding, but Aderyn wasn't inclined to be picky.

"Here," she panted, racing to the young man's side. "Stop wiggling it!"

"It's wiggling itself!" the young man said, but he lowered the branch and held it as steadily as he could.

Aderyn had been afraid she would need to waste actions doing the [Assess] command again, but it seemed her knowledge extended to all creatures of this type, because the blue lines and glowing dot were superimposed on this one as well. Not wanting to get too close to the venomous jaws in case the centipede suddenly let go and lunged for her, she swatted the blue spot with the end of the branch.

The creature squealed and released the branch the man held, but it didn't die. "Harder!" the young man said, and brought his branch down on the centipede's head with a cracking, shattering sound of breaking chitin. The thing jerked violently and lay still. Green ooze flowed from its shattered body, stinking more powerfully than the creature had when it was alive. Again, the system announcement appeared. Aderyn didn't know how she could have earned experience when she hadn't actually killed anything, but she wasn't going to turn it down.

The young man threw the branch away and turned to Aderyn. "Did they hurt you?"

Aderyn shook her head. "I'm glad you came along," she said, hating to admit to weakness to a stranger, but just as unwilling not to show gratitude when it was earned.

"What the hell are they?" The young man moved to prod one of the carcasses with his toe, then clearly reconsidered. His hair was cut in an odd style, shorter than any man's Aderyn had ever seen, and his clothes were strange, too—a short-sleeved shirt dyed a dark, rich red and heavy, stiff trousers of a blue so dark it was almost black. The shirt had a highly detailed painting on its front, an image of a hugely muscled man wielding a notched, serrated blade in one hand and a heavy club in the other, and ornate letters surrounding the image read FIVE FINGER DEATH PUNCH. Aderyn couldn't imagine how the paint didn't flake off.

"Giant centipede," Aderyn said. Now that the fight was over, she could take a breath and think about what had happened. She remembered [Assess] was one of the skills she'd been given to start, but she'd thought it was something an adventurer had to choose to access, not something the system prodded her with.

"Giant centipede?" The young man sounded skeptical.

"You can check the Monster Folio if you don't believe me," Aderyn said, irritated.

"Monster Folio?" Now he sounded confused.

"The index of monsters you've encountered? It grows as you fight things and learn more?" Aderyn let her irritation turn into sarcasm. Maybe he was stupid. The system didn't discriminate against people who were stupid; they could fight as well as anyone.

She remembered what her parents and her brothers and sister had told her about accessing the Codex or the Monster Folio, how you could use hand movements, but with a little extra practice you could open them with a twitch of your facial muscles, like a wink or a squint. Concentrating, she squinched up her right eye. It took a few tries, but eventually the Codex opened up in front of her.

When it wasn't actively displaying information or system messages, the Codex was obvious only as a blue glow outlining the edges of her vision. Aderyn said, "Um... Advancement."

Silver lines filled her vision.

Name: Aderyn

Class: Warmaster
Level: 1
Skills: **Bluff (1), Climb (1), Conversation (1), Intimidate (1), Sense Truth (1), Survival (1), Swim (1), Knowledge: Monsters (1)**
Class Skills: **Improved Assess 1 (1), Awareness (1), Knowledge: Geography (1), Spot (1), Discern Weakness (1)**

[*Improved* Assess 1]? And she was sure [**Discern Weakness**] hadn't been there before.

"What did you say?" the young man asked. He'd come to stand beside her and, when she focused past the Codex, she saw he was examining her, like he was as curious about her appearance as she was about his.

"Nothing. What's your name?"

"It's Owen. That's actually my middle name, but my first name is Jacob, and everybody's named Jacob." He smiled wryly.

Aderyn had never heard the name Jacob before. Or Owen, come to think on it. And what was this nonsense about first and middle names, and everyone having the same name? She decided not to press further. "I'm Aderyn. Thanks for helping."

"I wouldn't have known how to kill them without your advice," Owen said. "Blows just bounced off their scales. Or exoskeleton. Or whatever."

"Are you Staffsworn, then?" Owen didn't carry any weapons, and Aderyn couldn't understand how anyone could travel the wilderness, even the safe zones, without being armed, but a Staffsworn would be able to use any length of wood well.

Owen didn't say anything for a while. Aderyn was about to repeat her question when he said, "This is going to sound crazy, but —where am I?"

"In the forest outside Far Haven. Are you lost?"

"I'm starting to think no one's been as lost as I am right now," Owen said, again with that wry smile. The smile disappeared as Aderyn didn't return it. "Look, I don't know what else to ask, or what to say—you'll think I'm nuts. This isn't a RenFaire, is it? You're not an NPC? Someone to give me a quest?"

"What's a RenFaire?" Aderyn asked, puzzled as much by his desperate expression as by his words.

"Yeah," Owen said, sighing. "The centipedes were very convincing. I could explain everything away but those."

Aderyn's confusion increased. "I don't understand. If you're not Staffsworn, what class are you?" She squinched up her eye, trying to Assess him.

"No class," Owen said. "This is going to be hard for you to believe, but I'm from another world."

Aderyn sucked in a horrified breath and backed away, wishing she could run but afraid to turn her back on him. "Demon," she whispered. "Demon!"

"No!" Owen exclaimed. "I'm human, not a demon—don't run!"

Aderyn tripped over a loose branch behind her and fell. She kept backing away, scooting on her rear end. "Stay there," she said. "I'll... I'll banish you!" It was a total bluff. She had no magic that would dispel a demon. But Owen had acted so ignorant, maybe he didn't realize that.

"Would a demon have fought to protect you?" Owen said. "I promise I don't mean to hurt you. I—please, don't be afraid. I don't know what else to do."

He sounded so worried it stopped Aderyn's movements. She pushed herself to her feet and dusted the seat of her trousers off. "Demons are the only creatures who come from other worlds," she said, but not very certainly.

"Then maybe I'm the only one, but I promise I'm human." Owen didn't walk toward her, but he reached out a hand. "Just listen, all right? I was traveling cross-country by Greyhound, and last night I was jumped and robbed by some guys. They knocked me out, and when I woke up, it was morning and I was here in this forest. I thought I'd been kidnapped, because there wasn't a forest where I—anyway, that's not important. They took my phone and all my money and my debit card, and now you tell me this isn't even my world. Can you see how I'd feel lost?"

There were too many strange words in that little speech that Aderyn didn't know. He certainly sounded like someone not from around here, but he couldn't possibly be from another world.

Well, there was one way to prove it.

"Can you snap your fingers?" she asked.

Owen nodded. "Why—"

"Hold your right hand by your right temple, like this." Aderyn lifted her right hand with her thumb and middle finger pressed together. "Then snap your fingers, like this." She snapped, and the Codex came into view. Since all she wanted was to prove this stranger didn't have access to the system, she didn't bother teaching him the silent, faster way.

Owen did as she did. His eyes widened, and he took an involuntary step back. He waved his left hand in front of his face, flicking the fingers like he was trying to shoo away cobwebs. "What the *hell* is that?"

"It's the Codex, and it proves you're not an outsider, because an outsider wouldn't be able to see it." Aderyn felt a twinge of disappointment. The idea of a non-demonic outsider had grabbed hold of her. What might someone like this be capable of?

"Jacob Owen Lindberg," Owen said, his eyes shifting as he read invisible letters. "Class, Swordsworn. Level 1. Skills, **[Assess]**, **[Awareness]**, **[Bluff]**, **[Climb]**, **[Conversation]**, **[Intimidate]**, **[Sense Truth]**, **[Spot]**, **[Survival]**, **[Swim]**. Class Skills, **[Basic Weapon Proficiency]**, **[Knowledge: Monsters]**, **[Basic Armor Proficiency]**, **[Exploit Weakness]**. What is this? Are we in a game?"

"Why would you think it's a game?"

"Because—well, levels, classes, skills... it's like a roleplaying game.

And this heads-up display..." He waved his hand in front of his face again, but slowly this time.

"I don't understand half of what you say," Aderyn complained. "This is how the world works. It's not a game. And I don't know why you're still pretending this is all foreign to you. You accepted the Call, or you wouldn't have access to the Codex and the system."

"All right," Owen said. "All right. I haven't done any of that, but I'm part of your game—sorry, your world—until I can find a way back to my own world. Will you help me?"

Flashing letters blinked into view. Aderyn read:

You have received an invitation to join an adventuring team. Accept? Y / N

She hesitated. Owen might or might not be from another world. He might or might not be crazy. And her parents had made sure all their children knew how important the decision to join a team was. It wasn't hard to leave one, but the system penalized people who joined and left teams frivolously. Jumping into a partnership with a total stranger was crazier than Owen seemed to be.

But he'd saved her life.

Aderyn touched the Y.

CHAPTER THREE

The moment she touched the golden letter Y, the invitation disappeared, and a new display came to life. In the upper left, Aderyn saw Owen's name, level, and class, as well as a thick blue vertical line beside them showing his current health, which was at full. Her own name and level appeared at the bottom of her field of vision, above the thick blue line of her health bar, this one horizontal. She blinked, and the images faded but didn't disappear entirely. When she focused on Owen's name, the images grew brighter.

Congratulations! You have joined your first adventuring team. You have gained [100 XP]

Owen was staring into space. "Aderyn," he read.

"It's pronounced ah-DARE-in, not ADD-er-in, remember?" Aderyn said.

"Sorry. What class are you?"

Aderyn braced herself for an outpouring of scorn. "I'm a Warmaster."

"Wow, that sounds powerful," Owen said. "Is that why you knew how to defeat the centipedes? Where to hit them?"

"I—" Aderyn frowned. Then she called up the Codex again with a twitch of her facial muscles. It got easier the more she did it.

Name: Aderyn

Class: Warmaster

Level: 1

<u>Skills</u>: **Bluff (1), Climb (1), Conversation (1), Intimidate (1), Sense Truth (1), Survival (1), Swim (1), Knowledge: Monsters (1)**

<u>Class Skills:</u> **Improved Assess 1 (1), Awareness (1), Knowledge: Geography (1), Spot (1), Discern Weakness (1)**

[**Discern Weakness**]. That's what it had felt like—she'd seen the weak spot highlighted by the system. And— "What's that skill you have? Something about weakness?"

"I forgot," Owen said. "Wait." He snapped his fingers next to his right temple. "It says [**Exploit Weakness**], is that it?"

"Yes." [**Discern Weakness**], and then [**Exploit Weakness**]—it was almost like the two skills were meant to work together. But Aderyn had never heard of anything like paired skills. She suppressed a wild impulse to go farther into the forest and search for monsters to test her theory on. They were both still unarmed, and killing the centipedes had been about half luck.

She decided not to tell Owen what she'd guessed yet. He might still turn out to be crazy, or evil—no, she didn't think he was evil. She wasn't so stupid as to think handsome men couldn't be evil—and he was handsome despite being grubby from wandering through the forest—but it wasn't that so much as that he had a very open face. And he'd looked genuinely disturbed at being mistaken for a demon.

Her initial belief that no one from another world could access the Codex faded. Everything else said he was what he claimed: someone who'd been brought to her world, probably by magic. And if that wasn't the beginning of a quest, she didn't know what was.

As if the system had heard her thoughts, silver words appeared.

You have accepted the quest [Return the Otherworlder]. Set as primary quest? Y / N

She flicked the Y, and the words shrank into a golden dot that hovered in the upper right of her field of vision, on the other side from Owen's name.

"Did you see that too?" Owen asked. He gestured as she just had.

"Yes. That's our quest now."

"I don't suppose there's a glowing line that guides us toward completion of the quest?"

Aderyn gave him a withering look that made him blush. "That's ridiculous."

"I'm sorry. You said this isn't a game."

Aderyn shook her head. "I don't know how to get you back to your world," she said. "I don't know anyone who could. We'll have to search for someone who has that kind of magic."

Owen brightened. "Where is that?"

"Not in Far Haven. It might take time."

"I just care about getting home. My family's going to worry about me." Owen walked around one dead centipede to stand at Aderyn's side. "Is Far Haven your city?"

"It's more of a town. Big enough to supply us for a journey." Aderyn started walking, and Owen quickly joined her. "But you can't tell anyone you're from another world. They'll assume you're a demon like I did and won't stop for an explanation."

"Got it. Except, what about my clothes?"

Aderyn examined him again. He did look odd. His feet were cased in dirty white shoes that flexed in odd ways and tied up the top surface with strings. And there was the shirt. Aderyn plucked at it; it stretched slightly, like no fabric she'd ever seen before. "We'll say you're from beyond Greenacre," she said. "That's as far away as anyone here has ever gone who wasn't an adventurer, and so long as you keep quiet and don't answer questions or volunteer lies about your past, it will be all right."

She wasn't as certain as she sounded. But Rathven, one of her parents' former teammates and a Lightfingers who knew everything there was to know about the art of deception, had taught her that the best lies were either based in truth or were ones you didn't embellish. They couldn't base anything about Owen on truth, so they'd have to keep it simple. Aderyn hoped for the first time in her life her parents weren't as smart as she believed.

People stared at Owen as she and he walked through Far Haven's streets, though only the smallest children were rude enough to stare openly. As before, Aderyn ignored the stares, but she acknowledged the greetings she received with a friendly wave. Owen kept turning his head to stare at things until she said, "Don't do that. It makes you look ridiculous."

"I'm sorry, it's just that I've never seen houses like this except in pictures," Owen said. "Would they really attack me if they knew I was from another world?"

"Absolutely," Aderyn replied. "Demons are powerful fighters who can cast evil spells. Sanctuary cities like Far Haven are protected from them, but people know how dangerous they are and how much damage they could do if they somehow found a way inside. You'd be lucky to be killed instantly."

She went over options in her head. She had to go home before they left, not just to gather her belongings but to say goodbye. But Mother and Father would know something was strange about Owen, and it wouldn't be just his clothes they found suspicious. *But* they'd be even more suspicious if she didn't introduce her teammate to them... oh, it was all so confusing.

Aderyn scanned Owen from his shirt to his strange shoes. Owen needed boots, and he needed a sword, and they would both need traveling gear, all of which cost money Aderyn didn't have on her. She might not have enough even in her savings. She sighed. "We have to go to my house. It is really important that you not do or say anything strange in front of my parents, all right? They're level twenty adventurers and they've fought demons, so they might figure out that you're not from our world."

"Level twenty?" Owen said. "Is that high?"

Aderyn was relieved that he didn't have any more ridiculous questions, like what levels were or how someone gained them. "It's the highest you can get. The legend is that centuries ago, people could get to much, much higher levels, that there was no limit to advancement, but something happened that stopped all that. I don't know what. People in Far Haven don't really talk about it."

"Levels," Owen said, but didn't say anything more.

Aderyn took Owen around back, through the kitchen door. The floor was entirely scrubbed and dry and the bucket and scrubbing brush put away, which made Aderyn feel guilty at not having done all that herself. For a moment, she thought about sneaking into her room, gathering what few things were small enough and important enough to take with her, but she couldn't bear the thought of leaving without saying goodbye. Suppose she died out there and her parents never found out what happened to her?

To her relief, her parents were both in the small library, where bookcases filled to overflowing with books lined two of the four walls. <**Everburning Candles**> that smelled pleasantly of honey shed a bright, cool light over the worktable and the chairs for sitting and reading. Aderyn's parents were unusual in having many books that weren't either Spiritsmith research or sword fighting manuals. Some of them were histories, some were books about herbs, and a few were written versions of the system's Monster Folio. Aderyn's father was reading, and her mother was sketching something in a blank book.

"Mother, Father," Aderyn said, making both of them look up.

"This is Owen. He's, um, searching for his family. I've agreed to be his teammate on his quest."

Mother's eyes widened. "So soon?"

"It's good that you're taking on adult responsibilities now, Aderyn," Father said, rising from his chair. "Owen, where are you from?"

"Beyond Greenacre," Owen said.

"That's a long way off," Father said. "Do you know my old friend Pierse? He was from Greenacre."

Owen faced Father fearlessly. "I'm sorry, no," he said. "My family only rarely went into Greenacre."

Father didn't say anything. He regarded Owen closely. Aderyn's palms began to sweat. Finally, Father said, "It doesn't matter. Can we give you two a meal before you set out?"

"Dalin, surely we can't just let Aderyn go so abruptly," Mother said. "You should stay the night, at least. We'll help you gather supplies before that."

Aderyn tried not to wince when she considered all the stupid things Owen might accidentally say if they stayed more than an hour. Unfortunately, Mother's suggestion was reasonable, and she couldn't figure out how to reject it. "Um—"

"Lyzette, remember how eager we were to get out on the road," Father said. "Besides, if Owen is searching for his family, he won't want to lose any time. What can we do for you?"

"Owen needs a sword," Aderyn said, overriding her mother's next protest. "He's Swordsworn. He, um, lost his sword in his travels."

"Of course," Father said. He sounded so cooperative Aderyn was suspicious. But how could he possibly know anything was wrong? "Owen, come with me, and Lyzette, why don't you help Aderyn pack?"

Aderyn followed her mother into the store room. All her nerves were on edge at having let Owen go off alone with Father. She told herself it would be all right, and if it wasn't all right, there was nothing she could do about it.

The store room held all sorts of things, but what Mother dug through was adventuring gear, old but well-maintained. "There's not a lot left, not after your brothers and sister went," Mother said, "but what we can't supply, you can buy."

She piled Aderyn's arms high with a couple of bedrolls, a cleverly-designed cooking kit that all fit neatly into a single cast-iron skillet with a lid, a lantern whose paint had flaked away but was free of rust, and finally a flat packet made of oiled leather, stitched up the sides with fine leather laces and treated along the seams to be waterproof. "A map case," Mother said. "You won't gain access to the system's maps for several levels, and this will be useful."

They returned to the library, where they found Owen and Father. Owen was examining the blade of a sword. Aderyn had seen that one in the training room many times before. It was a slim blade, not so long as to require two hands to wield, but not short, either. The hilt was wrapped in leather that looked much newer than the rest of the sword, and its pommel was unadorned steel.

"I really shouldn't accept this," Owen said. "I can't pay." He handled it awkwardly, as if he'd never wielded a sword before.

"I don't need paying," Father said. "I can't let you go out into the Forsaken Lands unarmed. Your death would be on my conscience."

"Thank you, Father," Aderyn said quickly. All they needed was for Owen to blurt out something about not knowing what to do with it, though she couldn't imagine their worlds were so different that nobody in Owen's had weapons training.

"You're welcome," Father said. "Now, sit down, both of you."

Aderyn and Owen sat. Mother walked around them to stand next to Father. Father fixed Aderyn with the direct gaze that always made her want to squirm. She gazed back at him, hoping she looked innocently excited.

Father pursed his lips. "Well, now," he said. "Suppose you tell me what's really going on."

Chapter Four

Aderyn and Owen looked at each other. "What's going on?" Aderyn repeated, projecting even more innocence than before.

Father tapped his right temple. "I should be impressed that you both nearly fooled me," he said. "But you should have known better than to lie to an old adventurer. Neither of you have enough ranks in **[Bluff]**. What is he? A lost prince? A disguised nonhuman?"

Aderyn sagged. "Will you promise not to kill him?"

"It's that bad?" Father sounded surprised.

"I could remove his disguise," Mother said to Father.

"He's not disguised," Aderyn said. "But—he's from another world. Except he's not a demon, I swear!"

Before her parents could speak, Aderyn told the whole story of the fight in the forest and learning Owen's identity. "I don't know how it's possible, but he's not dangerous. He just needs help getting back to his own world. Please, don't attack him."

Father and Mother looked at one another. "Maybe we should intervene," Mother said. "If it's possible for humans to come here from other worlds—if there are even other worlds at all—"

"This isn't our quest, Lyzette," Father said. "Aderyn's an adult now. She's the one the system presented with this challenge. All we can do is give her support and trust that she's been prepared for this."

"Thank you," Owen said. "Your world is strange to me, and the fact that Aderyn is willing to help me means a lot. I promise I won't let her come to harm."

Aderyn's parents laughed. "That's generous," Father said, "but questing is dangerous work, and there's no reason any one adventurer deserves to remain unharmed rather than another."

"You'll watch out for each other," Mother said. Her smile faded as she looked at Aderyn. Aderyn guessed she was thinking about her daughter's useless class. Even if Owen was right, and Warmaster meant some kind of tactical support, it wasn't exactly something she could use to fight on her own behalf.

"You're going to need different clothes," Mother said to Owen. "What you're wearing is clearly foreign. How does the picture stay on?"

Owen looked down at his chest like he'd forgotten what he was wearing. "It's printed on."

"Printed? I have some printed books, but those don't have color. And the printing is just letters."

"So you do have printing presses. Cool." Owen hunched his shoulders, like that would draw attention away from his shirt.

"Why wouldn't we have printing presses?" Mother sounded curious rather than confused. But then, Mother had an inquiring mind and wasn't put off by things that didn't make sense immediately.

Owen glanced swiftly at Aderyn. Aderyn said, "I don't see that it hurts to tell them things, since they know your secret."

Owen nodded. "Your world looks a little like mine used to, centuries ago. We didn't have printing presses back then. I'm trying not to make assumptions about your level of technology based on how your world compares to mine."

Aderyn didn't know what "technology" was, but Mother didn't ask questions about it. Instead, she said, "Nobody's ever suggested that there are other human worlds than our own. Just the void where demons come from. Your experience is remarkable."

"I hope it's not insulting to say I want to get back to my world as fast as possible," Owen said.

"Of course not," Father said. He opened the packet containing the map and unfolded it to spread it on the library table. It was old enough that the creases had obliterated whatever had originally been drawn there, but most of the map was still intact. Father tapped a spot left of center. "This is Far Haven," he said. "Then here is Gardholm, and Asylum, and over to the east is Market Warding. The area around these towns is safe for beginning adventurers, though you shouldn't let that make you complacent—there are still plenty of monsters to challenge you."

He drew a line with his finger that crossed two of the points on the map he'd mentioned, running north and east to a larger dot. "This is where you want to go. Guerdon Deep. It's an actual city, bigger than Far Haven, and it's likely to have spellslingers capable of helping. Or at least who'll know where to start."

"But the road past Asylum leads through the Forsaken Lands," Mother warned, "so if you can't gain a few levels before starting that journey, see if you can attach yourselves to a caravan. There are always a few making the trip."

Aderyn examined the map, committing the route to memory even though they were taking the map with them. She'd expected to feel the excited fear she always felt when she considered entering the Forsaken Lands, but all she felt was eager anticipation.

"Thank you," she exclaimed, hugging her mother and then her father. Father folded the map and put it away, then handed the packet to Owen. Mother removed a small purse from her leather apron and gave it to Aderyn.

"It's not much, but it's what we gave your brothers and sister when they set out," she said when Aderyn exclaimed at its weight. "I know you'll be frugal in your spending."

"I will," Aderyn said. "I'll miss you both."

"Maybe you'll see Nollan or Borrus or Pia in your travels," Father said. It was said for form's sake, since the world was a big place and the chances of meeting anyone accidentally weren't good. But Aderyn took his words for what they really meant, as well-wishes.

They walked back down the street, carrying their supplies because Mother hadn't had any knapsacks for stowing things. "Should we get a pack horse, or something?" Owen asked.

"It's just an extra mouth to feed, and they tend to run away when monsters attack," Aderyn replied. "We won't carry much. This time of year, sleeping out of doors isn't a hardship."

She felt around in her pocket, stitched into the outer seam of her trousers by the seamstress Mariet as an experiment. A belt pouch could be slit or stolen, but it was a lot harder for a thief to reach inside the pocket without alerting Aderyn. In addition to her parents' money, which was actually a lot—mixed gold and silver coins that added up to the equivalent of twenty gold—she had some coin of her own, more than she'd realized. It was all enough to buy the rest of what they needed and have some left over.

Remembering Mariet made her decide on their next stop. "Let's get you new clothes," she said.

Mariet's shop was cooler than outdoors and brightly lit by <Everburning Candles>, though hers smelled of pine rather than honey. The front room was small, furnished only with a table against the left-hand wall and rows of drawers of different sizes attached to the back wall. Mariet pushed through one of the two curtained door-ways beside the drawers as Aderyn shut the front door.

"Aderyn!" Mariet exclaimed. "And... I don't know this young man."

"This is Owen," Aderyn said. "He's from beyond Greenacre. We're teammates."

"You've come a long way, then," Mariet said. Her head jerked in surprise. "Did you say teammates? Aderyn, did you get your Call?"

Aderyn braced herself. "I did. I'm a Warmaster. And Owen and I are leaving Far Haven soon to search for his family." It was a good, believable lie.

Unfortunately, Mariet focused on the one part of that statement Aderyn had hoped to bury. "A Warmaster? What's that?"

"A tactician," Owen said, startling Aderyn. She'd told him not to speak, hadn't she? "Warmasters see things like monster weaknesses and where to strike."

"Is that so?" Mariet sounded impressed. Aderyn wished Owen had kept his mouth shut. Sure, he'd made her useless talent seem valuable, but eventually someone who knew the truth would see through that lie.

"Anyway, Owen needs new clothing," Aderyn went on, pretending casualness. "What he's wearing is... is too formal for adventuring. He needs practical clothes. Do you have anything you could alter right away?"

"Well, someone's in a hurry," Mariet teased. "All you level one adventurers are the same. Any delay on the questing path feels like forever. Let's see what I've got in back."

When she was gone, Aderyn said, "Why did you lie?"

"I didn't lie," Owen protested. "Isn't that what your class is for? **[Discern Weakness]**, and pass that knowledge on to someone who can use it?"

Aderyn stopped with her mouth half open to argue. "Well," she said, then fell silent again. He was right. "Anyway, it's better if you don't say anything. You might give away your secret without meaning to."

Owen nodded. "Is she going to sew everything by hand, or do you have sewing machines?"

And there he went again, using strange words. "There are machines in the biggest cities, or so my parents say, but they're for pumping water or moving heavy objects. I've never heard of a machine that could sew."

Mariet came back with an armful of fabric she set on the table. "Try these on, and I'll see what I can do," she told Owen. "You can have some privacy there." She pointed at the second curtained doorway.

Owen glanced once at Aderyn, then took the pile of fabric into the changing cubby. Mariet winked at Aderyn. "Cute boy," she said with a suggestive smile.

"He's just my teammate. For as long as it takes to find his family." Aderyn tried not to blush. Why did old people always want to tease her about boys, and relationships, and falling in love? She was an adventurer now. All that stuff was unimportant. Even if Owen was handsome.

Owen came out wearing a pair of trousers whose waistband he held closed in front of him and a cream-colored linen shirt that fit him perfectly. "These pants are just a little loose."

Mariet plucked at the waistband. "It's a quick alteration. Seven silver for the shirt and trousers, and two silver for the alteration."

Nine silver. Aderyn had enough without tapping her parents' reserve. "How long?"

"Oh, half an hour. Is that fast enough for you?" Mariet winked again.

Aderyn paid, and she and Owen left the shop. "I keep having more questions," Owen said. "Where do we go now?"

They spent the half hour hurrying from shop to shop, buying simple things like <**Matchlighters**>, soap, a couple of waterskins, tin plates and mugs, and enough food for three days, the time it would take to reach the first of the sanctuary cities on the road to Guerdon Deep. That added up to seventeen silver. They bought knapsacks to pack it all in and a coil of thin rope, because Father always said he never regretted having rope on hand. That cost them only another twenty silver, thanks to Aderyn finding some used but still sturdy knapsacks the shop owner was willing to give them at a discount.

Aderyn wavered over a shiny steel compass in the shop where they bought the knapsacks. Its case was dented, but it worked perfectly, and eventually she bought it for forty silver. There were roads between the cities, but that might not always be the case. She told herself it was worth the expense. It was fun to daydream about a time when they would be experienced adventurers for whom spending forty silver was nothing.

The most expensive purchase was boots for Owen. Again on her father's remembered advice, Aderyn encouraged Owen to pick the best quality boots they could afford. That price turned out to be one whole gold coin, more than Aderyn had ever spent on an article of clothing in her life. She hoped it was true that good boots were worth their weight in gold.

When the half-hour was up, they returned to Mariet's shop and Owen changed into his new clothes. They made him look more normal, though Aderyn didn't know what to do about his unusual haircut. Still, now that the muscled man painting was gone, there wasn't anything about Owen that screamed "demon outsider."

Owen folded his old clothes neatly and put them and his odd white shoes in the bottom of his knapsack. He had a look in his eyes that said he didn't want to talk about it, so Aderyn didn't say anything. She guessed if she were dragged into a strange world, she wouldn't want to let go of the things that reminded her of home either.

Outside Mariet's shop, Owen said, "Is that everything?"

Aderyn scanned the street and the houses and shops. For the first time that day, she felt a twinge of nervousness. She was leaving her home, possibly for good, in the company of a total stranger, with a class her own parents had called useless. This might be the stupidest thing she'd ever done.

She hitched her knapsack higher on her shoulder and said, "Let's go."

CHAPTER FIVE

Aderyn leaped back as Owen thrust swiftly with his sword, skewering the last of the oversized rats. It squealed in pain and then slumped, sliding off the blade.

**Congratulations! You have defeated [Diseased Rat]
You have earned [10 XP].**

"I wish I knew why it thinks I defeated these monsters," Aderyn said, examining the four fallen corpses. "It's not like I have a weapon." It hadn't even occurred to her when they were shopping in Far Haven that she should buy a sword, or ask her father for one. Not having any ranks in **[Basic Weapon Proficiency]** meant she would be terrible at fighting for many levels, and she'd assumed there was no point in trying. Now she thought maybe that had been a mistake. Even a substandard fighter could get lucky.

"Your help means I can kill them quickly," Owen pointed out. "Maybe the system considers that a legitimate defeat." He wiped his sword on the sunburned grass, then tore up a handful of longer grasses to do a more thorough job.

"I guess that makes sense." Aderyn considered dragging the bodies away from the road, but remembered the "diseased" part of the monsters' name and decided not to risk contracting whatever disease it was. Monster bodies broke down fairly quickly, anyway, not like natural animals. If these had had useful body parts, and she had the right skill, she would have about an hour to harvest what she needed before the monster dissolved into nothing.

"I'm more worried at how slowly we're gaining experience," she went on. "You're improving rapidly with the sword, and we're getting better at working together, but that hasn't affected how much experience we get in these fights. I don't know how much it takes to get to level two, but I'm sure at the rate we're going, we won't achieve that level by the time we reach the Forsaken Lands."

"So, there's no absolute number of experience points for a level?" Owen threw the matted grasses away and sheathed his sword.

"There might be, but no one's ever figured it out—or at least everyone who's tried comes up with a different number. Father's theory is that the system wants level achievement to be a pleasant surprise, which is as likely as anything. So I feel like I shouldn't count experience like a miser hoards gold. But we still ought to be looking for other experience-earning opportunities. Like quests."

"Can we get those out here? Or do we have to be in a town?" Owen asked.

"A town. Well, that's not totally true. There are sometimes quest-givers on the road, but that's like, oh, fetch help for a stranded caravan, that sort of thing." Aderyn hefted her knapsack. "But mostly they're in towns. And if I'm right, we'll be in Market Warding by tonight."

They walked in silence along the dirt road that cut through the grassy plains. The road wasn't all that wide, and Aderyn felt she and Owen were the only people who'd ever used it, but she knew that wasn't true because the plains would swallow it up if there was no traffic at all.

The past three days had been mostly boring. They'd fought three more battles in addition to the diseased rats, all of them against vermin or small monstrous animals. Aderyn was grateful for how simple the battles—more like skirmishes—had been, because it turned out Owen really hadn't ever used a sword before. They'd also given the teammates opportunities to work together and understand each other's skills. Aderyn could use the **[Discern Weakness]** skill without needing gestures now, and Owen was always quick to respond to her instructions with **[Exploit Weakness]**.

Now she wondered, though, how much of the ease of those battles was a result of the paired skills. Maybe other adventurers wouldn't have killed those monsters so readily. Maybe her parents were wrong, and Warmaster wasn't so useless when working with someone whose skills complemented hers.

"Market Warding is about the size of your hometown, right?" Owen said.

"I don't know. I've never been there. But I think so."

"So we won't find a wizard—I mean a spellslinger there. Not one who can help me."

Aderyn shrugged. "Most spellslingers settle in big cities, where there's more of a market for their skills. The ones who retire from adventuring, I mean. But Market Warding will have inns, and we can buy more food and spend the night in beds rather than on the ground."

Owen smiled and rotated his shoulder. "I guess I'm soft, because that sounds wonderful."

Aderyn pointed ahead to where thin lines of gray smoke spiraled into the clear, cloudless sky. "That's it. Maybe we'll be there sooner than I thought."

They quickened their pace without discussing it, and by the time the sun hung low in the western sky, they had reached the walls of Market Warding. From the outside, the town looked exactly like Far Haven: walls of brownish-gray stone that rose to twice the height of a tall man, a broad oak door banded with iron, and two guards standing on the wall-walk to either side of the door, watching Aderyn and Owen approach. They appeared to be unarmed, but Aderyn knew they had crossbows loaded near to hand, and if they saw anything that might be a threat, they'd shoot.

Aderyn approached to where she could speak to the guards without shouting and waved. "We're adventurers from Far Haven, passing through Market Warding," she said. "May we enter?"

"Certainly," the guard on the left said. His eyes had the glassy, unfocused look of someone who was Assessing her and Owen to check the truth of what they said. She braced herself for some patronizing comment on their low level, but the guard only bent and worked a lever near his feet. The door swung open.

"Thanks," Aderyn said, and she and Owen entered Market Warding.

Once through the door, Aderyn stopped, staring. Market Warding looked so much like Far Haven it stunned her. There were the same thatch-roofed houses, the same narrow streets. Even the women sweeping the paths in front of the houses and the children running screaming after one another in some game were the same.

"What's wrong?" Owen said.

Of course Owen wouldn't know how the sight of Market Warding triggered unexpected homesickness in Aderyn. She shook her head and said, "Nothing. Let's find the market. We can buy food there, and if there are questgivers, they'll be near the town center or at the inn." Having seen the town, she was certain she knew exactly where the market and inn were.

Nobody paid them any attention, or at least no obvious attention. High-level adventurers were always noticeable by their gear, flashy weapons or elaborate armor and clothing, and aside from Owen's sword there was nothing that openly declared them adventurers. Aderyn didn't mind. Beginning adventurers could be prey for more than just monsters.

The street widened as they approached the town center, which was a small paved plaza with a fountain at the center. Market stalls filled the plaza, and the air rang with the shouts of vendors and the buzz of a hundred quieter conversations.

The fountain was more ornate than Aderyn expected based on her comparison to Far Haven. It was of white marble with brass trumpets crowning the central pillar and little carved fish surrounding the basin. Aderyn recognized the fish from a book in her parents' library; they were called dolphins, and according to the book they were murderous bastards who fooled humans into thinking they were harmless with their large eyes and permanent smiles. She didn't know why anyone would put them on a fountain, unless maybe to show that cuteness could carry even a murderous bastard far.

"Cute, dolphins," Owen said.

"Sure," Aderyn said. "Let's see what kind of opportunities are available before we stock up. If we find a good quest, that might influence what we buy."

"There's the inn," Owen said, pointing. "I—hey, I can read the sign!"

"I should hope so," Aderyn said. Then, in a lower voice, she added, "Oh, you mean because you're... what you are."

"It only just occurred to me that maybe I only think I'm speaking English, and I was given your language when I arrived," Owen said in the same low voice. "Since there are words I can say that you don't know the meaning of."

"Doesn't that make it more likely that we both speak the same language and there are a few concepts we don't have in common? I mean, you don't have Swordsworn in your world, so that's a new word, but you understand it."

"Yes, but 'sword' and 'sworn' both have meaning in English..." Owen's voice trailed off. "Maybe you're right. If our languages *are* different, and the system replaced mine with yours, I wouldn't be able to remember words for concepts your language doesn't have. Like RenFaire or toilet."

"It seems like the simpler explanation to me, that we speak the same language."

"Anyway, I was thinking, if they aren't the same language, suppose I wasn't given reading skills?" He laughed. "And now I remember I can read the Codex, so I don't know what I was thinking. Making me fluent *and* literate... yeah, that's a stretch."

Aderyn had gotten used to Owen's odd gaps in knowledge during their journey, and his words reminded her forcefully that they needed to be careful in what he said now that they were in a town again. "All right, but try not to stand out, yes?"

"I know. I haven't forgotten, Aderyn." He sounded annoyed, and Aderyn felt bad at how often she'd told him variations on that warning. He wasn't stupid, and he would be fine.

They passed through the market, ignoring the cries of the vendors, and eventually reached the inn on the plaza's far side. *Inn of the Dancing Damsel,* the sign read. Owen pushed the door open, but stepped aside so Aderyn could enter first. It took her a moment to realize what he intended, and then she couldn't figure out what the point was. Yet another strange custom. At least this one wasn't so strange as to draw attention.

The inn's taproom smelled deliciously of new beer and roast chicken, and Aderyn's stomach rumbled, though it had only been a few hours since their noon meal. Quite a few people sat at the bar or at tables throughout the room, drinking and chatting cheerily with their neighbors. The barman, a tall, burly fellow with a bald head that gleamed in the light from the windows, glanced once at them and then returned his attention to the pint he was pouring.

"How do we find quests?" Owen said in a low voice. "I was expecting... never mind."

"Expecting what?"

His face had reddened. "Game stuff. A question mark hovering over someone's head. I know, it's stupid."

"That would actually be really useful," Aderyn said. "I think we have to talk to someone. Let's sit, and take a look at who's here."

She took a seat at the nearest unoccupied table, and Owen followed a moment later. One by one, she Assessed each person. Most of them were without classes, men and women who'd opted to reject the Call to be laborers and tradesmen in the sanctuary cities. Aderyn's parents had taught her not to be dismissive of the non-classed, saying everyone served their purpose, but Aderyn still couldn't understand why anyone wouldn't want to accept the Call.

The few adventurers sat together in pairs or in one small group of three. Aderyn saw two Staffsworn, a Deadeye with his longbow leaning against the bar, a Flamecrafter whose scorched clothing was a good testament to his spellslinger class, a Spellcrafter, and a Moon-lighter who sat close beside her companion, a Stalwart bigger than any man Aderyn had ever seen before. She could easily imagine him breaking a line of goblins with his bulk alone. The least of them was a good five levels higher than Aderyn and Owen, some of them high enough the system wouldn't tell Aderyn their level—just "exceeds authority limit." Probably none of them had quests to offer, or if they did, they would be far too difficult for level one adventurers.

"I'll talk to the barman," Aderyn said. "We can at least have something to drink."

She had to push politely between the Deadeye and the Spell-crafter, and then the barman ignored her for a few moments, Aderyn guessed because he wanted to show he didn't think much of level one adventurers. She didn't get upset. There was no point. She did indulge in a moment's fantasy of coming back here when she was level ten or eleven and watching him grovel at her feet.

"What'll it be, missy?" he finally said, in a voice that sounded like rock grating on rock.

"Two pints," Aderyn said, "and if you know of any little errands that need doing around here, my teammate and I are looking for work."

The barman gathered up two pint mugs and started pouring. "Can't say as I do," he said. "There's a dungeon that spawns every fortnight or so just west of here, but it's dormant now. Sorry."

Aderyn hadn't expected such an unhelpful response. "Really nothing? Nobody needs vermin cleaned out of their basement or help collecting magical components?"

"I said there wasn't anything," the barman replied, sounding annoyed. "That's two silver for the drinks."

Aderyn paid and took the mugs back to her table. Owen, who had clearly been listening, muttered, "That was useless. He could have been more help."

"He doesn't seem to like beginners much," Aderyn said.

Owen took a drink and made a slight face he controlled almost immediately. "So, now what?"

"I don't know." For the first time since setting out on this adventure, discouragement threatened to overwhelm Aderyn. How could they gain experience and levels if no one would give them a chance?

She drank thirstily, though Owen was right, the beer wasn't great. Still, it relaxed her somewhat. They'd figure something out if it meant knocking on every door in Market Warding.

CHAPTER SIX

The door opened, and a woman strode in. She was short and stocky, with fair hair cut bluntly to frame her face and a stance that made her look like she could give the enormous Stalwart a fair fight despite their size differences. She ignored Owen and Aderyn as she walked past their table to the bar.

The barman saw her coming. "You again," he said, sounding even less friendly than when he'd spoken to Aderyn. "I told you you're on a fool's errand. Find some other bar to peddle your losing cause in."

"It's not a losing cause, not so long as I have breath in my body," the woman said. "I'm looking for partners to help me clear out a goblin nest. You can keep all the treasure—I just want what they stole from my brother. It's an easy job."

Swiftly Aderyn Assessed the woman. She was a level one spell-slinger, not even high enough level to have gained a magical specialty like Flamecrafter or Bonemender. A beginner, like them. Not someone who ought to be able to issue a quest, but...

"How much treasure?" one of the Staffsworn asked.

"I don't know. You know what goblins are like—they collect everything. I'm sure there's enough there to make it worth your while." The woman sounded tired, like she'd repeated this speech a dozen times before.

"You're not selling yourself high, sweetheart," the other Staffsworn said with a chuckle. "Could be we go out there, and there's no treasure worth the effort."

"Then experience," the woman said.

"A drop in the bucket at our level," the first Staffsworn said. "I don't think so. Good luck finding someone, though." He turned back to his mug.

"It's not hard," the woman insisted to the room at large. "I just need a few more adventurers, that's all. It won't even take half a day."

"What's this thing they stole from your brother?" asked the Spellcrafter. "Is it worth anything?"

"To me, yes. It's not valuable otherwise." The woman's gaze became shifty, and Aderyn didn't need **[Sense Truth]** to know she was lying.

"Huh." The Spellcrafter pursed his lips in thought. "Hasn't it occurred to you that if you partner with a couple of much higher-level adventurers, they'll just take it and leave you behind?"

The woman didn't say anything. The Spellcrafter laughed a nasty laugh and turned his back on her.

"We'll do it," Aderyn announced.

All eyes fixed on her at once. The woman's gaze unfocused as she Assessed Aderyn and Owen. Aderyn braced herself for scorn over their low level, or questions about what a Warmaster was, but instead the woman said, "All right. What do I have to lose?"

"Your life," the Deadeye drawled, and the others all laughed.

Aderyn ignored them. A new system message had popped up.

A new quest is available: [Recover the Lost]
Accept? Y / N

When she'd accepted, a second message appeared.

Set as primary quest? Y / N

"Choose Yes," she told Owen, interpreting his confused look correctly. "That will keep our other quest from interfering with this one, and for now, it's our main quest."

More silver words gleamed in her field of vision:

You have received an invitation to join an adventuring team. Accept? Y / N

She wasn't sure she wanted anything so permanent a connection with the odd woman, but they had to be a team to complete the quest, so she accepted that one, too.

The faint display that was always there at the edges of her vision brightened, and below Owen's name, level and class was a new block of text:

Name: Livia
Class: Spellslinger <undetermined>
Level: 1

The woman, Livia, examined Aderyn and then Owen. "Let's go," she said, and turned to leave.

"You kids are going to die out there," the barman said. He didn't sound as if this worried him. "Don't be stupid. No trinket is worth your lives."

"We're not going to die," Aderyn assured him, though she didn't feel as confident as she sounded. "And you're buying us a round when we come back."

Outside the tavern, Aderyn stopped Livia before she could take more than a few steps toward the plaza. "Shouldn't we introduce ourselves formally? I'm Aderyn."

"Owen," Owen said.

Livia looked them over. "I'm Livia," she said. "Let's get moving. If we hurry, we can reach the goblin nest before nightfall."

Aderyn grabbed her arm, bringing her to a halt again. "Aren't goblins nocturnal? We should wait until morning."

Livia wrenched away. "This is my quest, and I'm in charge," she insisted. "Waiting is stupid. I want this over with."

Aderyn was about to reply sharply, something about getting killed through impatience being even stupider than waiting, but Owen overrode her with, "I can tell this means a lot to you. Maybe we should go somewhere and you can give us more information. Because Aderyn is right that we need to make a plan. I know waiting is hard."

Livia's hard, angry expression evaporated, and tears sprang to her eyes. She wiped them away roughly. "I'm sorry. I just—I've been trying to retrieve my brother's brooch for weeks, and the longer it takes, the more it feels like he's slipping away from me again. Come on. I'll buy dinner. But not here. That barman is a bastard."

Aderyn regarded Owen closely as they followed Livia across the plaza. They'd known each other three days, and she'd come to respect his fighting abilities, but she wouldn't have guessed a Swordsworn to be so insightful.

Livia found them an inn off the plaza on one of the side roads, a small two-story establishment called the Adventurers' Rest that was just rundown enough to discourage most potential patrons. Only three other men and one woman sat at tables spaced far enough apart they didn't have to pretend to be friendly. The taproom was clean, though, and the inn smelled of pine and not rotten food or sewage, and when they found a table, the serving maid brought them food without being prompted: big, greasy turkey legs and potatoes baked in their skins and fresh green beans. Aderyn hadn't thought she was all that hungry, but she ate enthusiastically.

"I adored my brother Lusian," Livia said. "He was seven years older than me and I thought he could do anything. We all believed he'd end up a spellslinger like Dad, he was that good at understanding magic even before he got the Call, but then the system made him a Moonlighter. There's never been any kind of a rogue in our family, so we thought it meant something special." She let out a short, harsh laugh. "Maybe it did. I don't know anymore. He's dead now, so it doesn't really matter."

"I'm sorry for your loss," Owen said.

"Thanks. It was a shock to hear he'd been killed, and by goblins, of all things. He was level five, and his team was ambushed." Livia blinked away more tears and took another huge bite of turkey. When she finished chewing, she added, "My mother gave Lusian our family emblem, since he was the oldest child and the first to leave for adventuring. It's a brooch with the family seal on it. It's magical, but not very—one of our ancestors was a Spellcrafter who enchanted it with a minor aura of protection. So it's not valuable except to me."

"And that's what you're after," Aderyn said.

"Right." Livia nodded. "I don't know what the quest bonus for helping me will be, but Market Warding has a bounty on goblins, so I know you'll get something. And, as I said, goblins are hoarders and I'm sure there will be treasure."

"We're interested in the experience," Owen said. "We're trying to gain levels before we set out for Guerdon Deep."

Aderyn nearly choked on her mouthful of turkey. They hardly knew this woman, and spreading their business out for anyone to hear could be dangerous. She chewed and swallowed hastily, but it was too late.

"Guerdon Deep?" Livia said, sounding surprised but not horrified. "That's a long way off. What's in Guerdon Deep for you?"

"I'm searching for my family," Owen said, just as Aderyn said, "It's nothing." They glared at each other. "It's not a secret," Owen said.

Aderyn thought of all the things about Owen that *were* secrets. In her opinion, he was far too cavalier about his identity for someone who risked being misidentified as a demon. Well, maybe if he was open about the false story, it would keep people from digging to find the truth. "We're hoping to find a high-level spellslinger who can cast a locating spell," she said. This was one of the "facts" she and Owen had agreed on over the days they'd traveled together.

"You're right, you won't find many spellslingers of that level in the sanctuary cities," Livia said. She didn't sound at all suspicious, and Aderyn relaxed. This could work, after all.

She drained her mug and looked around for the serving maid to bring her another. Her gaze passed over the man sitting at the nearest table. The plate in front of him was half-empty of the same meal she and her companions had gotten, and he was just tipping back the last of his drink. He didn't seem to notice her, but Aderyn felt the sudden tingling sensation of being closely observed and guessed he'd been listening to their conversation.

On a whim, she Assessed him:

Name: Weston

Class: Moonlighter

Level: 1

She made herself look away as if she'd only been mildly interested. He didn't look like a Moonlighter, master of infiltration and stealth. He was enormous, for one, tall even when seated and broad in the shoulders and chest. If not for her Assessment, she would have guessed him to be a Stalwart or maybe a really bulky Swordsworn. On the other hand, he *had* been listening in without any of them noticing. And right now he was doing a good job of pretending a lack of interest.

"That Moonlighter is paying us too much attention," she muttered, quietly enough she was sure he couldn't hear. "Don't look at him. The man at the nearest table."

To her relief, Owen and Livia both managed not to react. "How do you know he's a Moonlighter?" Livia asked.

"I Assessed him. Do you think he intends to rob us? Because it's three against one, and I don't care how big he is, those aren't good odds."

Livia's expression was a strange mixture of confusion and surprise. "You saw his class? That's impossible. You'd have to be at least level six."

Aderyn opened her mouth to protest and then shut it, considering Livia's words. "I...think it's an aspect of my class skill. I didn't realize it was unusual."

"Worry about it later," Owen said. "What should we do?"

The serving maid finally caught Aderyn's eye and nodded. Aderyn watched her hurry behind the bar to pour another mug of ale. "We should do something unexpected," she said.

The serving maid approached with the foaming mug. "Anything else I can get for you?"

Aderyn glanced once more at the Moonlighter and made a decision. "Why don't you ask our friend there what he's drinking, and get him another?"

She spoke loudly enough that the Moonlighter was startled into looking their way. "Me?" he said, the picture of confused innocence.

"Sure," Aderyn said. "Why don't you join us, since you were so interested in our conversation? Save you the trouble of eavesdropping."

Owen raised his eyebrows. "And you got on *my* case for sharing secrets," he muttered.

Aderyn didn't understand the phrase "got on my case," but Owen's expression and tone of voice were clear. "I think this gentleman has a proposition for us," she said, hoping her guess was right. At worst, they'd spend money on drinks for someone who intended to rob them.

The big man stood and bowed, too gracefully for someone his size. Given that he was still only level one, he couldn't be much older than the rest of them, but his height and muscles and heavy beard made him look older. He swept an unoccupied chair from beside their table, spun it around, and said, "I'm Weston. And, believe it or not, I'm a Moonlighter."

Now that Aderyn knew low-level adventurers wouldn't be able to discover someone's class through Assessment, she'd half expected Weston to lie about his class. All the classes that depended on stealth and cunning, the Lightfingers and the Moonlighters and the Spiders, had reputations for being sneaky and treacherous as well, and she could almost sympathize if he'd wanted them to get to know him without any preconceptions. Of course, he could have lied to fool them into complacency so he could attack them, and that won him no sympathy at all.

But he'd been honest, and Aderyn relaxed, though not by much. She let Owen and Livia introduce themselves, then said, "I'm Aderyn, and I'm a Warmaster."

Weston's eyes widened, and he let out a little snort of amusement. "No," he said. "I had you pegged as another Moonlighter, with as good as you were at noticing my interest. A Warmaster. Haven't seen many of you around."

He looked like he wanted to laugh harder, and Aderyn flushed an angry red. "It's not a useless class," she said, realizing as she spoke that that was exactly the sort of thing someone with a useless class would say.

"Of course not," Weston said. "Sorry. I've only ever heard stories, and those can be wrong."

"You should watch your tongue if you don't know what you're talking about," Owen said. "Just because someone doesn't deal damage directly doesn't make them useless."

"It's not important," Aderyn said, getting herself under control. "I want to know why you were listening, if it wasn't to rob us."

"Rob you?" Weston sounded genuinely astonished. "Of course not. Moonlighters aren't thieves, or at least they don't have to be. I don't rob people."

"Sorry," Aderyn said, about as genuinely as he'd said it to her moments before. "So, what was it you wanted?"

"It sounded like you were planning a quest. Eliminating a goblin nest, is that it?" Weston leaned in close, prompting the rest of them to do the same. "It happens that I'm looking for a way to earn some money, and experience would not be scoffed at. I'm thinking three people is a little light for a raid on a goblin nest. Four would be safer."

"You want to join us?" Livia said.

"Why not? We're all just starting out, and nobody else is likely to give any of us a chance." Weston shrugged. "And it's not like it's forever. We do the job, we earn our reward, and we're all a little closer to fame and fortune as adventurers."

Aderyn caught Owen's eye. It was too bad they didn't have some sort of paired skill for communicating mind to mind. But he nodded, and Aderyn could tell he wasn't worried about giving his secret away. Of course, he was *never* worried about that, given her observations of him over the past three days, so that didn't reassure her. She, on the other hand, worried about it all the time, and even so, she didn't think Weston was any more a danger to them than Livia.

"It's your quest," Aderyn told Livia. "Your decision."

Livia nodded. "It's sound logic. All right. You're in."

The faint display that hovered at the edge of Aderyn's vision flickered rapidly, and Weston's information joined Owen and Livia's at the upper left of her range of sight. Weston looked relieved. He might have been more anxious for this opportunity than he seemed.

"Let's drink to our partnership," Livia said, waving down the serving maid again. "May it be successful in every way!"

Aderyn drank with the others. An adventuring team. It wasn't exactly what she'd dreamed of—her dreams had involved close friendships, the kind where you'd give your life for the others, and maybe a romance—but you had to start somewhere, right? And she liked Owen, and Livia and Weston seemed all right. For a first team, this wasn't bad.

CHAPTER SEVEN

Aderyn woke at dawn the next morning to the sound of someone rapping loudly on her door. "Let's go!" Weston called out. "Daylight's wasting!"

Aderyn groaned and rolled out of bed, which was unexpectedly comfortable for the quality of the inn. She opened the door, but Weston had already moved on to Livia's room. "Aren't Moonlighters supposed to, you know, be alert at night? Why are you such an early riser?"

"Always have been," Weston said cheerfully. "Asleep by ten-thirty, that's me, and up with the sun. Come on, let's go! The goblins will all be asleep by now."

Aderyn groaned again and shut the door. She pulled on trousers and shirt over the shift and drawers she wore to sleep in, slid her feet into her boots, and swiftly packed the few things she'd taken out of her knapsack last night. When she left the room, Weston was heading down the stairs. "I'll see about getting us food," he said with a wave.

Aderyn followed him, but stopped when a door opened abruptly in front of her and Owen came out. "Sorry," he said. "And I thought I was a morning person. Weston has enough energy for three people."

"He's right about getting an early start," Aderyn said, "but I don't think it's fair that he should be so cheerful about it."

The door beyond Owen's opened, and Livia slouched out. Her eyes were open the merest slits, and her short blond hair was messy in back like she'd just risen and hadn't brushed it. "How big a penalty is it if you kill a teammate?" she muttered. "I mean, if it's justifiable murder."

"He's not that bad," Aderyn said, amused.

"I beg to differ," Livia said. "Anyone that disgustingly cheerful at this hour deserves a knife in the back." She stomped down the stairs.

"She'll feel better when she's had something to eat," Owen said, but he didn't sound certain.

Weston had some measure of self-control, because when Aderyn and Owen joined him and Livia in the taproom, the two were sitting opposite each other in silence, Livia with her arms folded on the table and her head resting atop them, Weston digging into a pile of hashed potatoes flecked with ham and dripping with melted cheese. "I told them to bring more," he mumbled through his food. "Livia says she only wants coffee."

"You have coffee in—" Owen blurted out. Aderyn stepped on his foot in warning.

"I know, it's a lot, but I believe in a healthy, filling breakfast to start the day," Weston said.

Aderyn and Owen sat and ate what the serving maid brought them. It was delicious, and Aderyn washed her hash down with new ale and thought maybe Weston had a point about hearty breakfasts.

The smell of hot coffee wafted toward them shortly after the food appeared, and Livia lifted her head when the serving maid set down not a cup of the aromatic beverage, but an entire pot. "Bless you to live a thousand years," Livia moaned, and poured herself a cup and drank it down black. The others stopped eating to watch as she downed a second cup, apparently unaware that it was steaming hot. "Better," she said finally.

"What do you do when you're adventuring and you're between towns?" Owen asked, sounding amused.

"I have a coffee pot, ground beans, extra water, and the ability to spark a fire anywhere I want," Livia said, sipping her third cup. "So far it's never been an issue. And don't *you* say it's a terrible vice I'll regret someday," she added, fixing Weston with a bleary eye. "Everybody needs one vice, my mother always says, and mine is coffee. Yours is clearly something awful like an exercise regimen."

"Exercise stirs the blood," Weston said, adopting a falsely prim attitude that his wicked smile ruined.

"So, where is this goblin nest?" Aderyn said, wanting to stave off an argument, however friendly.

"East of Market Warding, maybe a little south of east," Livia said. "I have a map the survivors drew me." She stopped smiling. "We might need to search for a bit, so I guess it's better we waited for morning."

"I have a compass, if that helps," Aderyn offered.

"It will, thanks." Livia sipped her coffee again. Her eyes were now fully open, and she seemed alert. "I was told the nest has four or five adult goblins and maybe seven adolescents. That's a challenge to a group our size and level, but not impossible, especially if we don't rush in screaming. The goblins were only able to... to kill my brother and most of his team because the goblins took them by surprise, at night." She wiped her eyes. "I'm fine. Let's get the bastards."

"What else do you know?" Aderyn asked. "Location, terrain, the size of the nest? Is it underground or on the surface?"

"There's a dead forest out that way," Livia said. "The goblins control parts of it, and they've reinforced the tree cover with brambles. We might be fighting in close quarters."

"Maybe," Aderyn said. "But that gives me an idea."

THEY LEFT MARKET WARDING AN HOUR AFTER SUNRISE
and walked east, following the guidance of Aderyn's compass. There
was no road, because there were no settlements east of Market Warding. Instead, grassy plains spread out before them, dusty and dry and
yellow. It was going to be a scorcher of a day, and Aderyn was glad
again that they'd left so early. She warned herself not to be too eager,
but it was hard not to imagine sweeping through the goblin nest,
slaughtering the monsters, and returning to Market Warding by
noon.

She made herself focus on the compass needle, keeping a straight
course, or mostly straight course, thanks to what Livia had said about
the nest being south of east. Ahead, a smudge along the horizon
showed the forest that was their goal. Her boots crunched through
the dry grasses, pleasantly echoed by the footsteps of her teammates.
A light wind blew from the north, not one that would warn the
goblins with their scent, but not one that helped them, either. It
didn't matter. The goblins were asleep; the team had the advantage.

"The nest is about a mile outside town," Livia said. "Maybe a
mile and a quarter. I'm not entirely sure."

"That's awfully close to town for monsters to live," Owen said.

"These goblins don't approach Market Warding, and they
haven't stolen any babies. I was told they aren't enough of a threat to
entice adventurers to do anything about them." Livia shrugged her
knapsack higher on her shoulder. "Not like the dungeon northwest
of here."

"We heard about that," Aderyn said. "That awful barman said it
was dormant now."

"It's popular, so you have to be quick if you want to clear it,"
Livia said.

"What makes it popular?" Owen asked. He was getting better at
not asking awkward questions, like "what's a dungeon?" and "why is
it dormant?"

"For one thing, it's bigger on the inside," Livia said. "It looks like a stone cottage, but there's a maze inside that changes frequently and at least five rooms. Which means it's different every time, so you can defeat it more than once and still gain experience. The treasure is different, too. Wildly different, as in sometimes adventurers find gemstones the size of a hen's egg and sometimes all they get is a tin whistle. There's a breed of adventurers who love that kind of gamble."

"I think I'd rather have a guaranteed payoff," Weston said.

"But you chose this quest," Owen said. "Isn't that a gamble, too, given that goblins don't always collect valuables?"

"The challenge isn't as high on this quest, so it's reasonable if the treasure isn't as good. That dungeon, though... it's much riskier, and I'm not the sort to risk my life for a tin whistle."

"You are definitely an atypical Moonlighter," Aderyn said, making Weston laugh.

"I don't know why classes have to fall into types," he said. "Of course, I don't know any of you well enough to know if *you* fit your class types."

Aderyn braced herself for him to say something about useless Warmasters, but he fell silent.

They walked a while longer, not talking, until the smudge on the horizon grew larger and more defined. After a while, it was clearly visible as trees, but not leafy and green as Aderyn was used to from the forest outside Far Haven. Leafless branches reached spiky arms toward the cloudless sky, looking more like dead sticks than living trees. At first, Aderyn thought a terrible fire had ravaged the place, the wood was that black and lifeless, but as they drew nearer, she saw no char or other evidence of burning. Whatever had killed the forest had left no sign of itself. That chilled Aderyn more than the thought of a raging forest fire.

"I don't see any brambles," Owen said. "Nothing that indicates the goblins have fortified a spot."

"We'll have to go deeper," Livia said. "Maybe no adventurers come here, and the goblins think they're safe, but they're not so stupid as to live right out on the edge of the forest."

"Stay close," Aderyn suggested. "But not too close."

"I'll go first." Weston shrugged out of his pack, keeping only his sword, which was a broad-bladed weapon shorter than Owen's, and a long, thin knife sheathed at his other side. Aderyn and the others followed his lead. Their gear made a small heap that looked terribly defenseless all by itself in the grass, but nobody was going to disturb it, and they needed not to be weighed down by bedrolls and cooking gear if they might end up inside a goblin nest.

Aderyn felt unexpectedly uneasy without her pack. She had no weapon, which now definitely seemed like an oversight, given that she did have some skill with a sword despite weapon use not being one of her class skills. When they got back to Market Warding, she'd buy one. Until then, there wasn't anything she could do but assist Owen and maybe Weston, if he was willing to listen to a useless Warmaster's advice.

Weston led the way, slipping beneath the trees almost silently. He was good, Aderyn realized, despite his size; he seemed to have an instinct for where to step to avoid dry fallen branches, and while he wasn't invisible, he managed not to draw attention to himself. Maybe his class wasn't such a joke, after all.

They walked through the forest for several minutes. With no foliage to deflect the sun's rays, the heat grew more intense as the sun rose. Soon Aderyn was sweating lightly beneath her arms and around the back of her neck at her hairline. She kept her attention on the bases of the trees, looking for signs of goblin activity, but every so often her gaze swept the sky and the branches. She couldn't stop to examine them closely, but the branches seemed drained of life entirely, as if their sap had been sucked away. Was it a natural effect, or a monster's attack? She didn't know of any monster that could do something like that, and she hoped, if it had been a monster, that the thing was well away by now.

Weston's steps slowed just as Owen said, "Brambles. I think we've found it."

"I'll scout the extent of the nest, see if I can find the entrance," Weston said.

"Look for more than one," Aderyn suggested. "They probably have some hidden exits."

Weston nodded and strode toward the thicket, his steps slowing the nearer he got to it, and vanished around its far side. Aderyn examined the brambles. They weren't what she'd expected, which was dead, prickly bushes heaped up like a barrier. Instead, they were tree branches probably lopped off dead trees elsewhere in the forest. The goblins had arranged them far more intelligently than she'd thought the little monsters capable of, slotting branches together to make rounded walls of spiky wood. Aderyn couldn't see farther than the first layer. She relaxed. It was the perfect setup for her plan.

After what felt like an hour, but which according to Livia's pocket watch was only twenty minutes, Weston appeared around the far end of the nest and loped back toward them. "Three entrances, one of them very well hidden," he said.

"That's the one we'll leave open," Aderyn said. "They might not be smart enough to reason well, but if they are, they'll believe we missed that one because it was concealed, and that will make them underestimate us. We'll set fire to the other entrances and position ourselves at the third entrance, and then... it's just a matter of waiting for them to flee."

"You're sure this will work?" Weston said, not hiding his skepticism.

"Of course," Aderyn said. She wasn't sure, but it was the solution that made the most sense, given that there were three times as many goblins as there were teammates. She spoke confidently, though, so nobody would pick up on her doubts.

"Aderyn understands tactics," Owen assured Weston. "This will work."

Weston shrugged. "It makes sense. We ought to light both fires at the same time, though, so let me show you the entrances and we can split up to do that first."

They all moved as quietly as they could, though Weston still made much less noise than the others. The first entrance was just out of sight from where they'd approached, but it was obvious once they rounded the side of the nest: a hole in the thicket about three feet across, gaping and black and smelling of rancid goblin sweat. Aderyn regarded it with distaste. How fortunate that they wouldn't have to crawl inside, because if the whole nest had ceilings that low, they'd be fighting at a serious disadvantage.

"Owen and I will wait here, and Weston, you and Livia take the other entrance," she said.

Weston didn't argue about her issuing orders. "How will we know when to light the fire?"

"I'll send up a signal," Livia said. She held out her cupped hand and whispered a few indistinct words. A flicker of light like a tiny flame sprang into being, growing rapidly until it was a glowing orb two inches across. Livia tossed it into the air, where it gleamed brightly for a few seconds before going out. "It lasts only for a short time after I lose contact with it, but it's noticeable. I'll throw it high above the nest before I set my fire."

"Perfect," Owen said. He pulled a <**Matchlighter**> from where it was stuck into his belt and brandished it. "We'll be ready."

CHAPTER EIGHT

When Weston and Livia were gone, Aderyn watched Owen click the <**Matchlighter**> a few times. It was a long rod of oiled metal with a lever at one end that, when pressed, brought the striking surface of the <**Matchlighter**> into contact with the magic-infused steel and made a spark. The spark traveled down the length of the rod and ignited a flame, so the user's hand wasn't near the fire to risk burning herself. <**Matchlighters**> were the simplest magical items a Spellcrafter could create, which meant they were cheap and readily available. Aderyn's father had taught her to use an old-fashioned flint and steel as well, though, saying, "You never know when magic won't be there for you."

"You sure do like that thing," Aderyn remarked.

"We have lighters like this in my world, except they use lighter fluid, not magic." Owen clicked the little flame into life again.

Aderyn didn't chastise him for mentioning his own world. It wasn't as if Weston and Livia were within earshot. She watched the sky and listened to the erratic clicking noise. Soon, a tiny ball of light streaked overhead, rising to a point above the center of the nest and then winking out. "It's time." She grabbed hold of a thick branch and wrenched at it with her whole strength so it sagged, half-blocking the entrance.

Owen applied the <**Matchlighter**> to various points around the entrance, concentrating on the branch Aderyn had moved. The dry, dead wood caught fire readily, and in seconds, a crackling blaze tore across the branches, blocking the entrance. Aderyn and Owen backed away from the intense heat.

"Crap," Owen said. "Weston didn't say where the third entrance was."

"It's got to be on the far side. Let's circle around to meet them. And don't say 'crap.' Nobody in this world says that. I don't even know what it means."

They started running. "It's a politer word for 'shit,'" Owen said.

"Then say 'shit.' It's a swear word. It's not about politeness."

"Do we really want to have this discussion now?"

Aderyn shook her head. Weston and Livia were approaching from the other side. "It's not important."

Weston was pointing at the brambles. "There," he said when he was near enough for speech. "That little hole."

"That little hole" was much smaller than the entrance Owen had just burned. "Are you sure that's big enough for the goblins to escape through?" Aderyn asked.

"I've talked to adventurers who fought goblins. They said to watch out for the slippery little buggers because they can squeeze through cracks a cat wouldn't fit between." Weston drew his sword. "Let's stand where they won't see us right away."

"Livia and I will go over there," Aderyn said. "You and Owen stand out of sight on either side of the hole, and then they'll be drawn toward us and won't be expecting you."

Owen nodded. "But stay well back, all right?" he said. "If they escape us, you'll be in danger."

"I have a spell for that," Livia said, but she retreated with Aderyn so there were a few dead trees between them and the hole.

They waited. The crackle of the fire was audible now despite the flames being distant enough not to be visible. Then a high-pitched scream cut through the air, chilling Aderyn's blood. She forced her hands to relax out of fists and shook them to restore the blood flow. Beside her, Livia was flexing her fingers as well and muttering to herself. Despite her fear, Aderyn's excitement mounted. Her first real battle as an adventurer!

More screams, and a loud chittering noise, emerged from the nest, muffled by the branches. Aderyn had the sudden worry that her plan was stupid. They should have left people to watch the other exits—but there weren't enough of them to do that safely—but suppose the goblins put out the fire? Suppose they had an exit Weston hadn't found?

Movement at the hole dragged her out of her worrying, and a shape appeared, crawling through the tiny hole. It had a bulbous grayish-brown head roughly the color of the branches set on a skinny neck that surely couldn't support it. It wriggled free of the hole, faster than Aderyn could have managed, with long, wiry arms ending in claw-tipped fingers. It wore nothing but a loincloth that by the smell was made from uncured animal hide, and its toes bore the same sharp claws as its fingers.

Aderyn saw all this in the moment it took for the system to present her with information:

Name: Goblin, Juvenile
Type: Monstrosity
Power Level: 1
Assess?

It now took her only a long blink of both eyes to trigger her **[Improved Assess 1]** skill. Familiar blue lines of light swept over the creature, and a couple of blue dots converged on the goblin's throat and chest. Unexpectedly, a red glow shone over the back of the goblin's outsized skull.

"Aim for the—" she began, but Owen swung his sword in that

moment, decapitating the creature. "Yes, that!" she said instead. "Or the chest. Avoid the head!" She thought that warning would be more useful to a Staffsworn, someone whose weapon did bludgeoning or crushing damage, but every bit of information was important.

Congratulations! You have defeated [Juvenile Goblin].
You have earned [25 XP]

Another goblin was emerging from the nest. It was chittering rapidly and didn't seem to notice its fallen nestmate. Weston's sword caught it in the middle of its chest, impaling it so it jerked like a fish on a line. Owen's sword was only a second behind, slashing across the goblin's ribcage. Again, the system message appeared, marking the goblin's death.

Owen dragged the headless corpse out of immediate sight of the hole and wiped his hands on his trousers with a grimace. No more goblins emerged. Aderyn's fears of having guessed wrong resurfaced. She took a step away from Livia, in the direction of the fire she and Owen had set.

The hole exploded in a silent burst of tree limbs scattering in every direction. Three much bigger shapes emerged from the newly-enlarged exit. They were still shorter than the teammates, but bulkier than the juveniles, with heavily-muscled arms and shoulders and necks corded with sinew. Their rough, grainy skin made them look like animate trees, except for their enormous round heads.

Name: Goblin
Type: Monstrosity
Power Level: 2

Aderyn's heart pounded so hard it hurt. She focused on Assessing the creatures, though she had some guesses about their weaknesses. Sure enough, the neck was no longer a weak point. "Belly or chest!" she shouted.

Owen didn't acknowledge her. He parried a powerful blow from the nearest goblin, who wielded a much-notched meat cleaver that looked like it might more easily break bones than cut flesh. The goblin opened its fanged mouth and screamed in Owen's face, swinging again. This time, Owen dodged the blow entirely and thrust his sword at the goblin's midsection, impaling it. The goblin folded up over the sword. Owen booted it off the length of steel and moved to intercept the next goblin.

**Congratulations! You have defeated [Goblin].
You have earned [50 XP]**

"They're coming after us!" Livia shouted. Aderyn realized a group of the juveniles had left the nest and were headed toward them. The goblins screamed and waved their clawed hands and made those horrible chittering noises like thousands of insect legs skittering across a marble floor.

Aderyn froze. No helpful Warmaster information sprang to mind. Then Livia took two steps forward and chanted loudly a string of words Aderyn didn't understand, gesturing with one hand like sweeping a pile of crumbs off a table.

The ground in front of Livia rippled as if she was a stone dropped into a pool of water. The ripples extended outward, sweeping past the juveniles. In the next moment, the goblins had stopped moving. They screamed horribly and tried to lift their feet, but they were stuck fast as if in mud, or tar.

"It won't hold them for long," Livia said, shouting over the noise. "We should move." Weston had spotted the group of juveniles and was headed toward the trapped goblins.

A couple more notices of goblin deaths and gained experience had popped up while Livia was casting her spell. Aderyn wished briefly there was a way to suppress those messages while they were still fighting. "This way," she said, grabbing Livia's arm and hurrying her to a spot behind Owen. Owen spitted a smaller goblin and booted its body away. He had some long claw marks down his face that bled heavily, and his shirt was torn, but no blood showed there.

"How many more?" Owen shouted. He moved to put himself more directly between Aderyn and another of the big goblins.

Aderyn frantically counted back. "Three goblins and five juveniles killed," she called out.

Owen nodded, but didn't reply. He was too busy fighting the goblin, who had an actual sword and seemed to know how to use it.

Livia suddenly screamed and ran past Aderyn. "That's Lusien's sword!"

"No, stop!" Aderyn yelled. She flung herself on Livia, bringing the shorter woman to the ground just as the goblin's next swing would have taken her head off. "You'll be killed!"

Livia struggled under Aderyn's weight, screaming obscenities at the goblin. She was gradually wiggling free, and just as Aderyn knew she couldn't hold Livia down anymore, the goblin's chest erupted in a spray of blood as Weston impaled it from behind. Livia collapsed, sobbing.

The goblins who'd been mired in mud started to extricate themselves. Aderyn sat by Livia and made the spellslinger look at her. "Livia, there's still too many of them. What can you do to stop them?"

Livia stared at her blankly, not even blinking. Aderyn hauled off and slapped Livia across the face. "Wake up! We need to stop them or Weston and Owen will be overwhelmed!"

Livia shook her head as if coming out of a dream. "I don't," she said, then looked at the oncoming mass of goblins. She raised her hands and spoke more nonsense words. These sounded soothing, like a mother singing a lullaby to her baby, and so it didn't surprise Aderyn when the goblins again stumbled to a halt, this time with their eyes glazed over like they were dazed.

With that, the tide broke. Weston and Owen moved through the trees, finishing off goblins left mesmerized by Livia's spell, and in only a few minutes, the teammates were the only living creatures in that part of the forest. Silence descended, broken only by the crackling of the still-burning fires.

No one spoke. Aderyn looked around at the fallen goblins. She wanted to feel victorious, but all she felt was cold. It was stupid, because goblins were vicious killers who preyed on human children, and these goblins had killed Livia's brother and his teammates. But it still felt strange, having gone so deliberately into the wilderness to defeat monsters. Aderyn hoped it didn't mean she was too soft to be an adventurer.

"Is that all of them?" Weston said.

Livia collected her dead brother's sword and held it loosely in one hand. "I was told five adults and at least seven juveniles," she said. Her voice was distant. Maybe she felt the way Aderyn did.

"Let's count," Owen said. Then he froze. "Do you smell that?"

Aderyn sniffed. She smelled blood, and gore, and the stink of goblin. And, more distant, the hot scent of burning trees. On the far side of the nest, where she and Owen had lit their fires, a brighter light burned.

"Crap," she said. "I think we set the forest on fire."

Chapter Nine

S he ran for the fire, but Owen and Weston quickly outpaced her, and by the time she reached the burning entrance to the goblin nest, they were already there, staring. Golden fire outlined the stark, dead branches, leaping from tree to tree, but in a slow, lazy way. The growth of the fire reminded Aderyn of honey dripping off the end of a knife, gathering itself before making the languid jump to its neighbor.

"It's going to set the whole forest on fire," she said.

Livia came up behind her. "Do we care?" she asked. "It's not like anything but monsters use this place."

"Once it gets to the grasslands, there'll be no stopping it," Owen said. "I've seen prairie fires before. They burn everything in their path. It will set Market Warding on fire."

"We have to stop it," Aderyn said. "I don't know how."

"A fire break," Owen said. "That means a gap between the fire and the rest of the flammable stuff, a gap where there's nothing to burn. A trench, or a bare place—sometimes firefighters start a different fire to cut off a wildfire. Something empty."

"We can't dig a trench," Weston said. "Even if we had tools, there's no time. And we can't cut trees down, because swords are all wrong for that."

"I have an idea," Livia said. "There's a spell called *break* that, well, breaks fragile things. It normally doesn't work on trees, because they're not dry enough, but these trees might be vulnerable."

"Let's see," Owen said. "Aderyn, where's the best place to make a fire break?"

Aderyn couldn't stop staring at the fire. "This is my fault," she said. "I should have known what would happen."

Owen grabbed her by the shoulders and shook her. "Stop," he said. "We all agreed on the plan, and you're not the only one who should have guessed this possibility. You want to blame yourself, do it later. For now, let's fix this mistake."

Aderyn blinked. She'd never realized Owen's eyes were blue, a sort of greenish-blue, but with his face inches from hers, his eyes were all she could see. "You're right," she said. "All right. I think... the fire's not spreading fast, because there's no wind, so I think if we get just a little ways in front of it, we can make a line where there's nothing to burn."

They ran, glancing over their shoulders at the spreading fire, to where Livia took up a solid stance like she intended to wrestle the trees instead of breaking them. With a few muttered words, she gestured as if she was throwing an invisible rock at one of the slimmer trees. A loud crack echoed through the dead forest, and stark black lines radiated out along the tree's trunk like a fracture. Weston took hold of the tree and pulled, bringing it down and uprooting its base as well.

"That works," Owen said. "We'll drag the trees away, and Livia, you keep doing that, all right?"

For a feverish half hour, they worked without speaking as the roar of the fire drew nearer and the crack of breaking wood filled the air. By the time the fire reached them, they had created a bare zone ten feet wide that curved around the burning trees. Aderyn watched, feeling numb, as the last tree before the gap burned, reaching out its limbs to—nothing. The smell of char clogged her nostrils, but she was too tired to care.

The appearance of a new system message startled her:

Congratulations! You have completed the quest [Protect Market Warding].
You have been awarded [300 XP]

"I'm not sure we should gain experience for doing something to reverse a problem we caused," Weston said, but he was smiling.

"Hey, it's a win, and I'll take it," Owen said. "Now, let's go see what the goblins left behind."

They trudged back through the forest, which was truly dead now, burned and stinking and gray with ash. As flammable as the trees were, they hadn't been much in the way of fuel for the fire, and by the time the teammates returned to the goblin nest, the fires had burned themselves out. Now the nest looked fragile, like a kick would bring it down. Owen kicked it, then stepped back, coughing and choking on the cloud of ash he'd stirred up. "Well, that was stupid," he said.

"Not as stupid as setting the fire in the first place," Aderyn said. "I'm really sorry. That could have been disastrous."

"Owen's right, we all had the chance to realize what could happen," Livia said, "and the plan worked, so I don't think there's any reason to place blame." She took hold of a charred branch and wrenched it away, less vigorously than Owen had. "We have to take this thing apart. There's still a chance there could be more goblins in there."

By the time they'd opened enough of a passage that they could fit inside without crouching, it was past noon, they were filthy, and Aderyn was painfully aware that no amount of chores at home had prepared her for this kind of physical exertion. But she didn't suggest they rest and eat something. She, like all of them, was increasingly eager to find out what treasure they'd earned.

The goblin nest was, thankfully, empty of goblins. It also wasn't as big as Aderyn had thought, looking at it from the outside. There was one big central chamber, and four smaller rooms that looked like they might have been sleeping rooms from the heaps of garbage and torn cloth piled into loose hollows like nests.

They searched all the rooms, taking their time though Aderyn, for one, was disgusted at the smell coming from the sleeping rooms. There weren't many possessions in those chambers, let alone valuable ones; they found a scattering of coins that amounted to ninety-three silver, as well as a scratched copper medallion set with a poor-quality amethyst and a silver serving spoon with some lord's device engraved on the handle.

The goblins had stored most of their hoard in the central chamber, some of it in a wooden chest with the lock broken off, the rest of it piled at random throughout the room. Again, most of it was junk. Broken odds and ends, books whose pages were torn out, most of a wooden chess set that had once been painted red and white. Aderyn's eyes filled with tears when she found a child's wooden rattle stained with blood. Her earlier misgivings about having killed the goblins vanished.

Livia knelt before the wooden chest, sifting through the contents. She made a pile to one side of possibly valuable objects and a larger pile of garbage on the other side. Finally, she stopped. "I found it," she said, holding up a silver brooch. Aderyn and the others joined her. The brooch had a simple clasp and wasn't much more than a circle of silver, on which was engraved a stylized greyhound leaping across the circle, surrounded by a garland of oak leaves.

"It's beautiful," Owen said. "I can't tell if it's magical, though."

"I can," Livia said. "But that's not the important thing."

Suddenly, a system message flashed in front of Aderyn's face.

Congratulations! You have completed the quest [Recover the Lost].
You have been awarded [500 XP]

And a moment later, more letters appeared.

Welcome to Level Two

Aderyn gasped. "Did you see that?"

"Level two!" Owen exclaimed. He sounded tired and out of breath, but cheerful.

Livia didn't say anything. Her eyes were unfocused as if she was looking at the Codex. "Did you gain a level too?" Aderyn asked. She thought about Assessing Livia to find out for herself, but for once she felt awkward about doing so, as if that was too intrusive.

"I did," Livia said. "I achieved a specialization. I'm an Earthbreaker."

"That makes sense, given all the earth-related things you did," Aderyn said, trying to sound encouraging. Spellslingers could be sensitive about the specializations the system gave them, particularly since from what Aderyn could tell, there was a ranking among them based on one's elemental affinity.

"It's fine," Livia said. She didn't sound like she was faking enthusiasm. "It's not that. I didn't have a specialization I was hoping for, so I'm not disappointed. It's just that now I don't know what else I can do. I've had this goal for so long, I never really thought about what would come after."

Weston, crouching beside Livia, gripped her shoulder in reassurance. "You don't have to decide right away," he said. "Let's go back to town and sell the rest of this stuff and split the proceeds. Take a night to rest. Tomorrow will look different."

Livia nodded. "It's a good plan. I'm not sure how to sell these things, though. I'm actually bad with money. Never really had to worry about it before now, to be honest."

Aderyn had started to wonder, after seeing the family brooch, whether Livia came from wealth. She decided not to pry, not now. "If we were back in Far Haven, I'd know who would give me an honest deal."

"Don't worry about it," Weston said. "I love haggling, and I'm good at it. I'm sure I'll get us a good rate." He began collecting the trinkets. "Let's gather our gear—oh, actually we should clean that wound, Owen."

Owen touched the side of his face and winced as his fingers encountered the long claw marks. They'd stopped bleeding, but the edges looked black. "Damn. I hope these aren't infected. Do we have antiseptic or something?"

Aderyn gritted her teeth as Weston and Livia exchanged confused glances. "I left my waterskin with our gear, so let's hurry and I can wash those gashes. And maybe someone in Market Warding will sell us a healing salve," she said, pretending not to have heard the alien word he'd used.

Owen didn't seem to realize his mistake. He gathered up his share of the treasure and followed Aderyn out of the forest, back to where they'd left their knapsacks, and submitted patiently to her washing his wounds without wincing more than a few times. Aderyn didn't like the raw look of them, even after they were cleaned. A healing salve would be important not just for healing the wounds without leaving scars, but for keeping them from festering. There was no telling what kind of filth goblins might have on their claws.

By the time they returned to Market Warding, Aderyn's worries had multiplied. Owen was walking more slowly, and his eyes were glassy and his face flushed with fever. Her intention had been for all of them to go to the market to sell their treasure, but when they reached the inn they'd stayed at the previous night, Owen sat at the first table inside the taproom door and dropped his knapsack like he couldn't carry it any further. "I just need a rest, and some water," he said.

"You stay with him," Livia told Aderyn. "I know where I can find a healing salve."

"And I'll go sell this stuff," Weston said.

They were both gone before Aderyn could protest. Sighing, she left her knapsack on the floor beside Owen's and walked over to the bar to ask for a pitcher of water and some cups. When she returned to the table, Owen was leaning over it, the unwounded side of his face pressed against the none-too-clean wood. "Sit up," she said. "You need water."

"I feel awful," Owen said, but he sat upright and accepted a tin cup with both hands. He drank thirstily, set the cup aside, and lay down again. "My head feels like it's on fire, and it's throbbing, too. Do you people have antibiotics?"

"Stop using strange words," Aderyn hissed. She put her hand on his forehead and winced at how hot his skin was. "Livia will find something to heal the infection."

"You know about infection, but not about antibiotics," Owen murmured. "Your world is weird."

"Just don't talk, all right?"

Owen closed his eyes. "What if Weston steals all that stuff and runs?"

"What if—no. He wouldn't do that." But now Aderyn couldn't stop considering it. It wasn't like they knew Weston all that well, and now that the quest was over and he had the experience from it, there was no reason for him to stay with the team. And he *was* a Moonlighter, after all.

Aderyn focused on the faint images at the edges of her vision. Weston's name was still there, so he hadn't legged it yet, but more worryingly, the thick blue vertical line next to Owen's name was half as long as it had been before the fight, and as she watched, it quivered and shrank a little further. Without thinking, she clasped Owen's hand and was reassured to feel him squeeze hers in return. "It will be fine," she said. "And the treasure isn't important."

"You're scaring me," Owen said with a weak smile. "Am I dying?"

"No," Aderyn lied.

CHAPTER TEN

They sat together as Owen's health bar continued to shrink, the tiniest fraction at a time, and Aderyn cursed Livia, then Weston, then Livia again. Where was the woman? Maybe she'd seen the pointlessness of continuing with this team now that the quest was over, too, and she wasn't coming back. The whole brutal senselessness of Owen dying in a world that wasn't his own over a stupid goblin scratch made Aderyn want to scream. Owen's breathing continued strong, but his eyes were closed and his cheek looked even more inflamed than before.

The door to the taproom banged open, startling Aderyn into looking up. Livia hurried toward them, followed by a lanky young man whose reddish-brown hair flopped forward across his face as he ran. "I'm sorry it took so long, but the Spiritsmith was gone, and this fellow insisted he wouldn't just give me the salve," Livia panted.

The lanky young man dropped to his knees beside Owen and gently lifted his head. Owen didn't resist, but he didn't move like he was unconscious, and Aderyn's heart ached again. "That's because goblin claws carry disease, and a salve might not be enough," the young man said. He prodded at the claw marks. "Right. Can you sit up?"

Owen slowly pushed himself upright, wobbling as his hands pressed against the table. Aderyn hurried to put her arm around his shoulders, steadying him. Owen licked his dry lips. "That's nice," he said in a distant, dreamy way. "The EMTs are here. I didn't hear an ambulance."

"What is he saying?" the stranger said.

"He's delirious," Aderyn said quickly.

"I'm not delirious, I've been poisoned," Owen replied. His head wobbled like he was having trouble supporting it. "Ten cc's of adrenaline to the heart if it stops beating."

Aderyn laughed, hoping it didn't sound forced, and hoped even more that Owen would shut up.

The stranger didn't comment further. He removed a thin length of polished wood from his waistband and held its tip about an inch from Owen's wounds. Aderyn waited, but nothing happened except the stranger closed his eyes and began breathing rhythmically, in through the nose with a faint whistle and out through the mouth with a sigh. She was about to demand he do something when he flicked the tip of the wand in a complicated squiggly motion that ended with it pointed at Owen's face again.

Green light glowed at the tip of the wand, not bright like Livia's ball of light, but a subtle glow that looked like liquid phosphorescence. It bubbled up as if the wand were a fountain of glowing green water that, instead of flowing down to the stranger's hand, flowed into the air and crossed the space to cling to Owen's wounds. Owen's head jerked, and his eyes flew open, looking colorless in the green radiance. The green light flowed along the gashes, pulsing like a heartbeat three times, and then vanished. Aderyn gasped. The wounds were gone. Owen's cheek was completely unmarked.

"What kind of spellslinger are you?" she whispered.

"No kind," the man said. "I just know how to activate a wand." He stood and tucked the wand away in his waistband. "And I'm glad I came when I did. Those wounds could have killed your friend."

"I know," Aderyn said. "Thank you. What do we owe you?"

"Wait," Owen protested. "You said I wasn't dying! Why did you lie to me?"

"Would it have helped if I'd told the truth?"

"Well, no, but—"

"Then next time, don't try to die if you don't like being lied to," Aderyn retorted. "How much, sir?"

"My master Nessia charges a gold for the use of the wand," the stranger said, "but I can see you're all just starting out, so—"

"We can pay." Aderyn fished in her pocket for the coin. "Thank you—and this five silver is to recompense you for coming."

"That's not necessary." But the stranger was looking at Owen curiously. "Where are you from?"

"Beyond Greenacre," Owen replied.

"Really," the stranger said, drawling out the word like he didn't believe Owen. Aderyn stuck her hand back into her pocket. Maybe another handful of silver would convince this man to stop prying— but Livia was watching all this intently, and if Aderyn quelled the stranger's curiosity, she could only do so by rousing Livia's.

"Beyond Greenacre," the man said. "Far beyond, would you say?"

"I suppose," Owen said warily. So, *now* he was feeling cautious, was he? Aderyn wished she could grab him and run away.

"And you're a Swordsworn," the man went on. "Dancing on the blade's edge."

Now Aderyn was confused. "That's an awfully poetic way of putting it," she said. "How do you know his class? Did Livia tell you?"

"I didn't say anything, no," Livia said.

"It was a guess." The man looked around the taproom in an ostentatious, let's-see-who's-listening way. They were the only ones present, with even the barman not in the room. "There's a legend," he said. "A story about someone who will break the curse on this land—"

"What curse?" Aderyn said. "Market Warding is under a curse?"

"No, the world," Livia said. "You know. The stories of the Fated One."

"I've never heard of that," Aderyn replied.

The stranger raised both eyebrows. "Never heard of the Fated One? The one who will break the level cap and allow unlimited progression for all?"

Aderyn shrugged. "I've heard that there was a time when there was no level cap, and some people say that could end, but my parents always said those were fantasies, believing that the world will ever change."

"Not fantasies, not as far as the Heralds know," the stranger said. "There are many stories of the Fated One, that he will come from far beyond the lands we know, that he will dance on the blade's edge." He stared at Owen, whose slack mouth echoed Aderyn's shock.

"I'm not the Fated One," Owen said. "And I know about prophecies. They're all generic enough to be twisted to apply to any situation that suits you."

"Yes, but you're different regardless," the stranger said. "Jacob Owen Lindberg—what kind of a name is that? And you know things you shouldn't, and you use phrases that are alien to my ears—"

"That's enough," Aderyn said. "Thank you for your help. We can't express our gratitude better than we have. Owen and I are leaving now."

"To go where?" The man didn't move even when Aderyn got right up into his face. "Back to whatever world he came from?"

"He's not a demon," Aderyn said before her brain could get control of her mouth.

"Aderyn," Owen said.

"I didn't say he was," the stranger said, not sounding upset. "And that was another guess, but it seems it was a correct one."

"Another world?" Livia exclaimed. "What are you talking about?"

Aderyn felt the conversation racing out of her control. She snatched Owen's sword from its sheath and brandished it at the man's chest. "I said we were leaving. Don't try to follow us."

The man raised both hands to show he was unarmed. "I know he's not a demon," he said. "You've never seen one, or you'd realize that was impossible."

"And I suppose you have?"

"Yes," the stranger said flatly, and the force in that one word was enough to shut Aderyn up.

The taproom door opened, and Weston entered. "I got a good— Aderyn, what are you doing? Who's this fellow?"

"Stop, Aderyn," Owen said. He gently took the sword away from her. "There's no point. He knows the truth."

"Well, I don't," Livia said. "What's all this about other worlds? What does that have to do with the Fated One?"

"Is this man the Fated One?" Weston exclaimed. He walked forward to where he could examine the stranger. "I thought the Fated One would be taller."

Aderyn closed her eyes and let out a strangled groan that shut everyone up. "Fine," she said, not opening her eyes. "Fine. There's no point pretending anymore. But if you try to kill Owen, I swear I'll find a way to stop you."

"Nobody's going to kill anyone," Livia said.

"Is someone going to explain all this?" Weston said plaintively.

"Let's all sit down and talk," the stranger said. "My name is Isold, and I'm a Herald."

Aderyn opened her eyes and sank into her seat. "I thought you were an apothecary, or a Spiritsmith's apprentice, or something."

Isold sat on Owen's other side and waited for the rest to take seats. "I am, but it's a long story, and to be honest, I left my noon meal to come here. Shall we eat, and I'll explain? Including how I can be so sure Owen is from another world when that should be impossible?"

Weston let out a sharp breath. "Another world? A demon?"

Aderyn groaned.

Owen said, "I'm not a demon. It's... actually, another long story."

Weston shook his head. "Then we're definitely going to need food. Where is that barman?"

Once the barman was summoned, and all of them had trenchers of crusty bread drenched in melted cheese in front of them as well as mugs of ale, Isold began speaking. "I accepted the Call six months ago, after I'd been working with Nessia the Spiritsmith for about four years. I couldn't be a real apprentice, because I wasn't a Spiritsmith, but I like herbalism and I enjoy helping to cure the sick." He laughed. "The truth is, I only accepted the Call because I was certain it would make me a Spiritsmith. Becoming a Herald—I'm afraid I was resentful, and I avoided going adventuring thanks to that resentment."

Aderyn nodded understanding. Heralds had the widest range of knowledge among the classes, and her mother had said they gained skills of persuasion and charm that verged on magical, but until Aderyn had learned of the Warmaster class, she'd considered Herald the least useful of all the classes. Well, if she could be wrong about Warmasters, she could be wrong about Heralds, but she still understood what Isold must have felt when faced with this development.

Reflexively, she Assessed Isold and discovered he was level two. "But you did gain experience," she said.

"When I couldn't avoid it. Nessia has been kind to me, but I know she thinks I have the wrong attitude. And I can admit to myself that I do have the right predisposition for a Herald. I love stories, and learning things, and I'm good at convincing people of the rightness of my position." He chuckled again. "But I don't want to convince you because I'm a smooth talker. I want you to see the facts."

"I'm lost. What facts are these? I thought you were the Fated One." Weston washed down a large bite of bread and cheese with ale and burped. "Not that I believe in the Fated One as anything but an interesting story."

"I'm not. I think *he* is." Isold pointed at Owen, who reddened.

Weston arched one dark eyebrow. "Because he's a… wait, no one's explained how Owen can be from another world and not be a demon. What other worlds are there?"

Owen and Aderyn exchanged glances. Owen's mouth was full, and he was chewing so deliberately Aderyn interpreted it as him wanting her to do the talking. "Let me interrupt you, Isold, because if this isn't a secret anymore, you all might as well hear everything."

She told the short version of meeting Owen in the forest outside Far Haven and the quest they were on together. "But nobody knows there are worlds other than ours and the demon void," she concluded, "so you can't spread this around, all right? Please?"

"Of course not," Weston said.

"You could have gone on pretending," Livia said. "Thank you for trusting us."

"But that's why I think Owen is the one all the stories and prophecies mention," Isold said. "I admit I've made a hobby of collecting all those legends, but the truth is, I didn't actually believe they referred to a real person. My theory was that they reflect a future moment in time when the level cap will vanish and true advancement will be possible again. The notion of one person who's more special than anyone else, who can change the world? That struck me as wishful thinking. I mean, you know what adventurers are like. They all want to be famous, and what would make someone more famous than that?"

"That's what I always thought," Weston said.

"I won't bore you with the specifics," Isold went on. "There are hundreds of stories and at least three dozen prophetic poems—why do prophets always feel like they have to rhyme? Anyway, a lot of them talk about the Fated One coming from beyond the lands we know, and most people who try to interpret them think that means from far outside civilization. Only no one agrees on what that means —is it the edges of the sanctuary cities, or the borders of the settled world? Or even the lands that are closed to us because they're too dangerous for those of lower than level twenty?"

"And you think it means from another world," Livia said.

"I do now. It seemed impossible, but my instincts told me that all those little things about Owen added up to him being from outside this world. And since he's not a demon—"

"Are you sure?" Weston said. "No offense, Owen."

Owen shrugged and took another bite.

"I'm sure," Isold said. "I've seen demons. *A* demon, anyway. It's not something you forget, and they aren't mistakable for anything else, certainly not for a human. Anyway, once I guessed at that, it didn't seem like much of a stretch to think the prophecies and stories might be true."

"Owen, you're being quiet," Livia said.

Owen swallowed. "I didn't think there was much point to me saying anything, since you've all made up your minds." He sounded angry.

The rest fell silent. Livia looked embarrassed. Aderyn examined Owen, how tense his jaw was, and said, "I'm sorry. This is a lot to take in, I'm sure, and to be honest I'm not convinced Isold is right. I've never heard any of these stories, and if Far Haven didn't talk about it, how important could it be? I mean—not that Far Haven is the most important place in the world, but if there really is a Fated One, shouldn't everyone know about it?"

"I don't know," Isold said. "It's a fair question."

"It's ridiculous," Owen said. "This is all sounding like a bad '80s fantasy novel. Do you have any idea how many stupid stories have been written about a Chosen One who saves the world? Even if I believed that was a real thing, I'm nobody special." He laughed harshly. "Which is, of course, what every Chosen One says about himself. But it's true. I just want to get back to my world and never think about levels or killing monsters or experience again." He shoved his chair back and stormed out of the taproom.

CHAPTER ELEVEN

Aderyn rose from her seat. "He shouldn't go off alone."

"I think he needs time, Aderyn," Livia said. "He nearly died today, and now we've dumped this Fated One thing on him... it was too much."

"I almost wish I hadn't brought it up," Isold said. "But one of the things everyone agrees on is that the Fated One draws the attention of the world, and if it is Owen, things will start to happen to him whether he believes it or not. Even people who only believe they're the Fated One see increases in monster attacks, unexpected quests falling on them... it's like the system is testing people for their suitability."

"Does the system care?" Weston asked. "We've had the cap at level twenty for so long the times before that are almost mythical. You'd think if that wasn't meant to be, the system would do something about it."

"Unless this is the system's way of handling it," Isold said. "Giving adventurers the opportunity to prove worthy of the ultimate challenge."

"I don't want it to be Owen," Aderyn said. "He just wants to go home. And that means you can't possibly be right. If the Fated One has to be someone from another world, and Owen is the first person who's ever come here from another world—"

"That we know of," Isold said.

"If it was happening all the time, *someone* would know about it. You saw how bad Owen is at concealing the truth," Aderyn insisted. "So if Owen's the first, can you really imagine the system being so... so cruel as to set up rules to make breaking the level cap almost impossible?"

"That's a good point," Livia said. "All quests have solutions. The system doesn't set us up to fail—we fail because we don't use our skills properly, or we take on a challenge we're not ready for, or even sometimes out of bad luck, but not because the quest is impossible."

"I don't have answers to those questions," Isold said. "And it's true that I don't know for sure that I'm right about Owen being the Fated One. Call it a strongly possible theory."

"Which means it's not fair to him to act as if it's definitely true," Weston said. "And from what I've heard, there's no way to prove someone is the Fated One. Otherwise you wouldn't have all these men and women running around claiming that title."

"That's partly true." Isold frowned. "That is, there are ways to *disprove* it. But my guess is what I already said—that the system allows someone to claim the right to pursue the title, and then it tests them to see who will make it to the end. So there really could be dozens, or hundreds, of potential Fated Ones that the system treats as genuine aspirants. If that makes sense."

"You mean it's like entering a race," Aderyn said. "Anyone who enters could potentially be the winner, but they're all still racers. That makes them different from the ones who didn't enter the race."

"That's a much simpler way of putting it. Yes." Isold pushed away the remains of his meal.

"But then Owen *isn't* the Fated One, because he doesn't want to be," Aderyn persisted. "Surely the system wouldn't make someone..."

Her voice trailed off. The system chose people's classes, didn't it? And assigned skills, and chose when they leveled. It was perfectly reasonable that the system might also pick individuals to be Fated Ones. "It's not fair," she finished weakly.

"Like I said, there are ways to prove someone *isn't* the Fated One," Isold said. "Maybe that would ease Owen's mind. You're right, he has enough to deal with already."

"We'd have to find him first," Weston said. "He wouldn't leave town, would he?"

"He's not stupid. He knows that's not safe," Aderyn said. "And I bet I know where he went. Let me talk to him." She pushed back her chair, then hesitated. "The quest is over. You all don't have to stay."

"After learning this? I don't think I could bear not finding out what happens next," Weston said with a grin.

"If I have a choice, I'd prefer not to leave just yet," Livia said. "I realize we're not really friends yet, but you helped me, and if there's anything I can do to return the favor, I'd like to help you."

Aderyn nodded. "Let's at least find out what Owen wants."

She left the taproom and ascended the stairs to knock on the door of Owen's room. Why she'd felt he wouldn't leave the inn, she didn't know, unless she'd formed more of a connection with him over the past four days than she'd realized. But she was certain of her guess.

After a moment, Owen opened the door. "What?"

Aderyn swallowed. "Can I come in?"

"I don't know. *Can* you?"

Owen's bitterness felt like a slap. "I'm sorry," Aderyn said, and turned to go.

"No, I'm sorry," Owen replied, sounding less angry. "That's a stupid joke my mother says—you know, because the proper phrase is 'may I?' She was an English major... and you have no idea what that is." He opened the door wider. "Come in."

Aderyn entered. His room was furnished identically to hers:

narrow bed covered by a scratchy gray-brown wool blanket, chair in one corner, flat-topped chest at the foot of the bed to stow belongings. It didn't lock, so a thief wouldn't be stopped by it, but it did keep the room looking tidy. Owen gestured for her to take the chair and sat on the chest. He stared at the floor. Aderyn stared at her hands.

"I really am sorry about all this," she said.

"Why? It's not like you're the one who dragged me out of my world to this one," Owen replied.

"Because I haven't been very sympathetic. I've been so worried about you giving your secret away that I've been impatient with you. I didn't think about what it must be like, being in a strange place all by yourself."

"You haven't acted impatient. And I haven't been all by myself. You've been a good friend." Owen's voice still sounded distant and unhappy.

"Have I?" Aderyn, startled, looked up at him. He was gazing out the room's one window, watching a flock of birds soar past.

"I know you've wanted to be an adventurer for a long time. You could have gone anywhere, done anything, but you're stuck with me."

"In case you missed it, my class isn't useful except as a partnership. I'd just have annoyed anyone else I joined up with." Aderyn knew she sounded bitter, and she didn't care.

To her surprise, Owen laughed. "Listen to us. It's like we're competing for the title of Most Depressed Person in Market Warding. When really, we should be grateful. I've found a partner who's patient with my ignorance, and *you've* found a partner who is too dumb to know Warmasters suck."

Aderyn gasped. Then she laughed. "I assume 'suck' is something bad."

"You don't use that expression? Crap. I mean, shit. No, I don't. 'Crap' is for times when 'shit' is too much."

"I like it. I'm going to start using it." Aderyn sobered. "Look, I really am sorry we made you feel like the fate of the world was on your shoulders. I agree that the idea of a Fated One sounds like some adventurer's fantasy. But the trouble is, I'm not sure the system knows it."

"What does that mean?"

Aderyn explained what Isold had said about many would-be Fated Ones and the possibility that the system encouraged it. "If Isold could interpret the prophecies to mean you, that means other people could, too, which means the system might have identified you as a possibility. And like he said, once someone chooses that destiny—"

"Or has it thrust on them."

"Yes, or that. After that, things start happening to the person whether they want to be the Fated One or not. So you could be in danger."

Owen grimaced and turned away again. "I suppose there's no point in me telling the system where to get off."

"If you mean reject your fate, no, there's no point." Aderyn still didn't understand half the expressions Owen used, but she was beginning to interpret their meaning from context.

He shook his head. "What do *you* think I should do? It's your world. Can we just pretend the Fated One thing isn't real, and go on finding me a way home? If Isold is right, and bad things happen as we go, well, it's not that much worse than if I was an ordinary person, right?"

"Yes, but I was also thinking—Isold says there's a way to prove someone isn't a Fated One. Maybe we should do that first. It might ease your mind."

Owen nodded. "It would, actually." He rose from his seat and extended a hand to Aderyn. "Thank you. I appreciate what you're doing for me."

His hand was dry and rough from the beginnings of sword

calluses, and Aderyn clasped it firmly. "I should thank you for taking my useless class seriously."

"It's really not useless," Owen said. "You shouldn't say that. Just because all the other Warmasters don't have the right partner."

Aderyn smiled. "I like the sound of that."

When they returned to the taproom, Isold, Weston, and Livia were still seated at the table. The mugs were there, but the remains of the food had been cleared away. Nobody said anything as Owen and Aderyn took their seats. Owen said, "I'm sorry for my rudeness earlier."

"You were justified, and I'm sorry I let my enthusiasm take over," Isold said.

"You said there's a way to prove someone isn't a Fated One," Aderyn said. "What is it? And will it take long? We're headed for Guerdon Deep to find someone who can send Owen back to his own world."

"That's a question with an ambiguous answer," Isold said. "The thing itself doesn't take more than a few hours, but getting in could take days."

"You're talking about that dungeon west of here," Weston said.

"You've heard of it? Then you might know it's dormant now, and even though it's been a couple of weeks since it was last active, and that means the next time is coming soon, there's no telling exactly when that will be," Isold said. "What's worse, if we aren't on the spot when it becomes active, some other team could go in ahead of us, and that would mean waiting another week or more for the next chance."

"Let's not worry about that just yet," Owen said. "How will that dungeon disprove anything?"

"The final boss gives out random treasure. Mostly random. I've heard that for a Fated One, it always gives out the same thing—a golden circlet that only the Fated One can wear. If you're not worthy, you might get anything else. So if we take on that dungeon, and defeat the final boss, and the treasure is anything but the golden circlet, that would prove you aren't the Fated One."

"Is that really the only way to do it?" Aderyn asked. "Isn't that a little coincidental?"

"There are variable dungeons all over the world that all do what I've described," Isold said. "Maybe it's coincidence that one happens to be right here, but not as big a coincidence as if it was the only one in the world. And it could be the system giving Owen a boost by taking that burden away."

"Or giving him a destiny," Weston said. Livia elbowed him in the ribs. "Sorry, but I think you should face the possibility so it isn't a huge disappointment if this turns out to be true."

"I agree," Owen said, surprising Aderyn. "And I've decided not to have any expectations. It's not like I can control what the system's decided, right? So let's figure out how we can be the first ones through that dungeon door."

CHAPTER TWELVE

T wo hours later, the five of them left Market Warding and headed west. This time, there was a well-traveled road Isold had said eventually led to Gardholm, four days' journey away. Aderyn wiped sweat from her forehead and squinted into the distance. The plains stretched on for miles, but she could see the forest springing up beyond. It was a true forest, not dead like the goblins' home, and lush with summer growth. Her steps quickened briefly before she calmed herself. They'd reach the coolness of the forest eventually, and there was no sense exhausting herself trying to get there sooner.

"This is all going to depend on me being able to Assess a dungeon," she said. "Which is really unlikely. I've never heard of anyone being able to know things about a dungeon without actually going inside and encountering the monsters and other challenges. Those have power levels people can see."

"If you can't, we'll try something else," Owen said. "But I have faith in you."

Aderyn blushed. "If it's not just one door that appears when the dungeon is active—"

"It isn't," Isold said. "That's part of what makes getting in so difficult. Every door but one is a false door, but they're all identical otherwise. Every team of adventurers tries tricks to identify the real door, but as far as I know there isn't any magical item or spell that can."

"Anyway, if there are lots of doors, and I can't tell which is real, we still have as good a chance as any other team," Aderyn continued.

She briefly focused on the image of her team's roster, as Owen called it. She didn't know what a roster was, but she didn't have a better word for it, and his other term, heads-up display, just baffled her. With Isold having joined them, the left side of her vision was crowded with names and classes and health indicators.

To the right, little dots that enlarged when she focused on them gave details on their quests. **[Return the Otherworlder]** was at the top, with **[Clear Dungeon Spiteful]** below marked as the current primary quest. Livia had suggested that this was hopeful, that they'd already received the quest even though they hadn't entered the dungeon and that meant they would succeed, but Aderyn didn't want to count on the system's sometimes erratic sense of what qualified as an adventurer's quest.

Dungeon Spiteful seemed like a dramatic name, maybe one that implied a serious challenge. That excited Aderyn. Killing goblins had felt strange; clearing a dungeon was more like what she believed adventurers did. She hoped they would enter on their first try, not just because she didn't want to wait around for a week or more doing nothing, but also because she wanted Owen to have the reassurance that his destiny wasn't determined.

When they finally reached the forest, it was midafternoon and Aderyn welcomed the shade of the thick leaves. She'd only been in the forest outside Far Haven a few times and knew nothing about trees and plants, because trees and plants were boring unless they were animate and trying to kill you. What these were called, she had no idea, but she could see differences in the leaves and the size of the trunks, and for the first time wished she'd learned names for plants, if only because it would give her something to do while they walked.

She did pay attention to her surroundings, listening for monsters. The areas around frequently-cleared dungeons were usually uninhabited, though no one knew why, but "usually" wasn't the same as "always." A fight would slow them down, so she hoped the forest would continue quiet. Birds sang in the branches, so probably there wasn't anything around that they considered dangerous.

"We're almost there," Isold said.

"I hear people," Weston said, coming to a halt. The others stopped to listen. Aderyn still didn't hear anything but the birds and the occasional gust of wind, but Weston frowned. "Three people. Not fighting, not arguing, no sounds of a struggle. I think another team beat us there."

"It's fine," Owen said. "Remember, we have an advantage."

Aderyn didn't point out again that it might not be an advantage. She was tired of how pessimistic she sounded every time she reminded them that her skills might not work that way.

A few minutes' more walking brought them to a clearing the road cut through. The clearing was enormous, a good two hundred feet across, and looked like a piece of the fields dropped in among the trees. A stone house crouched not quite in the center of the clearing. "House" was the wrong word, Aderyn thought; it had six irregular sides, several roofs tilting at different angles, no windows, and a single chimney stack rising from the steepest roof. It also had no doors, and the walls showed no sign of places where a door might be concealed.

Off to one side of the house was a campsite. It had the semi-permanent look of something that had been there for a few days, with a firepit and a couple of tents. Three women lounged around the fire, talking and occasionally tossing bits of dry grass into the flames. They glanced toward the team and then ignored them.

"Never mind them," Owen said. "Aderyn?"

Aderyn blinked once, slowly, to Assess the strange house. She wasn't expecting to see anything, so it was a surprise when a message rose up before her eyes.

Name: Dungeon Spiteful
Type: Basic dungeon, variable
Power Level: 4
Assess?

Aderyn focused. Instead of shifting blue lines of light, the entire house glowed pale yellow, with lines of brighter yellow light along the edges of the walls and roofs.

"There's something," she said. "Wait a minute."

The longer she looked, the easier it was to see variations in the pale yellow glow. Outlines became visible on the walls, rectangular outlines like doors. Aderyn's first excitement faded when she realized she couldn't tell any differences between the rectangles.

She was about to tell her team it was impossible when a thought occurred to her. She focused on the nearest rectangle and Assessed it. Instantly, it disappeared. Aderyn blinked. She tried again, and again, and on the fourth time she found a rectangle that didn't disappear under her Assessment.

Her eyes were watering from staring so hard at the light. She blinked rapidly and the yellow glow vanished, but when she looked back at the house, she could still see the one rectangle, a faint yellow outline on the wall to the right. "Well," she said, "it worked. But there's a problem."

"What problem?" Owen asked.

"I know where the real door will appear. And it's in the wall right next to those adventurers." She nodded, not wanting to point and draw the women's attention.

"So they'll reach it first anyway," Livia said. "That's terrible."

"No, I have another idea," Owen said. "Follow me."

He strode forward, pointing at a wall adjacent to the one Aderyn had identified. "That's the one, right?" he said loudly.

Aderyn had no idea what he was thinking, but she played along. "That's it. That's where the real door will appear."

The three women adventurers sat up and watched the team approach. Aderyn saw Owen come to an abrupt stop that made the women laugh. A second later, she ran into what felt like a firm cushion that stopped her going forward. She put out both hands and felt around. An invisible barrier. Maybe the dungeon's name was more literal than she'd thought, if it spitefully made people wait at a distance so they'd all have to scramble for the doors when they appeared.

"Younglings," one woman said. She had bright copper hair and was dressed in flowing, dramatic robes. "Didn't even know about the barrier."

"You might as well go home, younglings," another woman said. She had black hair and wore leather armor covered with iron studs. "We'll beat you to the door."

"You don't know where it is," Owen said, ignoring their laughter. "We do."

"Those divination tricks are all lies," the third woman said, tossing her long blond ponytail over her shoulder.

"Our Warmaster Assessed the dungeon," Owen said. "She saw where the true door appears." He pointed at the wrong wall. "Right there."

The three women laughed so hard they sounded like they were choking. Even though she was starting to see what Owen's plan was, Aderyn's face still reddened with humiliated anger. "You can laugh," she said. "What level are we? Level two? Could an ordinary level two adventurer tell your classes by Assessing?"

The chuckling blond shook her head. "Impossible."

"You're Swordsworn," Aderyn told her. "Your friend in the robes is a Flamecrafter, and the lady in the uncomfortable armor is a Lightfingers. Tell me I'm wrong." She crossed her arms over her chest and glared at the women.

The women stopped laughing. "Warmasters are useless," the Flamecrafter said, but she didn't sound certain.

"Right. Fine. They're useless," Owen said scornfully. "Then you won't care if we camp over here. Seeing as how we couldn't possibly know where the door will open." He unslung his knapsack from his shoulder and stretched.

That was the signal for the rest of the team to look busy pretending to set up camp. Aderyn covertly watched the other team, who were now huddled together and whispering intently. She glanced at Owen, who looked tense. This could still fail.

Then the Lightfingers stood and approached their group, with the other two women close behind. "Move," she said to Owen. "We're taking this spot."

"Hey!" Owen exclaimed in well-pretended outrage. "We were here first!"

"And we're here now," the Lightfingers said. "Get out of our way."

Owen's hand went to his sword. The Lightfingers flexed her wrist and a knife dropped into her hand. "You want to make an issue of this, youngling?"

Owen glared a moment longer. "Let's back up," he said finally. Everyone gathered the gear they hadn't really started unpacking and walked away. Aderyn waited with her team until the women had settled their things in the spot Owen had vacated, leaving their fire pit and tents behind. Then Owen led them to a spot behind and slightly to the right of the women. Aderyn wished they could camp opposite the real door, but the women would realize something was up if they didn't at least make a show of trying to get near the fake door. This position left them ready to race for the real door when it appeared.

They sat without unpacking more than some dried meat and apples to eat. The sun sank lower in the sky, and the air began to cool. By the time the sun had disappeared behind the trees to the west,

Aderyn's early eagerness had worn off. It might still be days before the dungeon became active.

With nothing better to do, she Assessed the dungeon again. The glow was brighter than before, and the lines of light pulsed like a visible heartbeat. Aderyn watched for a while until she was sure the glow continued to increase. "I think it will be soon," she whispered. "It's glowing brighter."

"Let's quietly collect our things," Weston said.

"No," Owen said. "We need them to think they've outsmarted us again. They have to commit to the false door so they don't have time to beat us to the real one. Pack up, but don't be stealthy—just look like you're failing to be stealthy."

Aderyn nodded. Owen was turning out to be a real leader.

She went around gathering apple cores and throwing them back into the tree line. As she'd hoped, the activity drew the other team's attention, and soon the women were whispering again. Then they all stood and began checking weapons and adjusting armor and clothing, glancing now and then at Aderyn's teammates and laughing. Aderyn ignored them.

With her knapsack on her back, she sat watching the dungeon grow ever brighter as the sky grew darker. It was the strangest sensation. She knew the light wasn't real, because the clearing was unlit except for the other team's fire, and yet the house glowed with a yellow light that made her eyes water. By now, the yellow was closer to white, and the lines of light looked as solid and brilliant as iron bars in a hot forge.

Then everyone gasped as the light became real.

For a few seconds, the house glowed too brightly to look at directly. Then the glow vanished, and every one of the six walls had at least one door in it. To Aderyn's Assessment, the true door continued to gleam as if outlined in gold. "The one to the right," she whispered.

The three women shouted and ran for the false door. Owen said, "Wait... wait... *now!*"

The teammates ran full speed toward the glowing door. Isold outpaced the rest of them and slapped his palm against the wood two seconds before the others reached it. Aderyn heard one of the women scream something, but the door swung open inward, she tumbled through it on Livia's heels, and the scream cut off as they all found themselves elsewhere.

Chapter Thirteen

They stood in a long hall made entirely of dark, oblong stones, walls, ceiling, and floor. Torches flickered some distance down the hall, illuminating it well enough to show that it continued past Aderyn's range of vision. She turned around. The wooden door was gone.

Owen took a few steps forward and ran a hand along the stones of the wall. "Not wet," he said. "And the air feels dry and doesn't smell of anything but burning pitch."

"Does that mean something?" Livia asked.

Owen shrugged. "It's just less creepy than if the walls were covered in wet green slime and the ceiling dripped smelly water."

"If this is the maze, it's way too straightforward," Livia said.

"I only know that the maze is different every time, and that the final boss is always the last thing you encounter no matter which way you go," Isold said.

"Then let's get started," Owen suggested. "I'll take the lead, and Weston, you hang behind so nothing can creep up on us. Aderyn, right behind me. Okay?"

Nobody argued. Aderyn wasn't sure what the others thought of

Owen's newly-developed assertiveness, but she liked the change. It felt like he was more the person he usually was when he hadn't been dumped into an alien world where he didn't know the rules.

They moved slowly down the corridor, watching carefully for movement. The torches flickered more as they stirred the air with their passing, but didn't suddenly erupt into balls of flame. Maybe that was impossible, but Aderyn wasn't going to rule anything out, not in her first dungeon.

Eventually, they reached a crossroads, four halls branching in four directions. "Anybody have a preference?" Owen said.

Weston came forward and listened at each hall, then shook his head. "I don't hear anything to distinguish one from another."

"Then... left. Anybody have a lipstick?"

"What's a lipstick?" Aderyn asked.

"It was in a movie, where the girl marked her path through—"

"What's a movie?"

"I'm going to stop talking now," Owen said. "Left. We'll just have to remember the turns."

That was harder than it sounded. The hall turned left again almost immediately, then right, then right again. Still there were no sounds but their own footsteps, though Aderyn could barely hear Weston at the back of the group. There was nothing but endless corridors and occasional torches.

A change in the light made Aderyn gasp and spin around. Livia had just levitated a torch off the wall and extinguished it with a gesture. "There's still light if half the torches remain lit," she said. "This way, we'll know the corridors we've used."

"Excellent idea," Isold said, and Owen nodded.

Now they moved more slowly to give Livia time to work her magic. Aderyn watched her do it and realized she wasn't controlling the fire; she was wrapping the torch in a bubble of airlessness that deprived the fire of fuel and made it go out. "Clever," she said.

"It's actually the reverse of an *air bubble* spell," Livia said.

"Excluding the air from the bubble instead of containing it. I wasn't sure it would work."

"We're already learning," Aderyn said.

Then the hall they were in came to a dead end. They all searched for signs of a secret exit, but not even Weston found anything. "Back we go," Owen said, and they retraced their steps and took a different turning.

It wasn't long before they all heard it—heavy footsteps and guttural muttering. They were in a passage that made a sharply-angled turn just ahead, too sharp to let them see past it. "Let's prepare for an attack here," Owen said. "Back up just enough to give ourselves room."

"Let me cast a spell before you two attack," Livia told Owen and Weston. "I don't know how many of them there are, but I can entangle some of them and split their forces that way."

Owen nodded. He drew his sword and took up a position opposite Weston.

They waited. Aderyn wiped her sweaty palms on her trousers and wished she'd remembered to buy a sword. She felt helpless and isolated, standing behind Owen and waiting for whatever monsters these were to come charging around the corner. Though they didn't sound like they were charging. It sounded like marching feet, bare feet on stone—

Huge, seven-foot-tall shapes appeared around the corner, monstrous in the torchlight. Brown-furred, misshapen bodies loomed, their enormous floppy ears looking ridiculous atop their small egg-shaped heads. The two in front, clearly surprised. Livia shouted something incomprehensible, and a mass of wet brown earth the size of a small boulder flew past Aderyn's face, ruffling her hair with the wind of its passage. It struck the two monsters and engulfed them, thick mud running down their legs and pinning their arms with their huge spiked clubs to their sides.

Aderyn realized the **[Improved Assess 1]** message was flashing at her.

Name: Bugbear
Type: Monstrosity
Power Level: 2

She focused on what the blue lights of her skill were telling her as two more bugbears lurched forward, ignoring their trapped friends in favor of gutting the humans.

"Go for the belly!" she shouted, darting back to where Livia looked like she was searching for another spell, one that wouldn't hit her teammates. "Avoid the neck and throat, and hamstring them if you can!"

"They're pack creatures," Isold added. "Isolate them!"

Owen and Weston each went after one of the free bugbears. All four creatures howled wildly, making the corridors echo. Owen dodged a swipe of a spiked club and got behind the awkwardly stumbling monster, striking low at the backs of the bugbear's legs. The monster's howl sharpened with pain, and it collapsed, leaving its stomach open for a finishing blow.

Congratulations! You have defeated [Bugbear].
You have earned [75 XP].

Weston's slashes were less elegant than Owen's, but his blade found its mark just below the bugbear's breastbone, and he darted back to narrowly avoid being hit by the monster's death blow. Again, the victory message flashed.

Livia shouted, and a blast of dry earth shot past Weston and Owen to strike the trapped bugbears. Aderyn couldn't imagine that a rain of dirt could do any damage, but the bugbears shrieked and shook their heads as if blinded. "Hit them before they recover!" Livia said.

The second pair of monsters took less time to finish than the first, snarled in sticky mud and blinded as they were. Owen was barely breathing hard. "I'm afraid of getting cocky," he said, "but that was easy. And nobody got hurt."

"That's fortunate, because I can't imagine those spikes are good for anyone's health," Weston said with a grin.

"Should we search the bodies?" Aderyn asked.

"Bugbears don't carry valuables on them, and I don't want to dig through that mud in any case—not to be ungrateful, Livia," Isold said. "But I'd like to know what's in the direction they came from."

"Carefully," Owen said. "It could be their den, with more of them waiting."

They walked slowly and quietly down a series of bizarrely angled halls, some of them apparently doubling back on themselves, before they came to a larger chamber. It stank of bugbear and imperfectly tanned hides. It was also empty. Relieved, Aderyn joined in searching the room for hidden doors or panels, but again they found nothing. Unfortunately, they also didn't find any treasure.

"It's all right," Owen said. "It's the treasure at the end we care about. But this is another dead end, so we should retrace our steps."

This time, they had to go all the way back to the first crossroads to take the one turning they hadn't yet used. Immediately this took them into a strange zigzag corridor. "I wish the compass worked in here," Aderyn complained. "I know it's never certain whether a dungeon will obey the natural laws, but it would be nice to know which direction we're going."

A brighter light shone around the next zig of the hallway, and Owen put a hand on Aderyn's shoulder to stop her. "Anything?" he asked Weston.

"Still nothing," Weston said. "I hope I haven't gone deaf."

As they approached the corner, Aderyn wrinkled her nose. "That stinks worse than the bugbear den."

"It's disgusting," Livia said. She was pinching her nose shut and her voice sounded nasal. "Like all the worst foods in the world, but gone rotten as well."

Owen walked ahead and around the corner. "It's a dining hall," he called back to them. "And it pretty much is overflowing with rotten food."

The rest of them joined him. Aderyn breathed through her mouth to minimize the smell. A couple of mismatched trestle tables filled most of the space. Both of them were stained dark with unknown fluids—no, Aderyn was sure she saw dried blood as well. Flies buzzed over the second table, where the carcass of some unidentifiable creature rotted. Bones littered the floor, and Aderyn was grateful none of them were human.

"It's another dead end," Owen said. "And this time, there really isn't anywhere else to go. We need to find another exit out of this place."

"I do *not* want to spend that much time here," Livia said, but she joined in searching like the others.

Aderyn tried not to touch anything, reasoning that there wasn't likely to be a secret door, or even the trigger for a secret door, in a pile of rotting entrails. She took the wall nearest the door, not because it was farthest from the smell but because everyone else had scattered throughout the room and this was all that was left. She tried and failed to picture the maze they'd passed through already. Though... no, there wasn't anywhere in this wall for another passage to fit, given how much space the zigzag corridor had to take up.

"I found it!" Weston exclaimed. He was standing near the trestle table that didn't have horrible body parts on it, across the room from Aderyn on the diagonal. He pressed a stone that looked exactly like all the other stones, and a piece of the wall shifted, slid, and vanished.

You have discovered a secret door! Your reward is [50 XP].

Cool, sweet-smelling air puffed into the stinking dining hall. "Let's go quickly," Aderyn suggested.

But the secret passage was unlit, and the moment Isold, at the back of the group, stepped through the doorway, the wall slammed shut and they were alone in the darkness. Aderyn froze. She hadn't ever been afraid of the dark before, but now she knew that was because no dark she'd ever experienced had been this complete. There'd always been distant lamps, or moonlight, or even the stars. Here, the nearest wall might have been a yard away or inches from her nose. She made herself breathe calmly. She had a <**Matchlighter**> in her pack somewhere.

Livia chanted something too quiet to make out, and the little ball of light kindled in her palm. In its radiance, Aderyn saw her teammates' faces and breathed a little easier. Everyone looked as tense as she felt.

"This isn't practical," Livia said, gesturing with the light. "When I'm more advanced, I'll be able to separate it from myself and have it go on burning. But it doesn't shed much light this way."

"It's enough," Owen said. "Aderyn, did you have the lantern, or did I?"

Aderyn blushed. She'd forgotten her parents' lantern. "It's in here." Quickly, she dug through her belongings to find the small lantern. Owen lit it using his <**Matchlighter**> and trimmed the wick, and a golden glow shed light on their surroundings.

The secret passage was smaller than the other corridors, with a lower ceiling, but the dark gray stones were the same, and it smelled musty, like no one had entered it in years. The teammates proceeded down the corridor, with Aderyn in the center of the group holding the lantern so Weston and Owen's sword hands would remain free. The sounds of their boots against the stone were louder now, and Aderyn imagined she could hear them all breathing loudly—or something breathing loudly, at least. That was just nerves. She hoped.

CHAPTER FOURTEEN

The hall turned left, then left again, and soon the turns were coming closer together. "It's a spiral," Weston said, just as they made a final turn and entered a small, square room no more than fifteen feet across. Aderyn came to an abrupt halt to avoid running into Owen, and Livia bumped into her from behind.

At the center of the room, a round indentation three feet across glimmered silver in the lamplight. Aderyn stepped to one side to get a better look. It wasn't a circle of hammered silver, or a pool of liquid metal; it was more white with a silvery sheen to it. A waist-high stone pillar on the far side had a smaller matching circle set into its flat top.

Instinctively, she Assessed it and got the message:

Exceeds authority limit

"I don't know what it is," she said.

"I think I do," Isold said. "There are stories of magical artifacts shaped like this. They transport someone who stands in the circle to another circle that's linked to it. The distance between the linked circles can be vast, or it can be a few feet."

Owen and Aderyn exchanged glances. "It can't teleport us out of the dungeon, right?" Owen asked. "Isn't the point to defeat the dungeon while you're in it? So it's not going to send us somewhere deep in the Forsaken Lands."

"I have no idea," Aderyn replied. "But even if it—what was that word you used? Teleport?—Even if it teleports us somewhere else inside Dungeon Spiteful, that could be the middle of the final boss's lair. It could drop us unprepared on a monster that's waiting for us."

"But we've been everywhere else," Weston said. "I'm sure we haven't missed any other secret doors. This has got to be the way to the next level of the dungeon."

"I don't like it," Livia said. "That circle isn't big enough to hold all of us. Two at a time, maybe."

"That's a problem, yes," Owen said. "But are we all agreed that this is where we have to go?"

They all nodded.

"Then Aderyn and I will go first, and the rest of you follow as quickly as you can." Owen settled his pack more securely and extended a hand to Aderyn. "Just in case it tries to separate us."

Aderyn clasped his hand, and the two of them approached the edge of the circle. Owen's other hand was on his sword's hilt. "Count of three, and then we step on 'go,'" Owen said. "Ready? One... two... three... *go!*"

As one, they stepped forward onto the circle. Nothing happened.

Aderyn didn't let go of Owen's hand. "Maybe we need to touch that other circle to activate the transportation," she suggested.

"It's worth trying." Owen released her to hook his left arm around her right elbow, leaving their hands free. They took one more step forward so they were right next to the low pillar. In unison, they pressed their palms flat against the small silvery circle.

The world blinked. Aderyn's stomach churned as if someone had pulled it away from her body and let it snap back. The air was suddenly full of soft, greenish light, like sunlight through new leaves.

Aderyn tilted her head back to look up, and up, and up at a cavern roof that rose so high above its farthest reaches were shrouded in mist. Instinctively, she didn't remove her arm from Owen's as he tugged her forward.

All around them, the walls of the impossible cavern were brilliant with color, pinks and blues and eyewatering reds and the kind of greens Aderyn had only ever seen in picture books. The colors were soft, making the walls seem upholstered. Carpets of moss covered the many layers of the rough floor, and mushrooms of all shapes dotted the moss.

A whoosh of air behind them made Aderyn turn. Weston and Livia, their arms linked as Owen's and Aderyn's were, blinked in surprise. "Move away," Owen said. "What if it brings Isold through in the middle of you?"

Livia stepped away from Weston. Her eyes were wide. "It's a fungal forest," she said. "I've heard of these. Look, some of those mushrooms are as big as a man."

Aderyn had seen those, but only out of the corner of her eye, and she'd thought they were trees or very big bushes. Now she saw they were actually fungi, big broad-capped mushrooms with thick grey ribbing on the underside of the caps and stems bigger than she could put her arms around. The moss grew thicker beneath them, invitingly soft.

"I don't see an exit," Owen said. "Let's spread out and search."

Aderyn moved through the forest, marveling at its beauty. She stepped carefully so she wouldn't crush any of the tiny white mushrooms like fairy flowers within the moss. Rough stone steps led up to the next level, where a field of more mushrooms grew. These were about two feet high and purple with pink spots across their caps. They also smelled divine, more like butter and cream than mushrooms. Aderyn stopped to inhale the scent.

One of the mushrooms moved.

Startled, Aderyn froze. The mushroom lifted its cap, revealing lines in its stem that looked like eye slits, a narrow nose, a jagged-toothed mouth—and then the mouth opened, and the tiny eyes grew to red, malevolent embers. Aderyn stepped back, and the thing let out a puff of spores that enveloped her and were sucked into her throat as she screamed.

Aderyn stumbled, choking and coughing on the spores but desperately trying to get away. Her vision tunneled, and she felt dizzy and sick. Flashes of silver told her the system was trying to get her attention, but in her state, she could barely see the edge of the rocky ledge. Then she tripped and tumbled off the ledge, still trying to cough up the spores.

Hands were trying to lift her, but they were pulling in all directions and she screamed again, both in pain and in fear. "Don't breathe the spores!" she shouted, except she couldn't hear her words and she was afraid she'd only imagined it. The walls pulsed with colored lights that felt soft and plush like a stuffed toy she'd had as a child, a toy her sister Pia had taken and hidden to tease her. Maybe it was in this room.

She rolled to her knees and scrubbed her eyes, trying to see the missing toy. Her hands and feet were swelling, and so was her head, though it was a nice feeling and not painful. A tiny part of her knew this was all wrong, but that tiny part was stupid and needed to shut up.

Suddenly, water drenched her, freezing water that poured over her head and shoulders and ran in icy rivulets down her back and between her breasts. She screamed, and this time she heard herself. Someone was rubbing her face with a scratchy but still soft cloth.

"Sorry," Livia said. "I had to rinse the spores away. Can you see?"

Aderyn grabbed the cloth and scrubbed at her eyes, then coughed deeply and spat on the ground. Her spit tasted too sweet, like a dose of honeyed medicine. "The spores," she said. "They can't breathe the spores."

"Just sit here," Livia said. "Owen and Weston are taking precautions. There aren't very many of the monsters, but they're small and agile. It's all right."

Aderyn looked up at Isold, who was watching something in the distance. "Fungal gardeners," he said without looking at her. "I almost hate to kill them, but this isn't a real garden. It's all part of the dungeon."

Aderyn, shivering, got to her feet and squeezed water out of her hair. Owen and Weston were racing from rock ledge to rock ledge, pausing to stab at things near their feet. She couldn't see any of the fungal gardeners, but from the way the men moved, they had no such trouble. Both Owen and Weston wore cloths tied across their faces, covering their noses and mouths, but every so often they leaped backward as a puff of spores filled the air where they'd been.

**Congratulations! You have defeated [Fungal Gardener].
You have earned [25 XP].**

Aderyn was sure more of those messages had appeared while she was too confused to understand them. At the moment, she cared less about gaining experience than she did in seeing her teammates avoid her fate.

A *mudball* flashed past, slamming into a stand of mushrooms near Weston. The Moonlighter saluted Livia with his blade, then impaled something small that wiggled for a moment before sagging in death.

"Can you cast spells without stopping?" Aderyn asked.

"You mean, do I run out of magical energy?" Livia cast another *mudball*, this one in Owen's direction. "I'm sure I will eventually. I don't know how much energy I have in all, or how much it takes to cast each of the spells I know."

"That limit changes as you continue gaining levels," Isold said. "And the spellslingers I know say they can feel it in their bones when they approach the end of their reserves. I'd be careful if I were you."

"The monsters are all dead now, anyway," Livia said with a shrug.

Owen and Weston were approaching from opposite sides of the cavern. Owen hurried to Aderyn's side. "Are you all right?"

"I'm fine. Just wet. I can't believe I was caught like that."

"None of us were cautious," Owen said. "I'm just glad you're not hurt."

"Should I be worried that *none* of us are hurt despite two challenges?" Weston said. His normally cheerful expression was gone. "It feels like we might be coming up on something big."

"I doubt it works like that, like succeeding at two battles means we'll fail at the third," Owen said. "Aderyn, do you need to change into a dry shirt?"

The men turned their backs while Aderyn stripped out of her wet clothes and put on a dry shift and shirt. "Let's be more careful moving forward," she said. "Did we find an exit?"

"It's over there," Isold said. "Hidden behind a fold in the rock."

The teammates proceeded around the fold and found a corridor matching the ones they were now so familiar with. "That was a weird encounter," Aderyn said. "I guess I thought dungeons had some kind of unity. You know, like only goblins, or only magical beasts. Not bugbears and then fungi."

"The variable dungeons are truly random," Isold said. "Not just among themselves, but in terms of the challenges they pose with each new iteration. There's no way of knowing what you might face."

The hall turned left, then left again, and for a while they walked along a straight passage that again smelled of nothing but lit torches. Aderyn found herself walking close behind Owen. Instinctively, she wanted to be near enough to give him direction from her Warmaster skills the moment a new threat arose. But he'd done just fine fighting the fungal gardeners. He hadn't had her guidance at all. A moment's self-pity struck her and she dismissed it. She had value. Owen knew it, and she knew it. One missed opportunity didn't invalidate all the other times she'd been helpful.

The hall turned a few more times, then made another turn, at which point the passage opened up into a wider hall that curved out of sight about fifty feet ahead. On their left, a single wooden door stood closed and silent. It looked perfectly ordinary. It was also the only wooden door they'd seen in the whole dungeon except for the one they'd entered by.

CHAPTER FIFTEEN

They all gathered together and regarded the door closely. "Maybe it's an escape route. A last chance if people decide the dungeon is too much for them and they don't want to face the final battle," Livia suggested.

"In which case, we definitely don't want to touch it," Owen said.

"I don't know," Aderyn said. "My **[Improved Assess 1]** skill doesn't say anything about it. If it was a magic door, I think that would show up."

"Well, I'm curious," Weston said, and opened the door as they all let out various gasps of protest.

The room beyond was smaller even than the transport circle chamber. Its walls were lined with weapons racks on two sides and a narrow wooden table on the third side, and both weapons racks and table were covered with weapons and armor, shining and perfect. Aderyn gasped and stepped forward. "This has to be to prepare us for the final fight."

"I was thinking I've never seen anything that looks so much like a trap," Owen murmured. "What does **[Improved Assess 1]** tell you?"

Aderyn had reached out to pick up a short sword with a ruby embedded in the pommel. At Owen's words, she hesitated. She blinked both eyes to Assess the room.

Instantly, the room blazed with sickly green light.

Name: Trap of Greed
Type: Contact poison
Power level: 1

But that wasn't all. Below the block of text, the system letters read:

Touching one of these items will cause the object to adhere to the victim, causing slow acid damage until the object is removed. Removal requires a new victim to permit transfer to himself.

"Wow," Aderyn breathed. "That is a *nasty* kind of trap."

"So I was right," Owen said.

Aderyn explained what she'd learned. "I'm guessing my **[Improved Assess 1]** skill works on monsters, dungeons, and magical traps, but not items."

"I certainly didn't notice it, and I'm good at spotting non-magical traps," Weston said. "I think finding and disarming magical traps is something I gain later. Warmaster is sure turning out to be an interesting class."

Aderyn considered teasing him about how useless he'd originally thought her class was, but she was still too on edge about how close she'd come to having her skin dissolved by acid for levity. "Do we still get experience if we just don't touch the things? Or do we have to eliminate the trap?"

Wise choices lead to greater understanding.
You have received [100 XP] for avoiding the Trap of Greed.

Aderyn jerked. "Did you all see that?"

Owen nodded. He didn't look surprised, but all three of the others seemed as stunned as Aderyn felt.

"Did the system just talk to us?" Weston said in a hushed voice.

"It could just have been the expected message related to the outcome," Isold said, but he didn't sound certain.

"You mean, that's not normal?" Owen asked.

"It could be. It has to be. Why would the system talk to us?" Aderyn said. She backed up and shut the door firmly on the **[Trap of Greed]**.

"We have to be close to the end," Livia said. "That corridor curves. None of the others curved. Are we ready?"

They formed up again, Owen in the lead, Weston at the rear, the others grouped loosely in the middle. The hall continued to curve to the right, not quite spiraling, but definitely circling something. The lights were brighter now, and after a moment, Aderyn realized there weren't any torches and the light was coming from somewhere near the ceiling, which was high and white. The stones had gradually lightened until they were white, too.

"This looks like LED lighting," Owen murmured. "A kind of light in my world that doesn't come from fire or sun."

"It's bright. And it feels unnatural," Aderyn replied. Directly ahead, the glow increased until Aderyn couldn't look directly at it.

Owen slowed as they neared the bright end of the corridor. It looked like a door made of light. "Are we ready?"

Everyone nodded.

Owen squared his shoulders and stepped through. Aderyn followed close behind.

Immediately, the light was a more normal warm yellow, and the brightness faded. As Aderyn had guessed, the new room was perfectly round, with walls of pale gray stone and a high domed ceiling plastered white. There were no windows, but tapestries depicting mythical creatures like griffons and unicorns and dragons hung at intervals around the circle, with small round tables holding delicate porcelain vases between the tapestries.

A man rose from his chair—no, it was almost a throne—that stood on a dais at the center of the room. "Congratulations," he said. "Welcome to your reward."

Aderyn Assessed him immediately.

NaMe: Kem0n

ClAss: Sp3llcraFter

LeveL: 3

Aderyn blinked. The letters wavered, then spelled out:

Name: Kemon

Class: Spellcrafter

Level: 3

Kemon looked only a few years older than Aderyn, with black hair and striking blue eyes. He smiled in a friendly way as the other teammates joined Owen and Aderyn.

Owen didn't lower his sword. "Reward?"

"What about the final boss?" Weston asked. He, too, was brandishing his sword.

"This is a variable dungeon. The challenges you faced in reaching this place more than make up for a final fight. Therefore, there isn't one." Kemon smiled again and gestured at a chest beside his throne. "Go ahead and claim your treasure."

"Aderyn?" Owen asked.

Aderyn hesitated. She looked Kemon over. He looked perfectly ordinary. "It's another trap," she said, backing up. "He's not what he appears to be."

Kemon's smile became even more pleasant. "And what do you think I really am, young Warmaster?"

"Someone who shouldn't be able to identify my class at only level three," Aderyn said. "Owen!"

Kemon's body shivered, revealing a taller but still human form with a longsword sheathed at his side. His face slipped and slid like oozing mud, making Aderyn's stomach churn. Beneath the mud was —nothing, a wrinkled, featureless blank. Kemon drew his sword in time to catch Owen's first attack on the blade. "Good instincts," he snarled.

A new message appeared.

The Faceless One

Type: Abomination

Power Level: 5

"Abomination!" she shrieked. "I can't see any obvious weak spots!"

At the same moment, Isold shouted, "Don't let it touch your skin!"

The Faceless One blocked and parried and struck so fast he held off both Owen and Weston with ease. His lack of facial features made him seem even more terrifying, because he either didn't need eyes or perceived them through other means.

Livia raised her hands and shouted. A ball of sticky mud shot away from her. The Faceless One blocked Weston's next swing and then jumped impossibly high so the mud sailed past him to impact against a tapestry of a basilisk. He landed atop the throne and thrust at Weston's left side, slicing through his shirt and into the flesh beneath. Weston cried out in pain and staggered backward.

Aderyn once more Assessed the Faceless One, hoping some new shred of information would appear. She was vaguely aware of Isold rushing to Weston's side and of Livia throwing another *mudball*, but most of her attention was taken up by the unchanged block of text. The blue lines scrolled across the Faceless One's body, but no dots of light indicating weak spots appeared.

Owen was fighting alone now. Aderyn heard Isold muttering something as he dug through his pack and hoped it meant he had something that would heal Weston. The Faceless One bore down on Owen, pressing the attack, and as good as he'd become, Owen was no match for a skilled swordsman more than twice his level.

Aderyn cast about for something, anything that would help Owen. Her gaze fell on one of the porcelain vases nearby. She snatched it up and shouted, "Hey, monster! You!" before hurling the vase at the Faceless One's head.

It missed him completely, sailing above him with a good three inches to spare. But it made him flinch. Owen took the Faceless One's moment of distraction and used it to step away from the monster's attack, then swing a heavy, two-handed blow that caught the Faceless One across his midsection.

The Faceless One roared with fury and pain and thrust his blade at Owen. Aderyn threw another vase. This one shattered on the monster's shoulder, making him jerk so his sword thrust missed Owen completely.

Livia shouted again, and this time the floor rippled beneath Aderyn's feet as a wave of earth passed beneath her, rooting the Faceless One to the ground. He tried to pull free, and Owen's sword took him in the chest.

The monster jerked again, away from the sword impaling him. He dropped his sword and grabbed Owen's wrist, making Owen cry out in pain and try to wrench away. But in the next moment, he sagged and slid off Owen's sword. Immediately, the room's lights flashed three times, and system messages appeared in front of Aderyn's face:

**Congratulations! You have defeated [The Faceless One].
You have earned [500 XP]**

**Congratulations! You have completed the quest [Clear
Dungeon Spiteful].
You have been awarded [1000 XP]**

And then, the single line

Welcome to Level Three

"Level three!" she shouted, turning to Owen to share her excitement. He had slumped to the floor and had his wrist tucked under his opposite arm. "What happened?" she exclaimed, dropping to her knees beside him.

"Skin to skin contact," Owen said through gritted teeth. "I think he drained some of my blood." He held out his hand, and Aderyn hissed in shock. A ring of four evenly spaced blood blisters, with a fifth a little distance away, marked Owen's wrist.

"Should we bandage it?" she asked.

"Isold will know," Owen said.

Aderyn helped him stand and supported him as they walked to where Isold knelt beside Weston, who was just sitting up. Weston looked pale, and blood stained his shirt, but he didn't move like he was in pain.

"I will have to thank Master Nessia for the gift of this healing wand," Isold said. "Though to be honest, I think she was glad to see me move on. Glad for my sake, I mean—she's not a bad person." He swept the wand to point at Owen's wrist, then lowered it. "Unfortunately it can't heal drained energy. That will have to return on its own."

Aderyn focused on the team display. Weston's bar indicating his health was almost at full, and Owen's wasn't much lower, but Owen's radiated a pulsing red light. "How long will that take?" she asked.

Isold shrugged. "I don't know anything about magical healing except that rest makes it happen faster. Maybe tomorrow the blisters will be healed?"

"It doesn't hurt," Owen said. Aderyn thought he was lying, but four days' acquaintance with her new friend had already taught her that he disliked being fussed over. "We won. Let's see what the dungeon has for us."

"This, for one," Livia said. She held the Faceless One's longsword and was examining it critically. "I'm no weapons expert, but I can see magic on it."

"It is a <**Sword of Striking**>," Isold said, taking it from Livia. "An enchanted blade that does increased damage. They are very common, and the damage increase isn't much, but for a level three Swordsworn, it will be effective." He bowed and presented the sword to Owen.

"Then I'm not the Fated One," Owen exclaimed. "Not if this is the loot I got."

"You see?" Aderyn said. "Nothing to worry about."

"Except that was the boss monster's treasure," Livia said. "The dungeon treasure is, well, probably in there." She pointed at the chest.

They all stared at the chest for a moment. Then Weston knelt beside it and fiddled with the lock. "It's open," he said, and threw back the lid.

"What is it?" Owen said. His voice was tense.

Weston removed a small velvet bag from the chest and opened it. "Looks like garnets. Ten of them." He set the bag aside and pulled out two potion bottles that clinked against each other. "No idea what these are. But this is interesting." He hauled out a bundle of threadbare gray velvet and shook it so it was revealed to be a cloak. "Is it magical?"

"Yes," Livia and Isold said in unison. Isold went on, "It is a <**Cloak of Mists**>. If the person wearing it pulls the hood up, they become indistinct. Not invisible, but—well, let me show you." Isold wrapped the cloak around himself and pulled the hood well over his face. Immediately Aderyn felt compelled to look elsewhere, as if Isold had just become the least interesting thing in the room. She made herself focus on him, but even then, he was hard to watch.

"Amazing," Owen said. "Then I think we should look for a door out of this place."

Weston was staring into the chest. "That isn't all," he said, his voice suddenly somber. With both hands, he reached into the chest and withdrew something that shone brightly in the brilliant light. Weston raised it high enough that all of them could see it was a circle of gold, about the thickness of a thumb, sized to fit a man's head.

Chapter Sixteen

Aderyn's breathing was loud and harsh. "That doesn't mean anything," she said, and felt instantly stupid. Of course it meant something. This was why they were here.

"It doesn't have to be Owen," Livia said. "Maybe it's one of us. We should all try. Only the Fated One can wear it, remember?"

Weston lowered the circlet onto his own head. He yelped and snatched it off. "It squeezed," he said. "Felt like it was trying to take the top of my skull off."

No one moved to take the circlet. Then Owen stepped forward. "I'm sick of waiting and worrying."

He roughly tugged the circlet over his blond hair so it sat unevenly atop his head. The gold shone with a sudden white light that smelled like lilacs. Everyone except Owen exclaimed and shielded their eyes. When the light faded, Aderyn saw Owen looking at the ground, his free hand clenched tight, his hand that held the <**Sword of Striking**> almost white in how tightly it gripped the hilt. The gold circlet fit him perfectly.

"Well," she began, and couldn't think of anything else to say.

"I guess this was always what was going to happen," Owen said. "It's not like I'm not the hero, right? Mysterious stranger from another world, good at sword fighting even though I'd never held a sword in my life before four days ago... it's like someone's written me a script to star in."

"You don't have to follow the path," Aderyn said. She put a hand on his shoulder and made him look at her. "There are all those other Fated Ones, right? One of them, one of the ones who actually wants it, let them take it on. You just have to get back to your world."

"Unless this world decides not to let me go," Owen said bitterly.

"Stop it!" Aderyn shouted. "I promised I'd help you, and that hasn't changed. We'll go to Guerdon Deep and find someone who can send you home. And if the system throws extra challenges at us, we'll show it we can't be intimidated. But you have to stop feeling sorry for yourself. That won't get us anywhere."

Owen's eyes met hers. Then he smiled, a sideways, self-deprecating smile. "You're right," he said. "Was that more Warmaster knowledge?"

"No, my mother's wisdom. She always says if you want things to change, start by changing yourself." Aderyn squeezed Owen's hand and let him go. "And maybe the circlet gives you amazing new skills! You don't have to be the Fated One to appreciate those."

"Unfortunately, no," Isold said, his gaze fixed on the circlet. "My Herald's knowledge tells me that it is a **<Circlet of Naming>,** and that its one magical ability is to identify someone with a given trait or traits. That is, there are **<Circlets of Naming>** that only certain classes can wear, or those with a particular skill. This one is intended to identify the Fated One, or rather someone the system has chosen as a possible Fated One."

Owen gingerly took hold of the **<Circlet of Naming>** and with some relief removed it. "I was afraid it was going to be stuck to my head."

"Put it in your pack and forget about it," Weston suggested. "And let's get out of here. Did anyone see a door?"

There hadn't been a door when they entered, just the unbroken wall with its tapestries, but now a plain wooden door identical to the entrance had appeared. After picking up and stowing the rest of the treasure, the teammates approached the door. It had no handle, but Owen laid his hand palm-first against the wood, and in a flash of light, they were outdoors.

The sun had fully set while they were in Dungeon Spiteful, and with only a fat sliver of moon in the sky, most of the light came from a nearby campfire. Three figures rose and approached the team.

"You stole our quest," the Lightfingers said. A knife appeared in her hand. "Hand over what you got, and we won't kill you all and take it anyway." The Swordsworn stood just behind her, her hand on her weapon.

"We outnumber you," Owen said without flinching. "And you're not that much higher level than we are now. Back off. You'll have your turn at the dungeon."

The Flamecrafter raised her hand, and a fiery glow surrounded her fingers. "It's not just about the loot," she said. "We were beat out by a bunch of younglings. You think we want that news to get around?"

"You mean the news that we tricked you with a ruse even a level one should have seen through?" Aderyn said. It might be a mistake, taunting them, but she had a feeling this was going to end in a fight no matter what she said. Assessment hadn't revealed any major weaknesses, so maybe **[Discern Weakness]** only worked on monsters. In any case, this fight would come down to skill against skill.

The Flamecrafter snarled, then shrieked as a mass of water twice the size of her head fell out of the sky, soaking her and dousing her flame. The Swordsworn woman drew her sword, and she and the Lightfingers lunged at Owen, who was the nearest target. Owen whirled out of the way of the knife and parried the sword, and then Weston was beside him, his own blade at the ready.

"That way," Aderyn told Livia. "Stop that Flamecrafter!"

Livia nodded and moved left, giving herself a better view of the enemy spellslinger. Aderyn moved to the right, saw more fire erupt, and flung herself to the ground so the fire blast passed harmlessly over her head. She didn't know where Isold had got to and hoped he would stay out of the way of the fighting. She pushed herself to her feet and kept going, scanning the ground for large rocks or tree branches or something she could fling at the enemy fighters the way she had thrown the vases at the Faceless One. She might not have a sword, but she could still do *something*.

She heard Livia chanting, and the Flamecrafter shrieked again, but Aderyn's attention was focused on the swordfight and she could only hope that shriek meant something good for her team. The grassy plain was totally free of branches and large rocks. Aderyn hissed in frustration. She couldn't dive into the fight without getting hurt and possibly getting her teammates hurt as well, no doubt the reason Livia was fighting the Flamecrafter instead of trying to immobilize the Lightfingers and the female Swordsworn with *mudball*. But Owen and Weston were barely holding their own against the two women, who clearly had not only experience with their weapons but practice in fighting as one.

Impatient, she tossed her pack down and rooted through it. Clothes... tin plate and mug... <**Matchlighter**>... lantern. Aderyn snatched up the lantern and swung it around by its handle. The lantern was small but heavy, a good blunt weapon if she timed her attack right. She edged close to the battle and, bouncing on the balls of her feet, waited for Owen to strike.

Owen swung his sword, forcing the female Swordsworn back a step. As the woman prepared to retaliate with a lunge, Aderyn whirled the lantern around her head and, without letting go of the handle, struck the Swordsworn in the back of her head.

The woman jerked, then slumped to the ground unconscious.

**Congratulations! You have defeated [Caprissa the Swordsworn].
You have earned [600 XP].**

Owen ignored her and pressed the attack against the Lightfingers, adding his strength to Weston's. The Lightfingers, armed with two knives—Aderyn hadn't seen where the other one came from—was forced into a defensive fight, and after only a few seconds, she flung down her blades and raised her hands in surrender.

**Congratulations! You have defeated [Edda the Lightfingers].
You have earned [600 XP].**

"Watch her," Owen told Weston, and walked back to the fallen Swordsworn. She was just beginning to stir when Owen took her sword and tossed it well away from her. "Isold?"

"Here." Isold's voice came from nowhere. Her eyes watering, Aderyn focused on where the Flamecrafter stood with her arms pinned behind her by no one Aderyn could see until Isold pushed back the hood of the <**Cloak of Mists**>. "Stop struggling, miss, or we'll have to restrain you more punitively."

Aderyn didn't know what kind of punitively he meant, but the Flamecrafter held still.

**Congratulations! You have defeated [Neala the Flamecrafter].
You have earned [600 XP].**

Owen walked back to where the Lightfingers knelt with Weston's sword lying against the side of her throat. "You made a mistake," he said. "But it's obvious you're opportunists rather than evil, so we'll let you go with a warning. And... we'll take all your money."

"What?" The Lightfingers, Edda, jerked and came up short against Weston's blade. "You can't do that!"

"Of course we can. Aderyn, take whatever coin you can find. Isold, bring the Flamecrafter to sit with her friends. Livia, collect their weapons and throw them far away across the field so they'll have to spend time hunting for them." Owen smiled pleasantly at the furious Edda. "Don't follow us. We don't give second warnings."

Livia collected the knives and the sword and used her magic to toss each into the darkness in a different direction. The Swordsworn, Caprissa, regained consciousness in time to see her weapon go sailing into the dark. Aderyn, who was retrieving the woman's belt pouch when this happened, avoided the Swordsworn's eyes. Owen might be confident that the enemy team wouldn't follow them, looking for revenge, but Aderyn didn't intend to taunt them beyond their limits.

She gathered three belt pouches and decided for the same reason not to rifle through the women's gear. Without counting her loot, she nodded to Owen, who said, "If you're patient, your time will come to face this dungeon. Until then, like I said, don't think about following us."

The women glared at him, but made no move to rise. Owen walked away toward the distant road, not looking to see if the others were following. Aderyn hurried to catch up, followed by the other three.

By the time they reached the road, the fire was a distant speck and the forest was a dark mass of trees moving gently in the gradually rising wind. "Don't stop," Owen said.

"Even I can't see in the dark, Owen," Weston said. "We need a light."

"I think I broke the lantern," Aderyn said.

"That probably saved our lives," Owen replied. "Livia, can you make a light?"

A tiny flicker grew to an *orb of light* cupped in Livia's palm. "It's not much."

"It's enough. We just have to get far enough away from that team to camp for the night. I saw a clearing when we were on our way here —it's about a mile back."

Aderyn watched what she could see of Owen's face, lit from the side by Livia's *orb of light*. He looked and sounded as confident as he had while they were clearing the dungeon, as if the <**Circlet of Naming's**> identifying him as a potential Fated One hadn't happened. She was sure he hadn't forgotten; he just had a knack for leadership and, she hoped, had put aside his fears and anger in favor of getting them all back to Market Warding safely.

It was less than a mile before Owen said, "It's that way," and steered them off the road to a small clearing. It wasn't totally empty; a few saplings grew in the space, but there was enough room for all of them to spread bedrolls. Aderyn lay back and gazed into the blackness. The moon had dipped low above the horizon, close to setting and invisible behind the tree line, and the trees still grew thickly enough that she couldn't see more than a handful of stars, not enough to shed any light over the clearing.

On a whim, she squinched one eye to bring up the Codex and whispered, "Advancement."

Name: Aderyn

Class: Warmaster

Level: 3

<u>Skills:</u> **Bluff (2), Climb (1), Conversation (1), Intimidate (1), Sense Truth (3), Survival (1), Swim (1), Knowledge: Monsters (3)**

<u>Class Skills:</u> **Improved Assess 1 (4), Awareness (3), Knowledge: Geography (2), Spot (3), Discern Weakness (3), Dodge (2), Improvised Distraction (1)**

[**Improvised Distraction**]. That was certainly a good name for what she'd learned to do. It was too bad there wasn't a Codex listing for what skills a particular class would eventually have—or did that mean each Warmaster, for example, gained different skills based on what she did as an adventurer?

The thought saddened her. As far as she knew, there weren't any other Warmasters who advanced far enough to find out what their skills were. The idea of being the only one was depressing. She made herself think of other things. She had friends. She had a partner. She *was* advancing. With all of that, there was no reason to stay discouraged. But the sadness niggled at her still.

CHAPTER SEVENTEEN

S he cast about for a distraction. Owen lay a short distance away. She glanced at him, though his outline wasn't distinct in the light from the orb Livia hadn't yet extinguished. His eyes were closed, but she didn't think he was asleep. She Assessed him, curious about how things had changed.

Name: Jacob Owen Lindberg

Class: Swordsworn

Level: 3

<u>Skills:</u> **Assess (2), Awareness (3), Bluff (2), Climb (3), Conversation (2), Intimidate (2), Sense Truth (2), Spot (1), Survival (1), Swim (10)**

<u>Class Skills:</u> **Basic Weapon Proficiency (4), Basic Armor Proficiency (3), Knowledge: Monsters (2), Exploit Weakness (3), Dodge (2), Parry (1)**

"Your sword skills are growing," she whispered.

Owen's eyes opened. "It feels so strange," he whispered back, not looking at her. "In my world, people have to train for months, maybe years, to develop fighting skills. Not that there are a lot of sword fighters where I come from. Martial arts, maybe."

"What are martial arts?"

"Fighting with fists and feet. Learning how to disarm someone. Pinning an opponent."

"That sounds like something a Swifthands would do, or maybe a Lone Wolf." The light went out, and Aderyn rolled on her side to face Owen more directly. "So, you really never held a sword before four days ago."

Owen nodded. "And you didn't know anything about fighting either."

"I studied sword fighting under my father for two years. I've never fought in a real battle. Or—did you mean **[Discern Weakness]**?"

"Both, actually. I was wondering if anyone can learn skills when they aren't given them by the system. Wouldn't that make it pointless for you to have studied sword fighting?"

"People can learn skills the hard way. Most don't see the point, no, not when class skills are so much easier to develop. But I imagine it's like your world—it takes years of practice, but you do develop the skills. My mother says if you work at a skill for long enough, the system will give it to you, but she didn't say how long was 'enough.'"

Owen nodded. Then he sat up enough to prop himself on his elbow. "Hold on. Did you see my skills list?"

"I did—" Aderyn gasped. "I couldn't see it before. Wait."

She sat up fully and scanned the clearing. Weston was asleep and snoring gently. Livia was lying some distance from Weston with her arms over her head, blocking the sound of snores. Isold was sitting with his back to a tree and his head thrown back. Aderyn Assessed him.

Name: Isold
Class: Herald
Level: 3

"I can't see Isold's skills," she said.

"I heard my name," Isold said. "Do you need something?"

"No, it's fine. Aren't you tired?" Aderyn asked.

"My mind is too busy to sleep, despite my body's weariness," Isold said. "I have been examining my class skills and making some decisions."

"That's funny, because I was just experimenting with **[Improved Assess 1]**." Aderyn lay back, but propped herself on one elbow. "I can see Owen's skills, but not yours. Do you have an idea why?"

"I have all the **[Knowledge]** skills as class skills starting at level one, but within those skill sets, the actual information is spotty. It seems my knowledge develops as I use it. That means I know a great deal about magical items and monsters and very little about the capabilities of each class. And Warmaster is particularly unknown."

"Too bad, because I was wondering what else I could look forward to," Aderyn said.

"Is there some distribution curve for the classes? I mean," Owen corrected himself when Isold and Aderyn stared at him in confusion, "do you know what percentage of adventurers become Swordsworn, or Earthbreakers, or Warmasters, or whatever?"

"That is an excellent question," Isold said, "and unfortunately it's not one I know the answer to."

"I don't know, either," Aderyn said. "I always thought most adventurers were Swordsworn, but that's because my father teaches them, so I saw more of them than any other."

"I guess it doesn't matter." Owen relaxed onto his bedroll. "Can I ask an insulting question, Isold?"

"Go ahead."

"Do Heralds ever learn to do anything but share knowledge with their teammates? Because, no offense, but that doesn't seem like a good adventuring skill, not when there are so many monsters trying to eat our faces."

Isold chuckled. "Heralds learn to sway individuals and crowds through speech and music. They—"

Owen shot upright. "I'm sorry, did you say you're a *bard?*"

"Whatever that word is, you say it like it's a bad thing," Aderyn said.

"It's not, but—" Owen put a hand over his mouth like he was containing a laugh.

"Well, I wasn't insulted before, but I'm starting to be," Isold said, but he didn't sound angry.

"I'm sorry, I'm not laughing at you, it's just that in roleplaying games in my world—"

"Owen, I told you, this isn't a game," Aderyn said irritably.

"I know, and I'm not saying it is, I'm saying there are games in my world that are similar to what this world is naturally. In those games, people usually play bards as joke characters, goofy or always making bad puns. Or they seduce everyone they come across."

"'Insulted' is looking like a better option all the time, Owen," Isold said.

"I apologize. I'm not saying this well. What I mean is that based on how valuable your class has been to our adventuring, I will never think of bard as a joke class again. I was laughing at myself."

"Herald sounds more noble than bard," Aderyn said.

"I hope Heralds are no more foolish than the average adventurer, but I admit we are known for our seductive ways," Isold said, smiling. "I personally am not good at romantic talk."

Owen chuckled. "Well, musicians generally don't need talk."

"This is also true." Isold's smile deepened, and he looked caught in pleasant memories.

"What instruments do you play?" Aderyn asked.

Isold tilted his head back again. "None."

"But I thought Heralds started at level one with a musical instrument," Aderyn said. "The adventurers in Far Haven who became Heralds made a ritual of choosing the instrument they're drawn to."

"And I didn't want to be anything but a Spiritsmith, remember?" Isold shrugged. "I might have an affinity for a particular instrument, but I never tried to discover it. As it happens, though, I don't need one."

"But you won't be able to exercise your skills fully without one," Aderyn protested.

Isold fixed her with his gaze. Then he began to sing.

His voice was a magnificent tenor, so beautiful Aderyn didn't at first realize she knew the song. It was a familiar lullaby, one Aderyn's mother had sung to her as a child. Isold made it sound haunting, perfectly suited to this tiny clearing that might as well be in the depths of the sea, the darkness was so complete.

When he finished, Owen said, "Ah."

"That was amazing," Aderyn said. "I don't think you need an instrument at all."

"Thank you," Isold said. "I didn't realize at first that my voice is an instrument, and that no matter how I resisted the Call, I was prepared for this class from the moment I sang my first duet with my father. I suppose it's true the system knows us better than we know ourselves."

The three fell silent. Weston had stopped snoring, and Livia had taken up the discordant snoring melody. Aderyn lay back and considered Isold's words. If it was true the system knew each adventurer well enough to choose a class that suited them, what did that say about Aderyn? What about her was fit to be a Warmaster, a tactician, someone who stood back and shouted suggestions?

"Owen," she whispered.

"Mhmm?" Owen replied, sounding groggy.

"Can I have your old sword?"

"What, right now?"

Aderyn giggled. "No. Tomorrow."

"Sure." Owen yawned audibly. To her relief, he didn't ask any more questions. She wasn't sure she knew the answers to them. But she was tired of being helpless. So what if [**Weapon Proficiency (swords)**] wasn't her class skill? She was going to make the system recognize her hard work. And maybe it would take her somewhere unexpected.

The following morning, Aderyn sat with Owen in the taproom of the inn she was starting to think of as theirs. Maybe spending a couple of nights there didn't really qualify it for that name, but it was the one familiar thing in this adventure since leaving Far Haven, and Aderyn, well, she wouldn't exactly miss the place when she and Owen left for Asylum, but she would have fond memories of it.

Owen had a mug in front of him he hadn't touched. "I'll be sad to leave this place behind," he said. "Though I'm sure some of that is I'm not much of a camper. I mean I don't love sleeping outdoors," he clarified.

"I like it when the weather is warm. Not so much when it snows. So I guess we have that in common." Aderyn put her hand on the hilt of Owen's old sword, now strapped to her hip. It felt good. Natural. Possibly that was because it had been her father's, and it was familiar, but she liked to think it was because she was meant to wield it.

"I thought Weston would be faster than this," Owen said. "Maybe we should all have gone to sell the treasure."

"Weston is right that a big group of people all trying to sell one thing just gives the buyer more opportunities to cheat them. We're not in a hurry, right?"

Owen shrugged. "I guess not."

The taproom door opened, and Livia entered. She looked more alert than she had when they'd all woken in the clearing that morning before returning to Market Warding. "He's not back yet?" she said. She took a seat and waved to the serving maid for a drink. "That's probably good."

"Is it? Why?" Owen asked.

"If he sold everything quickly, it might mean he didn't get the best deal. This means he did some good bargaining." Livia arranged her pack by the side of her chair. "Where's Isold?"

"He said he needed to talk to someone." Aderyn drank the last of her ale. She felt uncomfortable in Livia's presence. They hadn't yet dissolved the team, and Aderyn didn't know how to suggest it. They'd become close in their adventures, and it felt like rudeness to announce it was over and that was the end of their companionship. And yet no one had said anything about continuing on to Asylum and then Guerdon Deep.

Isold entered the taproom at that moment, followed by Weston. "Sorry about the delay, but I wanted to get the best price for everything, and that meant having those potions identified."

"It's fine," Owen said. "What did we earn?"

"That's the other thing," Weston said. He sat next to Owen and set a small, clinking bag on the table. "If you don't mind, I'll take the <Cloak of Mists> as my share. It's worth a little more than our individual earnings, so I'll be happy to compensate each of you—"

"Don't worry about it," Owen said. "I'm sure it's close enough."

"That will be so useful to a Moonlighter," Aderyn said.

"Thanks." Weston upended the sack carefully, pouring silver coins onto the table. "The potions provided boosts to skills none of us have, so I didn't think selling them was a bad idea. And of course the <Circlet of Naming> is worthless."

Owen grimaced. "What about the <Sword of Striking>? Shouldn't I take that as my share, and not get any coin?"

"The sword was your personal reward for killing the Faceless One," Aderyn explained. "It doesn't count against our treasure."

"That doesn't seem fair. You and Isold don't kill monsters directly, so you wouldn't ever earn personal rewards."

"We don't *yet*," Isold said. "Heralds gain powerful offensive magics as they advance in level, and who knows what Aderyn will learn to do with her new sword?"

Owen still looked skeptical, but he nodded.

"For the rest of you, the total comes to nineteen gold, and divided four ways, that's three gold and twenty-five silver each." Weston was dividing the pile into four smaller piles with deft fingers as he spoke.

"That's a lot," Aderyn said.

"It's not all." Weston upended another small sack, and coins rolled everywhere. "This is what we took from those adventurers. Another ten gold, divided five ways."

Livia gathered her money up in silence, but Aderyn caught sight of her face and her expression was blank, like she didn't agree it was a lot. Aderyn didn't think Livia was the type to complain about being cheated, especially when she hadn't been, but this was one more evidence that Livia came from wealth.

Owen tucked his coin away in his pocket—Mariet had made sure his trousers had that unique innovation of hers—and then looked each of the others in the eye, one at a time. "Well. It's been quite an adventure."

Nobody said anything. Weston glanced at Livia, who returned his look.

"Thanks for... well, for everything," Owen continued. "Good luck in your advancement."

Still, no one spoke. Then Isold cleared his throat. "The journey to Asylum isn't a hard one, I've heard. But Guerdon Deep is in the Forsaken Lands, and it can be a dangerous trip. At least five days from Asylum to that city."

"We'll be fine," Owen said.

"Better if it wasn't just the two of you," Livia said.

Owen's hand, which had been fiddling with the mug handle, stilled. "I suppose that's true."

"Oh, for the love—" Weston exclaimed. "Fine. Since none of the rest of you are willing, I'll say it. We don't think there's any point in breaking up this team. And I, for one, want to see your journey through to the end."

Owen blinked. "You do?"

"This is the best challenge I've ever heard of," Livia said. "I agree with the musclebound Moonlighter. I would hate to stay behind."

"And, to be clear," Isold said, "just because you don't want to be the Fated One doesn't mean you won't be at the center of excitement, and how better to win advancement and treasure than that?"

Owen turned to Aderyn. "Did you know about this?"

"No, but it makes sense," Aderyn replied. "We all worked well together, and my father says that's not a given, especially not with a chance-met team." She didn't add that she felt like the teammates were becoming friends. That seemed too sentimental. But it was still true.

"Well, I—" Owen smiled. "I guess I shouldn't argue."

"It would do you no good, as I think you wanted this outcome," Isold said, clapping Owen on the shoulder. "I've spent my morning supplying myself for a journey, and I for one am ready to go at any time."

"Then, if everyone's ready?" Owen surveyed the teammates. "Let's head out."

Aderyn shouldered her pack and followed Owen. She felt unexpectedly cheerful. Five days to Asylum, with who knew how many battles during that time...they might be as much as level five when they reached their destination! Or at least level four, which was still respectable. She listened to Weston and Livia's friendly argument over the merits and drawbacks to rising early and smiled. Teammates. Companions, even. And an unusual quest that might have a great reward. Not bad for just starting out.

CHAPTER EIGHTEEN

They left Market Warding behind and followed the well-trodden road north and slightly west, clear enough they didn't need Aderyn's compass. Aderyn was about to ask Owen to tell them something about his world when she saw him stiffen and briefly slow his steps. Ahead, four travelers came into view, headed their way. "They're probably not dangerous," she told him.

"After fighting those three women at Dungeon Spiteful, I'm not inclined to take chances," Owen said. "They're too far away for me to Assess them, though I wouldn't learn anything but their levels anyway."

"We're still within sight of Market Warding," Isold said. "They won't attack us without provocation because the guards might ban them if they think they're dangerous."

"Besides, we outnumber them," Weston said.

"Not by enough to matter," Livia objected.

"It's fine," Owen said. "We'll just keep moving and ignore them. But—Assess them anyway, Aderyn, when you can."

Aderyn had already made up her mind to do that.

She wasn't sure how far away **[Improved Assess 1]** worked, so she tried every couple of seconds as the foursome approached. When the familiar display finally appeared, she thought the travelers might be fifty yards away. Closer than she liked, but she'd take anything.

Name: Rhadion
Class: Deadeye
Level: 5

Name: Virten
    Class: Pathseer
    Level: 4

Name: Seren
    Class: Swifthands
    Level: 5

Name: Nesta
    Class: Spellcrafter
    Level: 4

"They're close to our level," she said. "A Deadeye, a Pathseer, a Swifthands, and a Spellcrafter."

"You said a Swifthands does martial arts. Hands and feet fighting," Owen said, "and a Spellcrafter imbues objects with magic. What are the other two?"

"A Deadeye fights with a bow, most often a longbow," Isold said. "Pathseers have skill at tracking and moving silently, as well as with attacking from the shadows. Their abilities overlap somewhat with a Moonlighter's."

"A monk, an enchanter, an archer, and a ranger," Owen said, mostly to himself, which was good because Aderyn never knew what to say when he started talking nonsense. "Try to look confident, just in case the threat of being banned from Market Warding isn't enough."

Aderyn didn't know what "looking confident" would look like, but she strode more briskly and kept a hand on the swaying hilt of her sword. She glanced at Owen now and then out of the corner of her eye. He always looked confident, or almost always.

She watched the adventurers' approach with what she hoped was a Warmaster's sense of tactics. They were grouped too closely together to effectively fight, as the Spellcrafter would be in the Swifthand's way. The Deadeye lagged behind his group, but his bow was unstrung, as was the Pathseer's shorter bow. "They won't attack," she murmured. "I'm sure of it. Or the bows would be readied."

Owen nodded. "Good observation."

By this time, they were close enough for the Swifthands to shout, "Hey there! Are you heading for Asylum?"

Owen hesitated, glanced at Aderyn once more, then called back, "We are. Did you come from there?"

Neither group stopped walking, and in only a few seconds they were face to face. "Yes, we've just made that journey," the Swifthands said. She had a cheerful, friendly expression and looked perfectly relaxed, the way Aderyn felt she herself would look if she had weapons at the ends of her arms and legs. "Bad luck for you, though."

"Why is that?" Owen asked.

"We encountered quite a few monsters on the trip. The route is mostly clear now. So if you were counting on fights to boost your advancement..." The Swifthands looked genuinely regretful. "Still, it's not like we could have let the monsters win, right?"

"Don't worry about us," Owen said, matching her friendly tone. "We'll gain experience somehow."

"Good attitude. And good luck to you!" The Swifthands and her team saluted them with waves and passed on in the direction of Market Warding.

Owen didn't move at first. Weston shifted his weight. "That's not great," he said. "I thought we'd encounter enough monsters that we'd be at least level four when we reached Asylum."

"And we ought to be level five before we head for Guerdon Deep," Isold said.

"Maybe she's wrong, and more monsters will arise," Livia said, but she didn't sound confident.

Owen shook his head as if coming out of a daydream. "There's nothing we can do about it, unless there's some spell for summoning monsters for us to kill?" Livia shook her head. "Then we'll travel, and maybe this will be a pleasant, boring journey, and we'll all be grateful for it later."

Aderyn thought this was the most optimistic thing anyone had ever said.

AT NOON FIVE DAYS LATER, THEY REACHED THE GATES OF Asylum. After all that time walking through the grassy plains, interrupted occasionally by stands of trees too small to be called forests, Aderyn was glad to see something different to stop the boredom.

And it had been boring. They'd fought only two battles, neither of them terribly challenging. One was with a couple of corrupted brown bears Isold said had been infected with a magical disease and driven mad. Aderyn felt sorry for them and was glad her team could put them out of their misery.

The other battle had been against a gang of boggarts inhabiting one of those miniature forests. At first, Aderyn had been worried, because the boggarts had been hard to see and the team had thought there were twice as many of them as there were. But Livia's mudball had outlined them as well as fairy-light would have, and after a few seconds of terror, the companions killed the boggarts easily.

But that was it. They hadn't encountered anyone on the road who'd needed help in the form of a quest to bring aid, they hadn't come across any dungeons, and they were all still level three. Aderyn hadn't quite fallen into despair, because it wasn't as if they were forced to strike out for Guerdon Deep at level three. They'd just have to find opportunities for advancement in Asylum. But her earlier assumptions were all shattered.

"We'll have to earn experience here before we can move on," Owen said as if he could read her mind. "What are some ways we can do that?"

"Quests, mostly," Weston said. "We should find an inn and then spread out, looking for questgivers."

"I'll wait at the inn," Livia said.

She'd sounded so abrupt, almost angry, that Owen stopped. "Is something wrong?"

Livia shrugged and wouldn't meet his eyes. "No."

"You sound like something's wrong," Weston said. "Not afraid of a little hard work, are you?"

Livia shot him a withering glance. "Asylum is my home town, if you must know. And I might have said some things about not coming back until I've made a name for myself. I don't want to run into anyone who might tease me."

"Then what happens if one of us takes a quest from someone who knows you?" Aderyn asked. "You're not going to sit it out just to avoid being teased, right?"

"Being teased is uncomfortable," Owen said, "but it's not the end of the world. And it's not like we'll be here long. Level five, and we can head for Guerdon Deep."

"And didn't you want to go to your parents to tell them you avenged your brother?" Weston said.

Livia perked up. "I hadn't thought about that. Do you mind if I do that while you're looking for quests?"

"It's a perfect opportunity," Owen said. "And you can suggest a good inn first."

The guards let them through the gate without more than a few rote-sounding words warning them to keep the peace. If Market Warding had looked exactly like Far Haven, Asylum couldn't be more different. The buildings were mostly two-story, half-timbered construction, with the first story being small red bricks and the second smooth plaster crossed by dark wooden beams. It was bigger than either Market Warding or Far Haven and more crowded, with more adventurers walking the streets than those other towns. Aderyn stared in amazement. If Asylum was still just a big town, she couldn't imagine what a city like Guerdon Deep would look like.

Livia led them to the marketplace, which was filled with stalls doing a brisk business of selling, and down a side street to an inn with a sign depicting a jolly pig wearing a flat cap. "The Inn of the Merry Boar," Livia said. "I've never stayed here, but my parents' friends talk about how good the beer is. I hope that means the rooms are clean as well."

They let Weston negotiate for rooms and ended up with three of them, the inn being too full for each of the teammates to have their own. Aderyn stowed her pack in a room alongside Livia's and returned to the taproom to join the others.

"Livia, what do you suggest?" Owen asked.

"The crafters are always looking for runners to collect magic components," Livia said. "Those can be dangerous, and thus mean high experience rewards. Crafters' Alley is a good place to start. We might also find someone with a pest problem. There are farms outside the town wall—they're close enough that wandering monsters aren't a threat, but smaller creatures can infest their property, and if you get enough of those, they're worth experience to adventurers at our level. The farmers advertise at the Grange when they have that kind of problem."

"I wouldn't mind visiting Crafters' Alley," Isold said. "I have experience with crafting enough to recognize what will be an especially good reward."

"Weston, why don't you go with Isold," Owen said, "and Aderyn and I will find this... Grange, you said?"

"It's on the way to my parents' house, so I'll show you before I go there," Livia said.

"Meet back here for dinner," Owen added. "And go ahead and commit to whatever quest you find. Don't worry about all of us agreeing. We all know what the goal is."

Weston and Isold nodded. "Good luck," Isold said.

The Grange looked more like a barn than any of the more elegant buildings surrounding it. Its planed wooden walls supported a thatch roof bigger than any Aderyn had seen before, and the only windows were small, square ones tucked nearly under that roof's eaves. Even the door looked like a barn door, two enormous halves flung open so people could go in and out freely. She and Owen stood outside, staring at it, after Livia left. "It's intimidating," Owen said.

"I wonder what else it's for," Aderyn mused. "It can't just be for farmers to talk about their vermin control problems."

"I guess we can find out," Owen said, and led the way inside.

The darkness of the interior meant Aderyn couldn't see much. She heard Owen let out a grunt, and a deep voice said, "Watch it, youngling."

"Sorry, sir," Owen said.

The deep voice laughed. "'Sir,' huh? Where are you from that you think fancy manners will impress me?"

"Somewhere where that's how we show politeness. No fancy manners." Owen made as if to step aside from the still-unseen figure.

"Hold on there a moment, youngling." The darkness moved, and finally Aderyn could see the stranger. He was bigger even than

Weston, with a huge belly and thick fingers, but he didn't look angry despite his words. "You adventurers?"

"We are." Owen stared up at him fearlessly.

"You looking for work?"

"Yes. The right kind of work."

"Huh." The man scratched his short hair, making a shower of dandruff flakes fly. "You got any friends? What I have in mind will need more than two of you."

"We do."

"Huh." The man appeared to come to a decision. "All right. I'll hire you."

"You haven't said what the job is," Aderyn pointed out. "And we haven't agreed to it."

"Oh. Right." The man nodded. "I want you to find the man who cursed my property and make him reverse the spell. And if he won't do it, I want him dead."

CHAPTER NINETEEN

"We aren't murderers," Owen said. "Thanks anyway."

"No, wait!" the man exclaimed. He put a meaty hand on Owen's shoulder to stop him walking away. Owen wrenched free. "I didn't mean I want *you* to kill him. I was just planning to scare him into reversing the spell if you adventurers can't convince him to do it."

"That still sounds like aiding and abetting murder," Owen said.

"Huh?"

"He means we'd be guilty of putting that man in a position for you to hurt him," Aderyn clarified.

The man sighed. "If I swear I won't kill him no matter what he does, will you help? None of the other farmers are willing, and the longer this goes on, the less chance there is of me regaining my property. And then it will turn into a dungeon, and all my possessions will be gone."

Aderyn had a good idea why none of the man's fellows were interested in helping. He sounded like someone who thought violence was the best option for solving problems, and while Aderyn currently made her way in life by applying violence, that was against monsters, not other humans. Except those three adventurers outside Dungeon Spiteful. All right, *mostly* against monsters. Aderyn was still sure her team had the moral advantage over this fellow.

"I need more details," Owen said. "Then we'll think about it."

"I'm Ellias. Come with me, and I'll buy you drinks," the man said.

The tavern Ellias took them to was rundown, but busy, and Ellias waved at the barman like he was a regular and found them seats at a dirty table by way of nudging its occupants to leave. Three mugs of dark ale appeared in front of them, and Aderyn sipped hers and was surprised at how good the ale was.

"I got a farm outside town," Ellias said. "Wheat and corn, mostly. But I'm known for my beehives. Or I was."

Owen didn't say anything, though Ellias's silence suggested he was waiting for a prompt to continue. Finally, Ellias said, "It's the bees that are the trouble. I went out to harvest honey one morning about a week ago, and they were aggressive. My sweet girls are never aggressive, not to me and not to anyone. Then I realized they were bigger than usual. They kept getting bigger until three days ago, when they were fist sized and angry. They left the hives and swarmed all the buildings. My farmhands and I had to leave to keep out of danger."

"And this couldn't have happened naturally?" Owen said.

Ellias gave him an incredulous look. "You're an adventurer and you don't know a curse when you hear about it?"

"We don't know anything about bees," Aderyn said, kicking Owen under the table. "We just want to know how sure you are that someone did this."

"Very sure. I got enemies. People who are jealous of my success. And I'm pretty sure it was Delaila who did this. She's hated me for years."

Owen frowned. "I thought you said you needed us to find the person. If you already know—"

"Delaila's a farm owner like me. She doesn't have a class, so she doesn't have magic. But I know she hired someone to curse me. That's the man I need found."

"Then go to the—" Owen glanced at Aderyn, looking frustrated. She had no idea what was wrong, but he had the expression he wore when either something about her world confused him or he wasn't sure if his own world's experience applied. "You can't work this out between you and Delaila?"

"Do you want this quest or not?" Ellias sounded confused. "Delaila won't admit to anything, and the truth is, everyone's on her side. If I can't get the curse removed, I'll lose everything."

A system message appeared in Aderyn's vision.

A new quest is available: [The Honey and the Stinger]
Accept? Y / N

She looked at Owen. Owen still looked skeptical. She wished they could speak mind to mind, because she didn't want to reveal in front of Ellias that this quest was complex enough to be worth a lot of experience, and they needed experience. Instead, she nodded slightly, hoping he would understand.

"All right," Owen said.

Aderyn selected Y, and a new message appeared:

You have accepted the quest [The Honey and the Stinger]. Set
as primary quest?

"Let's see what the others come up with first," Owen said when Aderyn raised her eyebrows in a silent question. Aderyn nodded, and the quest appeared briefly on the right side of her vision before shrinking into a blue dot.

She rose when Owen did. "Where's your farm?" Owen asked.

"Anyone can give you directions. You can find me at the Grange when you've got the fellow." Ellias swigged down his ale in a series of gulps and set the mug aside. "Thanks. There's coin in it for you too when my property is restored."

Outside, Owen said, "I hope you know what to do. I don't even know how people here track someone down, let alone coerce a magic-user into working magic."

"We'll figure it out," Aderyn said. "It's got to be worth a lot of experience, is all I can think."

"Back to the inn, then." Owen cast one final glance at the tavern. "I can't believe you drank that stuff. Aren't you afraid of catching something?"

"Catching what? Like a mouse? It was good ale. I don't see what that has to do with catching anything."

Owen sighed and set off down the street.

They were halfway back to the Inn of the Merry Boar when Aderyn's display of her team's information brightened, and a system message appeared.

You have accepted the quest [Rose Hips and Feverfew]. Set as primary quest?

Aderyn blinked. The notice flashed once, then shrank to join Ellias's quest in the list. "I guess we're going to be busy," Owen said with a smile.

Rather than returning to the inn, Aderyn and Owen strolled through Asylum, becoming familiar with the town's layout. "There's a Crafters' Alley, so maybe there's a Wizards' Alley too," Owen said.

"We don't have wizards." Aderyn glared at him. "And you need to not sound foreign."

"Sorry. But you know what I mean. A place where spellslingers set up shop."

"Far Haven was too small for something like that, but Asylum is enough bigger—though I doubt we'll find anyone who can help you return home." Aderyn scanned the shop signs as they walked. This part of town, at least, didn't have any unifying theme to who sold what. In fact, it wasn't only shops, there were houses too, with householders male and female sweeping their stoops and calling out to the running children playing their games up and down the street.

"These towns are all so small and friendly. I'm not used to it," Owen said. He was watching one pack of children kicking a ball made from a pig's bladder.

"Are you from a big city?" Aderyn asked.

"The suburbs of a big city. Like... the outer limits, where the buildings are shorter and more widely spaced." Owen stopped to let the children run past. "Imagine if Asylum was dropped right next to Guerdon Deep. Though Cincinnati might be bigger even than that."

Aderyn tried out *Cincinnati* silently, moving her lips, and concluded Owen's world must have very different names from hers. On a whim, she said, "What do you miss most?"

"I would have guessed the internet," Owen said, "but the truth is, I miss indoor plumbing. It's so basic I never really thought about how much of modern life—my world's life—is based on it."

"What's indoor plumbing?"

"I don't think I can explain without giving you more questions. It's a different way to handle bodily waste. No chamber pots." Owen made a face. "Those were a surprise."

"Those are just for emergencies. Outhouses are much more sanitary."

Owen chuckled. "Indoor plumbing is like if you could use a chamber pot and have the waste vanish with the touch of a button."

Aderyn gaped. "You said you didn't have magic!"

"We don't. We have technology. And engineering."

"Well, I don't blame you for missing indoor plumbing, then." Aderyn shook her head in wonder. She couldn't help thinking about what it would be like if she'd been the one snatched away to Owen's world.

They rounded a corner, and Owen said, "I don't know what that sign represents." He pointed at a wooden plaque hanging over a door by two short chains. The outline of a fire was burned delicately into it. "Does it mean a Flamecrafter?"

"Yes. And that's a Windwarden's emblem two shops past it." Aderyn walked a little faster. "This isn't exactly a Spellslingers' Alley, because there are other non-magical shops, but I count five shops— two Bonemenders and a Tidecaller in addition to the others."

"Should we start looking for the one who cursed Ellias's bees?" Owen shook his head. "No, that's foolish. Even if we knew which kind of spellslinger could do such a thing, we shouldn't go up against someone that potentially powerful without all of us."

"There's more," Aderyn said. "Curses aren't illegal, but they're frowned on, and it's possible the curse bestower is hiding his true class. He might be a Lightsnuffer or even a Diabolist."

"I didn't know hiding your class was possible. Isn't that something you'd be able to see through, as a Warmaster?"

"Maybe." Aderyn shrugged. They'd kept walking as they talked and had nearly reached the end of the short street. "Usually there are limits to how much [Assess] will tell you. Like if someone or some monster is much higher level, it says 'exceeds authority limit.' And I think [Improved Assess 1] is the same. Though..."

"Though, what?" Owen prompted.

"I almost forgot, but when we fought the Faceless One in Dungeon Spiteful, when I assessed him the first time, the display was strange. Some of the letters were wrong. I wonder now if that was my skill fighting the Faceless One's false presentation, and I almost saw through it?" She shrugged again. "Anyway, the point is that evil classes have a skill that lets them disguise their presentation, so [Assess] will reveal the wrong thing."

Owen stopped. "Are you saying the system lets people have evil classes *and* allows them to lie about them? That's awful!"

"No, it's—" Aderyn stopped as well. "I never really thought

about it. It's not like the system assigns someone an evil class, starting out. People make choices that steer them toward becoming evil. So it's more that, say, someone starts out as Swordsworn, kills a lot of innocents, and if they're not captured and executed, they become a Brigand. Only the original class is still there, and if you're too low a level, you see that one instead of the evil one."

"That's almost worse, Aderyn. That means low-level adventurers are vulnerable to men and women like that." Owen looked as genuinely disturbed as he had when Aderyn had called him a demon.

"I guess so. But anyone low level enough to fail to see the true class wouldn't see *any* class, right? Except a Warmaster. And they'd all see that the Brigand was high enough level to steer clear of. So it's really unlikely someone with an evil class could fool anyone into believing they're not dangerous." Aderyn's discomfort grew. She'd never considered that the system might be responsible for allowing evil to flourish.

"I don't get this world sometimes," Owen muttered.

"What, you mean your world doesn't have people who prey on the innocent?" His words had roused Aderyn's defensive instincts.

"We do. But it's different. They aren't slotted into a class that defines them. They can choose not to do evil."

"It's not like a class makes you good or evil, Owen," Aderyn protested. "It guides you, sure, but adventurers all have to choose what they'll do with their skills. And at least in our world, anyone has a chance of identifying someone who's chosen evil, so they aren't taken by surprise."

"That's true. I kinda wish my world had pop-up labels for criminals. It might save lives." Owen sighed. "Sorry. I didn't mean to be critical."

"You weren't critical. More like... considering. And I like hearing about your world."

"You do?"

His surprise made her feel uncomfortable, like there was something wrong with her interest. "Yes. It helps me know you better. Don't you feel we're fighting better as a team the better we understand each other?"

"Yeah, I do." He grinned. "I should ask you more questions about your life, then. So long as we're exchanging knowledge."

"My life is boring. Yours has things like magic chamber pots." She grinned back.

"And yours has magic everything," Owen countered. "Let's head back to the inn and see if the others have returned, and you can tell me about the different kinds of spellslingers. That's not boring."

"I still have trouble believing in a world without magic," Aderyn said. "How do you light your houses at night if you can't cast magical light?"

"Will you be satisfied if I say 'electricity'?"

Aderyn pictured lightning bolts flashing within a glass jar, captured by this mysterious technology. "Probably not."

CHAPTER TWENTY

They had to stop talking once they returned to the busy part of town. Aderyn could imagine the commotion if the wrong person overheard Owen talking about his world. When they returned to the inn, the others hadn't come back yet, and it was nearly dinnertime. They claimed a table in the gradually filling taproom and sat in companionable silence. One of the things Aderyn liked best about her growing friendship with Owen was how they didn't need to fill the air with talk to feel comfortable together. Maybe that was because Owen was an otherworlder, or maybe it was because Aderyn never worried about what Owen thought of her, whether he was silently judging her. Or maybe it was none of those things. She was grateful for it anyway.

Isold and Weston returned about twenty minutes later. "What, the spellslinger's not back yet?" Weston said, dropping heavily into a chair beside Owen. "I say we eat without her."

"I didn't think you disliked Livia," Aderyn said.

"Dislike? I don't dislike her. She's the one who disapproves of me." Weston said this with a grin. "I bet she feels guilty at how she doesn't rise early, and she turns that into criticizing my habits."

"I don't think you're right," Isold said. "You take every opportunity to needle her about sleeping late, so if there's anyone who should feel guilty, it's you."

"I refuse to dignify that with a response," Weston said loftily. "Besides, Moonlighters and Earthbreakers don't get along. Well-known fact."

"I've never heard that," Aderyn said.

"It's true! Earthbreakers are all direct and to the point, and Moonlighters are creatures of misdirection. Definite conflict, built in."

"Uh-*huh*," Aderyn said. She waved at Livia, who'd just entered the taproom and was scanning it. "Go ahead and tell Livia your theory. I bet she makes you eat it."

"I'm sorry I'm late," Livia said as she approached. "My parents had guests who wanted to hear about my adventures."

"It's fine," Owen said. "Were they glad to see you? Your parents, I mean?"

"Surprised." Livia didn't sound happy. "They weren't expecting me."

"Well, we did clear that goblin nest quickly," Aderyn said.

Livia shook her head. "I mean they weren't expecting me to succeed at all. I can't believe my own parents didn't have faith in my abilities."

"But you were only level one or two," Weston said. He looked serious now, with no sign of frivolous humor. "That was quite a feat for someone of that level. Their disbelief doesn't have to be personal."

"Don't defend them," Livia said. "I'm telling you they didn't think I was capable, regardless of level or skill."

"Hey, I'm just pointing out—"

"You can keep your pointing to yourself," Livia snapped.

"Stop," Owen said. "You both have the best of intentions and you need to not assume otherwise. That's not how teams work."

Livia wiped her eyes. "You're right. I'm sorry, Weston."

"I should have taken your side," Weston said. "It's not like I even know your parents. They might be awful people."

"They're not. They're just—I don't know what to call it. I'm the youngest, and I've never tried to make anything of myself. I'm sure they thought my desire to restore my brother's brooch was just posturing."

"But they were glad, right? You did something that brought them peace," Aderyn pointed out. "Even if they were surprised, they can't take that victory from you."

"That's true." Livia brightened. "Look, let's eat something. I'm starving. And I saw we took two quests. I want to know the details."

"Ours isn't complicated," Isold said. "We found a Spiritsmith who is trying to invent some new concoction. He wouldn't tell us what—very secretive—but that's why the quest is more potentially lucrative than gathering resources usually is, because he would only give it to a team that didn't know enough to figure out what rose hips and feverfew could possibly be used for."

"But you worked for a Spiritsmith," Aderyn said. "Don't you have knowledge a typical Herald wouldn't?"

"We didn't share that fact with him," Weston said with a grin.

"It doesn't matter, because in fact I don't have any idea what he's trying to invent," Isold went on. "The complicated part is that the rose hips must be harvested only from one of three types of rose, and the feverfew must grow within ten feet of the same. Aside from that, it's a basic collecting quest, and we have the promise of five gold in addition to whatever experience we gain."

"Then it sounds like what Aderyn and I agreed to is going to be the difficult one," Owen said.

The serving maid brought them dinner, a couple of roast chickens and new salt potatoes and the same kind of green beans they'd had in Market Warding, and Owen explained the encounter with Ellias as they all ate. He concluded by saying, "I was hoping one of you might know which kind of spellslinger can curse someone like that. I mean, it might not be a curse, it might just be, um, an enlarge bee spell or something."

"I've never heard of an enlarge bee spell," Livia said. "Nothing that specific, I mean. There's an *enlarge creature* spell, but I think that makes things a lot bigger. You'd have bees the size of hunting hounds, not the size of fists."

"And you said the change made the bees unusually aggressive," Isold said, frowning. "I wonder. Suppose it's two effects? Because I don't know how someone would change the bees' size, but a Herald can influence a creature's attitude, all the way to making a peaceful creature angry."

"And the size change might not be a spell at all." Weston leaned forward intently. "There are potions that increase a person's strength tremendously, including the size of the muscles."

"Do you have personal experience of that?" Owen asked, eyeing Weston's large frame.

Weston laughed. "I've been this big since I was fifteen, without benefit of muscle enhancers. But I had a friend back then who was jealous of how I outgrew him, and he stole one of those potions from a Spiritsmith's shop and, well, overindulged. For about ten minutes, he dwarfed me."

"And... after the ten minutes?" Owen prompted. He wore a look of appalled fascination.

"He was a lovely shade of lavender and his vomit killed a whole bed of petunias."

"So it doesn't last forever," Aderyn said, as horrified and fascinated as Owen.

"No. Usually—if you use it properly, that is—the effects last for a day."

"Which means, if you're right, someone has been going out to the farm daily to reapply the potion." Now Owen looked thoughtful. "That might be faster, staking out the farm to find the culprit."

"Why do we need stakes?" Isold asked.

"It's—never mind. Isold, how long does the effect of the emotion manipulation last?"

"The less intelligent the creature, the longer the effect lasts," Isold said. "For bees, it might be permanent."

Owen grimaced. "And it's back to being complicated."

"I don't think so," Aderyn said. "I think you were right about going to the farm to catch the Spiritsmith, or whoever bought the potion. That person will know the Herald who made the bees aggressive. Then we can approach the Herald and get them to make the bees peaceful again."

Owen nodded. "When you put it like that, I think we have a plan."

ELLIAS HAD BEEN RIGHT. THE FIRST PERSON THEY ASKED for directions said, "Oh, yeah, the crazy beekeeper. Take the northeastern gate and follow the road through the farmland about two miles. Each farmstead is marked by colored posts on either side of the path leading to it. You want the one marked by the red posts. You got adventurer business with Ellias?"

"Something like that," Owen said. "Thanks."

"Take my advice, ignore whatever he asked for," the man said. "There's a reason he got no friends in town. 'Bout the only friends he does have are those bees, way he talks about 'em you'd think they were real women!" He laughed, clapped Owen on the shoulder, and walked away.

"Should we be worried about that?" Owen asked the companions in a low voice. "Ellias's reputation isn't going to affect the results of the quest, is it?"

"The system is what rewards us, not the questgiver," Aderyn

explained. "We might end up with no money if he's tightfisted, but we care more about the experience than coin."

"That, and not setting anyone up for Ellias to hurt them," Livia added.

"I figure we can find out who's behind this, and then decide what to tell Ellias," Owen said. "Let's go. We'll want to be there around dusk."

"What difference does it make?" Weston asked as they walked. "Do you think the person giving the potion to the bees comes at night?"

"I saw a show once that said most bees are active during the day, and the ones that aren't are tropical, which this place isn't," Owen said. "They won't be asleep, probably, but I'm betting they aren't very active. So, yes, I think the person dosing them does it at night when he's less likely to be stung."

Aderyn decided not to ask about the words she didn't understand. "And we'll put a stake in him to stop him."

"No, that's not—a stakeout means watching a place to see what happens there, or who goes there. I don't know why it's called that. We'll set up where we can watch from hiding, and then we can catch the guy."

Leaving Asylum worked the way leaving Far Haven did. Weston laid his large hand over the glowing spot on the doorpost, and the door swung open. Neither of the guards paid the companions any attention. Guarding must be seriously boring work most of the time, right up until the town was attacked and it became seriously terrifying.

To the left, the sun sank toward the horizon, turning the clouds red and gold. Aderyn didn't think they'd see the moon tonight, not with as much cloud cover as there was. It might mean rain, which would help them—bees wouldn't fly in the rain, would they? On the other hand, it might mean their prey wouldn't pay a visit to the farm that night. Aderyn fell back on hoping the night would stay clear and dry.

The northeast road out of Asylum was larger than the southern one they'd approached by, wider and more well traveled. They saw the first of the colored posts about a quarter mile outside town, two brightly-painted waist-high poles the color of new grass. They stood on either side of a narrower but still obvious path branching away from the main road. In the distance, fields of green-gold grain blew in a light breeze. Aderyn didn't know any more about farming than she did about trees, but she did know green meant unripe.

"If I wasn't an adventurer, I'm not sure I'd have the courage to maintain a farm out here, outside the city walls," Owen said.

"Hard to have a farm *inside* the walls," Weston joked.

"You know what I mean. How dangerous is it, really?"

"I don't know," Isold said. "The protective aura generated by a town's wall extends some distance, varying according to the size of the town. If a farm is close enough, there's no fear of monster attacks. At the outer edges of the aura, you might find goblins or kobolds raiding. I've heard the real problem is vermin swarms finding an unwatched corner and breeding unchecked until they're too big a threat for a non-classed person to fight. Ellias's problem is unique in my experience, which admittedly isn't much."

"And then if the monsters aren't destroyed soon enough, the farm becomes a dungeon. That seems like good incentive to hire adventurers," Aderyn said.

"Yeah," Owen said, distantly. "I wonder about that."

"About what?" Livia asked.

"Probably nothing. I had an idea, but it's gone now. Must not have been important."

"Or it will come to you in a moment of crisis," Isold said.

By the time they reached the red posts, the sun was halfway below the horizon, and their shadows were long and gray and seemed to deliberately point the way to Ellias's farm. They hadn't seen anyone else sharing the road with them, and when they occasionally looked back, the road there was empty, too. "Hope that means we beat our prey here," Weston said.

"Unless he came and went already," Livia replied.

"You're incredibly pessimistic, did you know that?"

"I prefer to think of it as realistic. Not that I expect a Moon-lighter to be familiar with realism."

"Argue later," Owen said. He ran a hand across the leftmost pole. "This paint's in bad shape. I have the feeling Ellias isn't a very good housekeeper."

The narrow side path to Ellias's farmsteading wasn't in much better shape than the posts. It was deeply rutted, and tall grasses grew right up to its edges. The fields of crops, too, looked abandoned, and a couple of crows took off, cawing loudly, from where they'd been feasting unhindered on the grain. "Ellias said he and everyone who works here had to leave," Aderyn mused. "I know he cares more about the bees than the crops, but he can't want the harvest eaten by birds. Whoever did this really must hate him to want to destroy his whole life."

"Maybe," Owen said. He sounded distant again.

"I doubt anyone would go to these extremes for a prank," Weston said.

"No, I agree. I'm just wondering. Ellias has enemies, so one of them being the culprit is obvious. But it's like you said, Aderyn—someone would have to hate him, and most people's enemies don't harbor that kind of resentment and anger." Owen shook his head. "It doesn't matter. Right now we have to see about catching this guy and hope he knows something we can use."

CHAPTER TWENTY-ONE

A small stone house with a thatch roof came into view, standing in an open space surrounded by the grain fields. It didn't exactly look rundown, and the roof was in good repair, but the weathered wooden steps leading up to the front door were cracked, and the walls showed gaps where stones were missing. The windows were either missing their glass or had never had any.

A low hum filled the air, growing louder as they approached the house. "Hear that?" Weston said.

The rest of them nodded. Owen said, "Let's circle wide around the house and see what we can see."

"I'll do it," Weston said.

"Bees use other senses than sight and hearing. Your stealth won't be any better than ours." Owen gestured, and the companions made their way slowly to the right, circling the house at a distance big enough to keep them out of the bees' range.

Aderyn, walking behind Owen, put a hand on her sword's hilt before realizing that was stupid. The bees were small enough that a sword might not do any good. Then she gripped it again for reassurance. She wasn't afraid of bees, but she did worry that they'd guessed wrong, and the person they were after wasn't going to show up that night.

The first bees appeared when they were within fifty feet of the house. Ellias had said the enlarged, enraged bees had infested the farmsteading's buildings, not just their hives, and sure enough, several fist-sized bees circled the house's sagging eaves, darting beneath the gutters. As Aderyn watched, one sailed away from the house and disappeared past the nearest corner. "We need to be careful, if they've taken over the property," she whispered, and then felt stupid for whispering because it wasn't as if the bees cared.

"Let's get a look at the hives," Owen suggested. "I bet the bees go back there at night, like going home to roost."

The hives were at the back of the house, five tall white boxes whose paint was pristine white, not at all in the kind of disrepair as the posts and the house. Two of the hives looked broken, with their top sections fallen to the ground, and giant bees swooped in erratic loops around all five, bumping into the sides of the hives like they were trying to get in where they no longer fit. That thought stirred Aderyn to sympathy for the creatures, who'd been victims as much as Ellias, maybe more so.

Owen stopped outside the longest range of the bees' flight. "See? They're already less active. And there are hardly any bees around the other farm buildings."

"They're still active enough that I doubt anyone could get close to the hives to pour the potion over them," Weston said. "And with the size of those stingers, I wouldn't want to risk it."

Aderyn silently agreed. The stingers were the size of a darning needle.

"What about an aerosol spray?" Owen made an impatient noise. "Okay, I'm sure you don't have those, but suppose... what about perfume bottles that squirt mists of perfume? What about those?"

"Those aren't uncommon," Isold said. "That would be an ideal solution."

"Then let's hide and watch," Owen said. "Weston, can you conceal us, or find good hiding places?"

Weston was already scanning the farm's outbuildings, a stable, an outhouse, a couple of dilapidated sheds. "Come with me."

Aderyn still felt exposed beside the outhouse where Weston positioned her, but he said, "Trust me, as the sun sets lower, this side will be more in shadow and you'll be completely concealed," and thirty minutes later she had to admit he was right. She had a good view of three of the five beehives and the bees circling them. Idly, she Assessed them:

Name: Giant Bee

Type: Vermin/Vermin Swarm

Power Level: 2

It really did look like they were trying to get inside, and she had a horrifying image of too-large bees crushed inside the wooden boxes. But no, if it was a potion that did it, and if Owen was right that it was sprayed on, the concoction couldn't have reached inside the hive.

Sure enough, when she looked closer, she saw normal-sized bees clinging to the hives, ignored by their enlarged sisters. With that, the whole situation struck her as ridiculous and maybe even evil. Somebody hated Ellias enough to harm these innocent, useful creatures. She was more determined than ever to catch their prey and make him stop.

Full night fell. The skies had unexpectedly cleared, revealing the waxing moon. At that hour, it hadn't yet reached its zenith, but it was high and large enough to shed bluish-white light over the fields, the buildings, and the beehives. It was a perfect night for doing mischief—or catching someone intent on doing mischief. The shadows that had concealed Aderyn were gone, and she hoped she wasn't terribly visible.

From her position, she could see Owen, crouched beside the empty stables, and Livia, on her other side next to one of the sheds. She knew Weston was somewhere on Owen's far side, and Isold was on the other side of the outhouse. Her legs had started to ache, so she stretched them as best she could without moving and hoped this wouldn't take so long that her toes went numb.

Then she heard whistling. It wasn't very good; she only recognized the melody, "Morning by the River," because the whistler's notes were in tune for the first part of the chorus before becoming discordant. Whoever it was didn't sound like he was afraid of being caught. Aderyn smiled wickedly. He was in for a surprise.

A man came around the corner of the house as the companions had almost two hours before. He strode carelessly, like he didn't care that his presence made the bees more agitated. There were even fewer of them active than before, but those few buzzed and flew at the man in a frenzy. Aderyn held her breath. Suppose the enlarged bees' stingers were deadly?

Then she saw that the man was draped head to toe in a fine mesh that attached to a wide-brimmed hat and spread outward from there. It didn't interfere with his sight, because he continued to walk confidently, but the bees who brushed up against it veered away, staggering in their flight like they were drunk. It had to be coated with something that repelled the insects. Aderyn felt irrationally outraged, like this man was cheating.

From beneath the mesh, the man produced a glass bottle with a tiny hose and air bladder attached. Aderyn's mother used bottles like that to spray, not potions, but mists of water over the more delicate plants in her herb garden. The man aimed the bottle at the first hive, and Owen rose from hiding and ran at him. Aderyn leaped to her feet and followed, staggering slightly on legs that tingled.

"Put it down," Owen told the man, pointing his sword at him. "We want information, and we won't hurt you if you give it to us."

The man took a step backward, then another, at which point he nearly ran into Aderyn's sword. He squeaked, an unexpectedly childish sound. It was then Aderyn realized their mistake. They'd run right into the bee swarm's range. She gasped at the sight of three fist-sized bees diving on her.

Livia, behind her, shouted the words of a spell. Just as the bees were within a hand's breadth of Aderyn's face, a golden light like a curved wall sprang up around her. The bees hit the light and bounced off, spinning helplessly away in a random direction. Owen was almost invisible behind a golden light shield of his own.

"Stop!" the man said. His voice was high-pitched enough that Aderyn revised her estimate of his age downward. He was certainly younger than they were, not a child but not an adult, either. "Stop! Don't hurt me!"

"Back up, away from the hive," Owen said, his sword never wavering. The golden light flickered and dimmed, and Aderyn hurried to get away as well, fearing that meant the shield was failing. By the time the light vanished, they were all gathered about thirty feet from the back of the rundown house. Weston removed the hat and bundled up the mesh, revealing a boy no more than thirteen or fourteen, his face contorted in terror.

"I didn't hurt no one," he said. "Don't kill me."

"I told you, we just want information," Owen said. "Who gave you that potion?"

The boy looked at the bottle in his hand like he'd never seen it before. "This potion?"

"Don't play stupid," Owen warned, taking the bottle from him.

"Nobody gave it to me," the boy said. "I bought it with my own money."

"Your—" Owen's brow furrowed. "You bought it yourself? Who told you to use it on the bees?"

"That was my idea. Thought it would be funny." The boy smirked.

Owen glanced at Aderyn. "Who is this kid?"

Aderyn Assessed him. "He's nobody," she said. "Even if he

wasn't too young for a class, I could tell you that. His name's Flerrius."

Owen pursed his lips in thought. "Livia, keep an eye on him and immobilize him if he tries to run. Everyone else, over here."

He led them a short distance away to where they were out of earshot of Flerrius. "This doesn't make sense," Owen said. "He doesn't act like someone intent on revenge, and yet he also doesn't act like a psychopath. Someone who'd destroy another person just for fun," he clarified.

Isold looked past them back at Flerrius. "I wonder," he said. "If we are dealing with a Herald somewhere in this mess, Flerrius might be under that adventurer's control."

"You mean, a Herald could make him do things and believe it's his own choice?" Owen said.

"I mean precisely that. And that worries me. I don't know at what level Heralds gain that skill, but it is certainly much higher than our own. We may not be able to compel the Herald to do anything."

"Shouldn't we worry first about getting the truth out of the boy?" Weston said. "We can't do anything about the Herald if we don't know who he is."

"Is there a way around the compulsion?" Aderyn asked Isold.

"We have to ask questions that aren't related to the facts protected by the compulsion," Isold said. "Direct questions will be answered with lies."

"Then let's give it a try," Owen said.

They returned to where Livia watched over Flerrius. She looked like she wanted to know what they'd talked about, but she didn't say anything. Owen stepped to where Flerrius could see him. "Who made the potion?" he asked.

"Tobus, of course. There's only one Spiritsmith in Asylum," Flerrius said disdainfully.

"Is he the one who told you how to use it?" Owen asked.

Flerrius stiffened. "I figured it out myself. All my own idea."

Owen let out a hiss of annoyance. "Wait," Aderyn told him. "Flerrius, do you know whose farm this is?"

"Sure. It's old man Ellias's farmsteading."

"And does he have enemies?"

Flerrius shrugged. "A few. Miss Delaila, Mr. Laras, Mr. Winnet."

"Will they be jealous that you hurt Ellias's property first?"

"Nah, they'll just be glad someone took him down a peg." Flerrius's voice was clear and without a hint of resistance.

"So, not them," Owen said. Aderyn agreed. If one of Ellias's enemies was behind the plot, Flerrius would have gone back to claiming it was entirely his idea. "In fact, I don't think they have anything to do with it."

"I have a question," Weston said, stepping closer. "We're new in town, Flerrius. Any other new adventurers show up in the last week?"

Owen nodded approval.

"Always adventurers in and out of Asylum," Flerrius said. "I keep track. Gonna be an adventurer myself someday. I'm training to be Staffsworn."

"Then you know how many and what kind—oh, no, you wouldn't be able to Assess them to know their classes," Weston said, sounding regretful.

"I do so," Flerrius retorted. "Just because I can't see it—I have other ways of finding out. There was a Swordsworn, two Stalwarts, a Herald, a Bonemender, and a Deadeye. Not counting you lot. I didn't even know you was in town."

"We just arrived. We're staying at the Inn of the Merry Boar." Weston sounded so casual Aderyn would have known he was up to something even if she couldn't see his face. "I bet those other adventurers can't afford that kind of luxury."

"Hah! The Stalwarts are staying there!" Flerrius exclaimed. "The others are at the Golden Tankard. Shows what you know."

"You're right, you're much smarter than I am," Weston said.

"How about you run along home and forget about this prank. You've proved your point."

"But it's not done," Flerrius said. "It has to be done before I can stop."

"Damn it, I was right," Owen muttered. In a louder voice, he said, "What will make it done, Flerrius?"

Flerrius craned his neck to look at Owen and said, "It's going to become a dungeon."

Chapter Twenty-Two

"What do you mean, you were right?" Aderyn exclaimed.

"I had a suspicion," Owen said. "Listen, Flerrius, that's not going to happen. You've lost. Get back to town and stop pestering the bees, or we're going to drag you in front of a... a judge and everyone will find out what you tried to do. You don't want that, right?"

Flerrius frowned. "What's a judge? Like a magistrate? I can't face a magistrate, it'll kill my old Nana."

"Yes. A magistrate." Owen rolled his eyes. "If you don't want your Nana to find out, get back to town and forget all your plans. Got it?"

Flerrius's eyes widened. He shook his head violently. "Can't do that. Got to finish the job. I *got* to."

"Why is that?" Owen asked.

"I—" Flerrius started to shake, his whole body caught up in the motion.

Swiftly Isold gripped him by both shoulders, steadying him. "It's fine, lad, we're all friends here," he said. His voice, which was normally melodic, sounded different now—still beautiful, but humming with a low tone that sounded like the bees. Flerrius stopped shaking. He stared at Isold with his mouth hanging slightly open.

"Now, I know you had this amazing idea to create a dungeon," Isold went on, his voice still humming. "Did you tell anyone else about it? Get advice from anyone else? You can tell me. I'm your friend."

"Friend," Flerrius repeated. "Right. You and me and the Herald."

"That's right. I bet your Herald friend thought your idea was wonderful." Isold smiled. "Did he have any suggestions?"

"Just that the bigger the bees were, the more powerful the new dungeon would be," Flerrius said. He looked more relaxed, and his voice verged on cheerful.

"That was smart," Isold agreed. "Did you talk together about which farm to use?" His voice, by contrast, sounded tense beneath the humming.

Flerrius nodded. "He agreed old man Ellias had the right place. All those bees to become swarms, and poison attacks—"

"Oh, of course." The moonlight made it hard to make out details, but Aderyn thought Isold looked like he was on the verge of fainting. Isold swallowed visibly and said, "The thing is, Flerrius, this dungeon is too close to Asylum. It's not going to form properly even though you've taken all the right steps. I'm sorry to disappoint you."

"Oh." Flerrius glanced at each of the companions in turn. "I didn't know."

"That's why we came out here to tell you. That potion is expensive, and we didn't want you to waste your money." Isold released the boy and stepped back. "You hurry on home, and we won't tell anyone about this. We wouldn't want people to think it was your fault your plan failed, when really it was just bad luck."

Flerrius's expression cleared, and he smiled. "Wow, thanks! I'll see you later." He ran around the corner of the house in the direction of the road, and the sound of his running footsteps soon dwindled to nothing.

Isold put a hand to his forehead. "I need to sit," he proclaimed, and immediately collapsed. The others cried out and hurried to surround him, with Weston supporting him and Livia pressing water on him from her waterskin.

Isold drank deeply and said, "I'm all right now. I've never done that before and I didn't know it would take so much out of me."

"What *was* that?" Owen asked. "Mind control?"

"No, it's called **[Charm]**. It's an influence, a minor compulsion to make the subject believe I am his friend—though actually it's more subtle than that, because it can influence the subject to feel friendly or indifferent or angry depending on my performance." Isold wiped sweat from his forehead. "But I was combating the influence the other Herald had on Flerrius, and since that Herald is considerably higher level than me, it was a strain."

"It was more effective than me yelling at him, that's for sure," Owen said.

"But I don't know where it leaves us," Aderyn said. "We knew a Herald was involved before talking to Flerrius, and though we now know where that Herald is staying, we don't know why he wants Ellias's farm destroyed or why he involved Flerrius."

"Probably he wanted someone else who'd take the blame if the act was discovered," Weston said.

"And Flerrius did tell us what the Herald wants," Owen said. "He wants this place turned into a dungeon. The rest of you, take pity on an ignorant otherworlder and explain why someone might do that on purpose."

"Well, if he was in need of experience," Livia said. "But that's a lot of effort to go to for a dungeon you could only use once. And—how much higher in level is he, Isold?"

"I don't know for sure, but I assume level ten at the minimum," Isold said.

"Couldn't he make the dungeon any level he wanted?" Owen asked.

"It doesn't work like that," Weston said. "Dungeons are created from, well, whatever is in the area. In the safe zones, there aren't any monsters around high enough level to generate a dungeon that's more than maybe level five."

"Then a dungeon built from this foundation wouldn't be worth anything to a level ten adventurer, no matter how vicious the bees," Owen said. "Not to mention that the dungeon wouldn't form at all."

"Ah, well, that was more by way of being a bald-faced lie," Isold said with a grin. "Ellias's farm is close enough to the outskirts of the aura that a dungeon could definitely form here. But it's true that a dungeon forming this close to a sanctuary city wouldn't be very high level, so we're back to the problem of it making no sense."

Aderyn glanced over her shoulder. She could hear the bees buzzing, but they were currently out of sight. "The Herald made the bees angry," she said, "and Isold said the effect would be permanent. That sounds like an extreme version of what you did to Flerrius."

"I suppose, but I don't see what you're getting at," Isold said.

"Could he do it the other way, then? Make the bees friendly?"

"I thought we were counting on that, getting him to reverse what he did," Owen said.

Aderyn shook her head. "I mean that if he could change the bees' attitude, couldn't he do the same to other creatures? Like monsters? Like, higher level monsters that would make this dungeon powerful?"

Weston let out a low whistle. "I just had this image of a long line of trolls being piped or sung into complacency for the length of time it takes to lead them into a dungeon. He could seed the dungeon with much higher-level monsters than naturally occur in it, and that would raise the level of the dungeon."

"Could the Herald get experience for defeating a dungeon he created?" Owen asked.

"Sure," Weston said. "He'd only get it once..." His voice trailed off as he and Livia exchanged glances.

"And then he could bring in another set of monsters," Livia said, sounding both horrified and impressed. "Again, and again... he'd only have to travel ten or twenty miles to outside the safe zone instead of going all over the continent to different dungeons. *And* he might get experience for controlling them, too, if the system saw that as defeating them."

"Would that work?" Owen asked.

"If that was his plan, the Herald certainly believes so," Weston said. "I've never heard of it being done before, but this is the farthest I've ever gone from Market Warding in my life. Who knows what's possible?"

"Even if he seeded the dungeon with high-level monsters, it would still continue to spawn new low-level monsters based on the original contents," Isold said. "And if he didn't kill them because their power level is too low to be worth experience to him, those would eventually escape the dungeon boundaries and rampage through the countryside. All these farms would be destroyed."

"We won't let that happen," Owen said. "Let's get back to town. We have to stop that Herald."

"But how?" Aderyn asked. "He's at least seven levels higher than we are. Even if he didn't have mind-altering magic to turn on us, how are we supposed to force him to stop his evil plan?"

"I have a plan of my own. Or, part of a plan," Owen said. "But we're going to need one of those bees."

By ten o'clock that evening, the companions were sitting in the taproom of the Golden Tankard Inn, near the fireplace. The fire was unlit at this time of summer, and the musician tuning his fiddle could stand close to the hearth without being scorched.

"Another round," Weston called to the serving maid, waving his hand drunkenly in her direction. "I think we deserve it after all the work we did today."

Aderyn drank down the last of her ale in a gulp and resisted making a face. The drink was good, but the alcohol had hit her like a brick wrapped in a pillow. She'd have to only pretend to drink this third one or she'd be no use in Owen's plan. "I still can't believe it," she said in a voice loud enough to reach the fireplace and the nearest table. "Trying to create a dungeon that close to town. That takes nerve."

"Well, that's not going to happen," Livia said. "We caught the boy responsible and he'll face punishment."

"I don't know," Owen said loudly. "It was obvious someone put him up to it, and I have a good idea who."

"You mean, some adventurer?" Weston said. He burped loudly and added, in a slightly slurred voice. "It would have to be someone new to town. No resident would risk being caught."

"Somebody really convincing," Aderyn said, slurring her words as well. "Must be someone like that around."

"Well, we have the evidence, and in the morning we'll take it to the judge. I mean the magistrate." Owen drank down the last of his ale and let out a less-convincing burp than Weston's. "Let the magistrate deal with it."

The sound of a bow on fiddle strings drew Aderyn's attention to the musician. He was tall and lean and extremely handsome, and when his gaze roving the room lit briefly on her, she shivered despite herself. The man smiled as if he knew how he'd made her uncomfortable. The smile irritated her, but she remembered the plan and kept her irritation to herself.

The musician went into the first few notes of "The Farmer's Wayward Daughter," and cheers went up from the assembled crowd. Some drinkers began stomping their feet with the rhythm. Aderyn smiled and pretended to enjoy herself, but inside she was tense.

Owen swore this would work, but there was so much they didn't know, starting with the Herald's personality. If he was too calm, if he didn't take the bait—but Owen had said, "Bards can't be all that different in your world, and there's never been a bard who didn't have some measure of pride—no offense, Isold."

"I wish I could say you were wrong," Isold had said with a wry smile.

Now Aderyn listened to the music, and watched the Herald play, and wondered when the man would strike and in what way. She still didn't believe he'd have the nerve to attack them in the open. Well, if Owen was wrong, they'd find some other way to bring the Herald to justice. The more Aderyn thought about what the man had done, in coercing Flerrius to do evil and in having the raw nerve to think he deserved to take Ellias's property, the more she was convinced justice wouldn't be satisfied just by having the Herald reverse what he'd done.

The song ended, and wild cheering erupted. The Herald took a bow amid a hail of silver coins. "Something a little less raucous now," he said, and drew the bow across the strings once more. This time, the melody was hauntingly sad, and it touched Aderyn's heart despite her knowledge that the Herald was a villain and a bastard. She closed her eyes briefly and let the music fill her. When she opened her eyes, the Herald was once more looking directly at her, and this time, his smile was malicious.

She found it impossible to look away. To distract herself, she blinked one long blink and Assessed him.

Name: Hameth

Class: Herald

Level: Exceeds authority limit

She'd Assessed him once before to confirm he was staying at the inn, since they hadn't been sure a high-level adventurer would want to play for his supper, so to speak, in a low-level sanctuary city. She hadn't liked him then and she didn't like him now, arrogant and sure of himself and, now, giving her the look that said he was interested in seeing much, much more of her whether she liked it or not.

The slow, throbbing sound of the melody captivated Aderyn. It felt as if it joined itself to the beat of her heart, twining through her bones and flowing through her veins. She almost wasn't aware when the fiddle music stopped and the Herald began to sing. She knew he was singing words, but they slipped away from memory even as she tried to focus on them. The lyrics had something to do with forgetting, with letting her cares disappear. This business with Ellias's farm —it didn't matter. In a hundred years, it would be gone anyway, so why not give it immortality as a dungeon? It all made perfect sense.

She smiled at the Herald, and his returning smile warmed her. He *was* attractive, and sleeping with him would be wonderful. She pushed her chair back and started to rise. Nobody would mind if she kissed him in public, right?

CHAPTER TWENTY-THREE

"That's quite enough," a woman's forceful voice said, cutting across the song and bringing it to a stop. Immediately Aderyn's mind cleared, and she wanted to be sick at how she'd actually considered sex with that horrible man.

The Herald's eyes widened. "Is something wrong?"

"Don't play games with me," the woman said, standing up from the nearest table. She was heavyset and wore plain but well-made clothes, and her presence was as powerful as the Herald's. Unlike the Herald, who oozed charm, that presence felt confident and reassuring. "You want to explain why you thought you could get away with using your Herald's hypnotizing skill on a room full of non-classed citizens?"

"I did no such thing." The Herald sounded offended. "If I had, you'd have been affected too, miss...?"

"Magistrate Gemina," the woman said. "Level twenty Spider. And you're not the first Herald to try his tricks on me." She fished an amulet out of her shirt and displayed it so the blue jewel at its center winked in the dozens of magical lights illuminating the taproom.

The Herald stared. Then he dropped his fiddle and ran for the door.

He got only four steps away before a *mudball* struck him in the center of his back, propelling him into the wall and sticking him there. Gasps and laughter arose from the crowd, and then everyone was talking at once. The magistrate strolled forward and stopped next to Owen.

"You're clever," she said. "I admit I didn't think that plan would work, though seeing that bee convinced me you had something worth listening to. Are you sure you're not actually a Spider?" She winked.

"It was—that is, I heard of someone doing something like this before, and I thought it was worth the risk," Owen said. Aderyn remembered his earlier explanation on the way back to town, which had been full of words like "television" and "cop show" and "entrapment," and she was grateful he'd remembered to control his enthusiasm now.

"You were right. I'll send someone to collect the boy Flerrius in the morning and see about removing any lingering compulsions the Herald left. If you drop by the town hall in the morning, there'll be something there for all of you. As well as my personal thanks." Gemina nodded at each of the companions and continued on her way to supervise taking the Herald into custody.

"That was a risk," Weston said. "You know how I feel about risk."

"Yes, that the risk should be worth the reward," Owen retorted.

"Exactly. That was exhilarating. Well, not the hypnotism. That bastard made me want to sleep with him! And I'm not even attracted to men!" Weston laughed. "And we've succeeded, and the magistrate intends to reward us—I say we've had a really good day."

"Except the quest isn't over," Aderyn pointed out. "We haven't seen the system notification. What more do we need to do?"

They all sat in silence for a few moments while the noise raged on around them. "We stopped Flerrius enlarging the bees," Owen said. "We caused the Herald to be captured."

"But the bees are still enraged," Livia said. "And I get the feeling that Herald isn't going to reverse what he did."

"And it's not going to wear off?" Owen asked Isold.

"Unlikely. But—" Isold put a finger to his lips in thought. "The solution may be simpler than that."

"You know a spell?" Livia asked.

"No. But Flerrius's use of the strength enhancing potion reminds me that there are other Spiritsmith concoctions that alter other parts of the body, as well as a person's mood."

"You want to give the bees joy juice?" Owen said.

"That is an evocative name that is not what it's actually called, but yes. Its effects are temporary, but with insects, it's likely good enough to override the Herald's emotional manipulation permanently."

"In the morning," Owen said. "The Spiritsmith is probably asleep the way we ought to be." He rose from his chair. "It's been a long day."

Aderyn silently agreed. She wanted to sleep off the slimy feeling the Herald's hypnotism had left her with.

Her gaze fell on Isold, who was laughing at some joke Weston had made, and uncertainty filled her. Isold would have those powers eventually, and what was to stop him from using them the way that Herald had? She reminded herself that Isold was nothing like that bastard, but she couldn't help remembering being helpless under the Herald's power and imagining it happening again.

The Spiritsmith's shop smelled of peppermint and thyme and hot peppers, all of which mingled pleasantly instead of fighting with each other. Aderyn eyed the wall racks of bottles with a semi-professional eye. Her mother didn't own a shop, so she didn't display her work like this, rows and rows of colorful potion bottles in a hundred different shapes, but Aderyn saw some she recognized. Spiritsmiths who set up businesses had standards—healing potions in bulbs, for example, or potions to enhance someone's speed in a three-inch-long tube—so adventurers in the heat of battle could grab the right bottle in an instant.

"Didn't I talk to you people yesterday?" Tobus the Spiritsmith complained. "I'm sure I told at least two of you about my need for a particular plant. You can't possibly have found enough rose hips and feverfew after less than twenty-four hours. Why are you here?"

"We were called on to perform another task," Isold said pleasantly, ignoring the Spiritsmith's hostility. "I assure you—"

"I don't want assurances, I want those plants! Doesn't anyone appreciate the kind of trouble I go to to maintain this town's supply of potions and salves? You're adventurers—do you think healing potions and strength enhancers grow on trees? I have to have supplies to maintain my stock, you know."

"We do, and we intend to search for your ingredients immediately," Isold said, still in a peaceful tone of voice. "As it happens, the place we mean to begin searching has a pest problem we've been asked to deal with, and until we do that, we can't harvest the rose hips you wanted."

Tobus harrumphed. "And you can't search elsewhere?"

"Come now, master Spiritsmith, you don't trust us to give your quest the diligent care it deserves?" Weston exclaimed. "We spent yesterday surveying the area, looking for appropriate roses, and now that we're ready to begin collecting, you want to hold us back. All we need is the euphorium, and perhaps a misting sprayer. We're not even asking you to provide it for free!"

"Euphorium's not cheap," Tobus grumbled.

"We can pay," Owen said, reaching into his pocket. "How much?"

"Seventy-five silver," Tobus said.

"Seventy-five? You can't be serious," Weston said. "We are doing you a favor, after all. Sixty silver."

"Doing me a favor?" Tobus exclaimed. "I haven't seen any rose hips or feverfew. Maybe I'll get someone else to work for me, what with how demanding you lot are."

"I'm sad you feel that way," Weston said, sounding downcast. "But—"

"Seventy-five silver," Owen said. He'd been counting out coins on the table and now pushed the little pile across to the Spiritsmith. "We don't want special treatment."

Weston sputtered indignantly. Tobus glared at Owen as if he suspected a trick. "This is to clear the way to harvest plants for me?" he asked.

"Eventually, yes," Owen said.

Tobus's frown disappeared. "I'll throw in the mister for free," he said, and stumped through the door to his back room.

"I could have had the euphorium for sixty-five!" Weston hissed.

"Sometimes haggling isn't the solution," Owen said. "Getting this guy's cooperation isn't worth a ten-silver savings. And how much would the mister have cost?"

Weston opened his mouth to protest and then shut it again.

Tobus returned, carrying a large glass bottle with a sprayer attachment and a corked bottle shaped like a pyramid the size of Weston's large fist. The pyramid was full of greenish-blue translucent liquid. "Be careful how much of this you use," he said. "Too much euphorium, and you get so happy you don't care about pain. *Any* pain. You could lose an arm and bleed to death with a smile if you're dosed up on the stuff."

"We're not using it on ourselves, but thanks," Owen said, accepting both bottles.

"Right," Tobus said, tapping the side of his nose and nodding knowingly. "You're grownups, mostly, and what you do with it is your business. Enjoy!"

Out in the street, Livia said, "I can't believe he thought we were going to get blissed out on euphorium. What kind of adventurers does he think we are?"

"The boring kind," Weston said. "Don't tell me you've never indulged."

"I have not, and I don't think you have either, you big oaf."

"No name calling," Owen said. "Let's find out if this works."

The road to Ellias's farmsteading looked very different in daylight. That morning, the companions saw workers in the fields to either side of the road, moving through and around the other farms' crops like busy little ants. Nobody was close enough to acknowledge the team, but Aderyn felt less lonely now that it didn't seem they were the only people left in the world.

The buzzing coming from Ellias's farm buildings was louder than it had been the night before. "I didn't think about how much more active the bees would be," Aderyn said as they came within sight of the hives. Great brown-black clouds of bees, small and large, surrounded the hives and the outbuildings, and the eaves of the farmhouse crawled with bees in constant motion.

"We'll just have to move slowly," Owen said.

"Let me cast *force shield* on you before you go out there," Livia said. She chanted, and made some intricate gestures, and the glowing golden field of light sprang up in front of Owen. "I'm not high enough level to cast it as a sphere, so be careful to keep it between you and the bees."

Owen nodded. He took several long, slow steps until he was about ten feet from the nearest corner of the farmhouse, lifted the mister bottle, and squeezed the little bladder so a puff of strawberry-scented mist enveloped the eaves. It spread farther than Aderyn had expected, nearly covering ten square feet of eaves and roof.

The effect was instantaneous and dramatic. The bees stopped

their movement, clinging to the roof or hanging motionless in midair. Then they all took to the air, flying in great slow loops that looked to Aderyn like a drunkard's path, aimless and happy. Owen walked forward into the midst of them. They ignored him. "I guess it worked," he said, and sprayed more of the roof.

It took about an hour to spray all the bees. At the end of that time, the whole area stank of strawberries, there was about half an ounce of euphorium left in the mister bottle, and the bees were performing aerial acrobatics any Spider would envy. Owen returned to his companions' side. "I hope that was enough to fulfil the quest, because I'm out of ideas."

As if in response, a message appeared to Aderyn.

Congratulations! You have completed the quest [The Honey and the Stinger].
You have been awarded [750 XP]

Welcome to Level Four

And then, immediately following, the words:

Congratulations! You have completed the secret quest [Destroy the Herald's Selfish Dungeon].
You have been awarded [1000 XP]

Aderyn let out a cry of excitement that was echoed by Weston. Isold pounded Owen on the back. "A secret quest! That's better than gold."

"Which we will also probably get once we return to town," Owen replied. He carefully poured the liquid back into its original bottle and corked it. "We might need this someday," he said, and after a moment's hesitation handed the bottle to Isold. "And no, I don't mean we should get hopped up on joy juice to see what it feels like, Weston, which I can tell was going to be your next suggestion."

Weston grinned. "I am fairly predictable, huh?"

"Now, was the thing about harvesting rose hips here another bald-faced lie, Isold, or are the right rosebushes on Ellias's farm?" Owen went on.

"It was the truth, actually." Isold led them around the corner of the farmhouse to a small kitchen garden. A row of bushes heavy with reddening bulbous fruits defined one edge of the garden. Small white flowers grew at the bases of the bushes. "Tobus said to look for rose-bushes where the flowers have fallen off prematurely, and to harvest the rose hips that are not yet ripe. And I see feverfew growing there near the bushes."

"How are we supposed to harvest these plants?" Aderyn asked.

Isold showed them how to collect the feverfew by uprooting the whole plant, and Aderyn and Owen did that while he and Weston used their belt knives to cut the rose hips away from the stems. As they worked, Livia assembled a carrying pouch she soaked with her water summoning spell so the feverfew wouldn't wilt too much in the growing heat of a summer day.

Though the bushes had plenty of fruits and flowers, when they'd harvested as much as they could, Isold said it wasn't enough. "We have to fill this bucket to the marked line. Let's try the rest of these farmsteadings. Though we may have to pay for the privilege. Rose hips make a good, healthful tea anyone can make, not just apothe-caries or Spiritsmiths."

"You don't suppose Ellias will be mad that we took his plants?" Aderyn asked.

"We'll call it part of our payment if he is," Owen said, "but I bet he'll be so happy to have his farm back he won't care about a few missing handfuls of rose hips and some torn-up weeds."

They spent the rest of the morning and early afternoon trudging up and down the roads to the other farmsteadings, knocking on doors and explaining their quest. Aderyn was surprised at how genuinely pleased the farmers were to see them. Her parents' stories of adventuring included plenty of tales of clashing with non-classed men and women, farmers, traders, craftsmen, and the like. According to Aderyn's mother, the non-classed disliked adventurers because they felt adventurers looked down on them for not accepting the Call. "Which is sometimes true, don't get me wrong," Lyzette had told her daughter, "but really it's more that some people feel guilty about having declined the Call, and they take it out on adventurers."

But every farmer they spoke to was polite, if not enthusiastic, and if they had rosebushes, which not all of them did, they guided the companions to look at them and were disappointed if they weren't the right kind of bushes. Some of the farmers insisted on feeding them or giving them large glasses of new beer. Their welcome reconciled Aderyn to how long the stupid quest was taking. Why they'd agreed to it, she didn't know—except they needed any experience they could gain, and this could be substantial. She still wished they'd opted for something else.

CHAPTER TWENTY-FOUR

Finally, at nearly two-thirty according to Livia's pocket watch, Isold said, "That's enough." The rose hips filled Isold's carrying container to the brim, and Livia's makeshift basket was nearly as full.

"What a relief," Owen said. "I'm sweating buckets. How do people in your world get baths?"

"You can rent the inn's tin bath for a few coppers," Livia said. "In rich houses, there are heated cisterns so a hot bath is easier to draw. And in cities, they have bath houses with tubs you can actually lie down in."

Owen grimaced. "I miss hot showers. Practically endless hot water pouring down over you, rinsing away dirt and sweat... that's another indoor plumbing thing my world has."

"Indoor plumbing?" Weston asked.

"He'll tell you all about it while we walk," Aderyn said. "Especially the magic chamber pots."

"They're toilets, and it's technology, Aderyn, not magic."

"You couldn't explain how it works, so how is that not magic?"

"I—" Owen fell silent. "Huh. There's this saying in my world about how any greatly advanced technology is indistinguishable from magic, or something like that. And it's true I can't build a sewer system or plumb a house or install a toilet. So maybe in a sense it *is* magic, just magic founded on science instead of the system."

"Your world is so different," Livia said. "I wonder, if I went to your world, whether I would still be able to wield magic. Like, does magic come from who I am, or does it come from what the system does to run the world?"

"I wish we could find out," Owen said. "Though if it meant you getting trapped in my world the way I'm trapped here, I'd rather not know."

A pang of sadness struck Aderyn at his words. She'd been enjoying his company so much she'd forgotten the goal was to send him home. "Is that how you feel? Like you're trapped?"

She'd thought she'd asked the question lightly, but Owen jerked as if she'd punched him. "I don't—I mean, yes, I don't feel like I belong here, and I want to go home—maybe 'trapped' was the wrong word. I like you all, and I'm glad I'm not alone. And your world isn't awful, just weird by my standards."

"I want to know how your world ended up turning ours into a game," Isold said. "How would anyone from your world know about ours, if we didn't know about you? It seems really farfetched for that to happen."

"I don't know." Owen sounded relieved at the change of subject. "Maybe people from your world visited mine in the past, and they told some of my world's people about their world, and those people didn't want anyone to think they were crazy, babbling about magic and quests and monsters, so they turned it into a game. It's as reasonable a theory as any."

"If you could be transported to this world, it makes sense that the transport could go both ways," Aderyn said.

"It's too bad there's no way to control the transfer." Owen chuckled. "I can think of friends who would kill for a chance to live here. Play out the fantasies that in our world they can only, well, play. Pretend, I mean."

"I don't know how I feel about that," Livia said. "Would they even take this world seriously if they were thinking all the time about how much it resembled a game? They could get hurt or even killed that way."

"It didn't take more than one monster encounter to convince me this was real despite how game-like it seemed," Owen said, "but I was never really into fantasy RPGs. Not like some of my friends who play in three or four games at a time. So maybe it's just me, and you're right that most people wouldn't have the right attitude."

The repeated mention of Owen's world was making Aderyn's heart ache. "Maybe we should consider it—or, no, I mean be aware of the possibilities. Because someone who can send you home to your world could probably pull someone out of it."

"That raises another question I've had these past few days," Isold said. "How sure are you that the system is what brought you here? Suppose it was a spellslinger instead?"

"I don't know." Owen pursed his lips in a considering way. "I assumed it was the system because Aderyn didn't know of any spells or spellslinger specializations that could do that. But if we assume someone can send me back, that means it could be a spellslinger, and in that case, I'd really like to know why they did it."

"It doesn't matter, though, right?" Weston said. "System, spell-slinger, what matters is getting you back."

"Yeah." Owen still sounded like he was thinking hard about something. For the briefest moment, Aderyn saw a future in which they couldn't send him home, and it filled her with guilty happiness. Then she silently scolded herself. She was being selfish. Owen didn't belong here, and he had a family who had to be worried about where he'd gone. But if he went home, she was back to being a useless Warmaster—that, and she would miss her friend. She told herself to stiffen her spine. She didn't need just one partner, and she would find another, or she'd explode everyone's expectations and become the world's greatest Warmaster *without* a partner. It could happen.

The guards let them back into the town, and although they'd only eaten scant rations at noon rather than interrupt their search, they all agreed they would turn in the quest items before getting a real meal. Aderyn's mood lightened the nearer they got to the Spirit-smith's shop. If this was enough to push them over the edge to level five...

Tobus was no gladder to see them than before. "Back so soon? Let me guess, you need a speed enhancer so you can outrace someone who stole all the rose hips you harvested."

"You've got a very droll sense of humor," Isold said with a smile. "As it happens, we've finished your quest." He set the collecting container on the table as Livia laid her squishy wet bundle beside it.

Tobus's mouth fell open. "No," he breathed. "I can't believe it. You must have harvested the wrong ones. Nobody else was able to find the plants."

"I promise they're what you asked for. You can test them if you like." Isold sounded perfectly calm, but Aderyn had been watching him closely and his jaw had tightened as if he didn't like how Tobus had all but called him a liar.

Tobus plucked a rose hip from the container and sniffed it. Then he bit into it, not enough to do more than break the skin, and touched his tongue to the crack. "This might be it. I'll need to run more tests."

Aderyn felt something nagging at her as Tobus picked up the container and carried it into his back room. "We should have seen a quest complete message," she whispered. "Did anyone see that?"

"Something's wrong," Owen said. It was all he had time for before Tobus returned to pick up the feverfew. "Master Spiritsmith, is there something else we have to do?"

"What? Oh. No, I don't think so. Did you want more work? I'm sure I could come up with something for a handful of competent adventurers like yourselves." Tobus retreated into the back with the squishy bundle of plants.

Still no quest notice appeared. "I feel cheated," Weston said, his smile not as brilliant as usual.

Tobus came back into the front of the shop. "Let me give you something for your trouble." He pulled out a belt pouch and, rather than dumping its contents on the table, began picking through it.

"The quest isn't complete," Owen said. "What aren't you telling us?"

Tobus looked at Owen with narrowed eyes. "Are you accusing me of underhanded behavior?"

"I don't know what to accuse you of. We did as you asked, and the quest isn't complete."

"The system's rewards have got nothing to do with me." Tobus handed Owen five gold coins. "There. Be off with you."

Owen palmed the coins without looking at them. "What's the rose hips and feverfew for?"

"I'm certainly not going to tell you my secrets. Now, get out before I call the guards."

Owen didn't move. "I think I'm going to have to insist that you tell us, or I'll go to the magistrate and explain how you're creating a potion the system doesn't want you to complete."

"Owen?" Weston said. "How—"

Owen gestured for silence. "In fact," he said, "I'm guessing this potion of yours isn't harmless. Aderyn?"

Aderyn jerked. "Um... yes?"

"What do you see?"

Aderyn managed not to blurt out that she had no idea what Owen was talking about. Instead, she Assessed the Spiritsmith.

NaMe: T0bus

Clasz: SpiriTSmith

Lev3l: Exce3ds author1ty LimiT

"Something's wrong," she said. "He's not what he seems."

Tobus backed away, reaching for one of the bottles on the wall rack. "Stop him!" Owen shouted.

Isold dove for the Spiritsmith, who got his hand on the bottle only to have it slip, glistening with *grease* summoned by Livia, from his grasp to shatter on the floor. Acid began to burn a hole in the wood, and everyone recoiled. Owen drew his sword and pointed it at Tobus. "What are you really?"

Tobus struggled in Isold's grip. "You're insane. I'm a respected member of this community, not some criminal you can threaten."

Aderyn stepped closer and Assessed him again.

Name: Morrion

Class: Unknown

Level: Exceeds authority limit

She let out a hiss of shock. "It says his name is Morrion and it won't tell me his class. I think he's something evil."

Tobus, or Morrion, laughed. "Stop throwing wild accusations around and get out of my shop."

"I don't think so," Owen said. "We're going to Magistrate Gemina and she'll figure out who you are. In any case, you can forget about crafting that potion."

"Owen, have you gone crazy?" Weston demanded. "You're jumping to all sorts of conclusions. What makes you think this potion is dangerous?"

As he spoke, a system message popped up.

Congratulations! You have completed the secret quest [A Potion Brewed in Malice].
You have earned [1250 XP]

Warning: The quest [Rose Hips and Feverfew] has been invalidated by the completion of another quest. [Rose Hips and Feverfew] will be removed from your active list.

Weston gaped. "Lucky guess," he said.

"Instinct, and a Warmaster's skill," Owen said.

"I've never heard of a notice like that before," Isold said.

Weston had begun removing rope from his pack. "I think we should bind him, just in case."

Tobus/Morrion wrenched at Isold's grip again, but the lanky Herald was stronger than he looked. Between Isold and Weston, they got the Spiritsmith's hands tied behind his back, and the little group left the shop and headed for the plaza where the town hall was. It didn't take long for them to attract attention. After the third time someone shouted at them, wanting to know why they'd captured Tobus, Owen said, "Let's move faster. This could get ugly."

But it seemed no one liked Tobus enough to intervene, and they reached the town hall without incident. Inside, they waited as a girl ran off to fetch Gemina. Aderyn was starting to feel nervous, even though she'd seen Tobus's Assessment change and trusted her skill without question. It was still awkward, the thought of explaining it all to the magistrate who *hadn't* seen what Aderyn had.

A few minutes later, Gemina appeared, looking as unruffled as she had the night before. "What a surprise," she said, taking in the scene before her. "I expected you all this morning, but not in company with the Spiritsmith."

"I demand you make these ruffians let me go," Tobus said. "I won't be treated this way. I'm a valued member of the community, not a criminal."

"Magistrate, he's not who he says he is," Aderyn exclaimed. "His name is Morrion, and I don't know his class because Assess won't show it to me. He's concealing something."

"Yes, after further... conversation... with that Herald, Hameth, I discovered the two were conspiring together," Gemina said. "There isn't much call for strength enhancers in this community, and adventurers are the primary market. Since Tobus, or whatever his name is, doesn't sell to adventurers very often, I had to wonder why he had that potion on hand and in such quantities. And Hameth was quick to rat him out as co-conspirator in the dungeon-creation plan." The magistrate advanced on Tobus, regarding him closely. "I'll call the guards to take him into custody for interrogation—unless you want to confess what you intended to brew right now?"

Tobus/Morrion glared at her.

"I didn't think so." Gemina spoke quietly to the girl, who ran out of the room. "It seems this community owes you adventurers a debt. Uncovering not one, but two men bent on disrupting and harming Asylum—impressive work."

"So, the Herald's plan would have worked?" Owen asked.

Gemina chuckled. "Not really. Not more than once, anyway. Hameth is cunning, but he's not that bright. If he tried repopulating a dungeon with much higher monsters, over and over again, word would eventually get out about the new and oddly-powerful dungeon in the safe zone, other high-level adventurers would arrive, and they'd put a stop to it."

"I'm not sure how that works," Isold said. "We understood his plan was to create his own personal experience-generating dungeon, but wouldn't others have wanted to be complicit so they could reap the benefits, too?"

"You're so sweet at your level," Gemina said, but she sounded more amused than patronizing. "You haven't yet had the hard lessons knocked into you. Adventurers don't like cheats. They especially don't like other adventurers getting advantages they can't have. Any party who discovered what Hameth was up to would have taken him out of the picture. Permanently. That's why you never hear about this sort of scam. Granted, it's the first I've seen anyone try it in the safe zone—but, even so, you stopped it before monsters could overrun Asylum, and we're grateful."

She removed a belt pouch and poured a stream of gold coins into her palm, bounced the coins a few times, and added two more. Then she handed the coins to Owen. "A token of our thanks."

Owen didn't count it. "Thank you."

As he spoke, silver letters formed in front of Aderyn's face.

Congratulations! You have completed the quest [A Snake in Sheep's Clothing].
You have earned [2000 XP]

And, half a breath later:

Welcome to Level Five

CHAPTER TWENTY-FIVE

Aderyn gasped. They'd advanced so quickly it was like they'd skipped level four completely. She wanted to check her advancement and find out if she'd gained anything interesting, but now wasn't the time. "Level five," she said.

"Congratulations," said Gemina. "Do you intend to leave soon? I'm sure there are other quests we can provide."

"We'll talk about it," Owen said, "but I think we're eager to proceed to Guerdon Deep."

Gemina whistled. "That's a dangerous journey even for five adventurers of your level. Make sure you're properly equipped, and I wish you luck."

Once the false Spiritsmith was taken into custody by a couple of beefy guards, the companions left the town hall and walked slowly back the way they'd come. Now that they weren't prodding a bound man before them, the citizens of Asylum paid them no attention. Aderyn figured either they didn't look like adventurers, or they *did* look like adventurers, but low-level ones who weren't likely to provide excitement. Hah. If they only knew.

"We should spend some of that money on improving our gear," she said. "We need armor, at least."

"I don't," Livia said. "I have a new class skill I can't wait to try out. Shifting magical plates of metal providing me the same protection armor would." Her eyes were unfocused, and she kept drifting sideways as if she was drunk.

"How can you read your Codex and walk at the same time?" Weston exclaimed.

"It takes focus and practice," Livia said smugly. "And groundedness."

"Is that a dig at my lighthearted approach to life?"

"Well, if you—"

"Are you having fun or are you sniping at each other?" Owen asked.

"What's sniping?" Weston and Livia said as one, and both laughed.

"Earth and Air, if you consider Moonlighters being light on their feet," Aderyn said. "They can't help but clash."

"Yes, imagine if I was a Windwarden," Weston said. "We'd really be at each other's throats."

"Just so it stays friendly," Owen said. "Let's go back to the inn and divide this money up. Magistrate Gemina gave me a lot of gold coins, and we've still got the purse Ellias handed us to split between us."

Rather than spread their money out in the taproom for everyone to see, they all crowded into Aderyn and Livia's room, which was slightly bigger than the others. Owen poured all the coin into a pile on the clothespress lid and sorted it into piles. As he'd said, there was a sizeable lot of gold coins, and even more silver coins, with a few coppers mixed in because Ellias had essentially given them everything he'd had in his belt pouch.

"That's five gold each from the town," he said. "Very generous."

Aderyn couldn't stop staring at the little piles. This was more money than she'd ever had in her life.

"And... another forty-six silver and ten copper apiece, with three copper left over," Owen said. "What can you buy with a copper?"

"Half an apple," Isold said. "You keep them, Owen."

Aderyn gathered up her coin and put it in her pocket, then discovered the pocket bulged so much it was obvious. She'd need a belt pouch, after all. She scooped most of her money into her knapsack, leaving enough in her pocket to buy a few necessities.

The others collected their shares as well. "The magistrate said we should be well equipped," Owen said. "What does that mean? In practical terms?"

"Armor," Weston and Isold said in unison. "We've gotten lucky so far," Weston added, with no trace of his usual good humor. "Like Aderyn said, you and I at least need armor, Owen, because armor use is a class skill for both of us."

"How is that something that requires skill?" Owen asked. "It's not like it takes skill to put on your pants in the morning, or to walk while wearing them."

"My father says it's about knowing how to fight while having your movement hampered," Aderyn said. "Different weights of armor require different maneuvering. There are some that anyone can wear without much difficulty, but they don't provide as much protection."

"And the greater your skill with armor, the more effectively it protects you," Isold added.

"Okay, that makes sense," Owen said. "What else? I already have the best sword I'm likely to get in Asylum."

"Upgrades to the gear we already have," Livia said. "I know I need better boots. And I know a shop that sells odds and ends. Sometimes they have magic items."

"Shopping quest!" Owen exclaimed, making them all laugh.

They walked to the market as a group before splitting up to

search for specific items. Aderyn went with Owen and Weston to an armorer's. The smell of the shop, of metal and leather, reminded her so much of fighting practice with her father she had to lag behind so her companions wouldn't see her get weepy.

She watched Owen be fitted with a hardened leather brigandine that laced up the sides and had flaps hanging down in front and back to protect the tops of his legs. Owen chose matching vambraces, which Weston declined on the grounds that they reduced the flexibility his less-reinforced leather jerkin gave him. Owen was looking more like a Swordsworn all the time, Aderyn reflected, between the armor and the sword and the way he walked with greater confidence every day.

Then Owen looked up and caught her eye, and he smiled, a funny expression that clearly said he felt ridiculous, and her heart beat faster for a few seconds for no reason she could imagine. "You look good," she told him.

Owen glanced at the armorer. "This doesn't feel as unnatural as I thought it would, all things considered. What are you going to buy?"

She'd almost forgotten her purpose in coming. The armorer focused on her, eyes narrowing as she Assessed Aderyn. "What's a Warmaster?" she said.

"Tactical support," Owen said, "but her abilities are boosted by having fighting skills, which means she has to be in the way of an enemy attack sometimes. Aderyn, I think you should get something light so you can stay maneuverable."

"Tactical support," the armorer said, tapping her finger against her lips. "Can't say I've ever heard of that, but your reasoning is sound. Let's get you one of these jerkins."

The smooth, pliable leather jerkin fit Aderyn snugly but not so tightly she couldn't move her arms. It had a placket that overlapped in front where the lacing was and short cap sleeves protecting her shoulder joints. It was also dyed a very pretty deep blue.

"It won't defend you against a hard thrust from a dagger or

sword," the armorer said, "but it will deflect most slashing blows and take the brunt of a club or mace. The idea is still that your best defense is not being in a position to be hit, of course, but this will help."

"It's perfect, thanks." Aderyn paid with one of her gold coins; she had exact change, but this was the first time she'd spent actual gold on herself, and handing over the coin made her feel competent and well-to-do. Just like a real adventurer.

They walked from the armorer to a weapons shop, where Weston haggled for a brace of throwing knives. "I don't have the skill yet, but I know it's only a matter of time," he told the companions as he balanced one of the knives flat on his fingertip. "Level seven or level eight, according to my mother."

"Your mother was a Moonlighter?" Owen exclaimed.

"Still is. She retired at level thirteen to have children." Weston flipped the knife into the air so it tumbled once before he caught it and thrust it into its sheath in one smooth movement. "She taught me all sorts of tricks, though with me being as big as this we didn't think I'd end up following in her footsteps. My father is a Stalwart and built like a brick shithouse, like me, so it's understandable."

"A Stalwart—" Owen's mouth snapped shut. Aderyn could guess he'd been about to ask what a Stalwart class meant. She nodded and jerked her head sideways, indicating that they could talk outside.

"What about a knife for the lady?" the shop owner said with a smile and a wink. "You look like you know how to handle that sword, but nobody ever regrets having a backup weapon."

"I—" Aderyn glanced over the display cabinets. One of the blades caught her eye, and she stepped closer to examine it. It was only about a foot long from pommel to tip, sharp on both edges and with a bluish glint to the steel she liked. "Can I see that one?"

The man's eyes lit up. "A connoisseur," he said. He carefully retrieved the knife and extended it to her, lying flat across both his hands. "The blue steel is made by a special process I can't share with you—trade secrets, you understand, and the woman who forges these would have my head if I spread her business around like that. It isn't magical, and the bluing process doesn't make the steel special, more like it's her signature on the weapon. So everyone knows a Jasena piece on sight."

Aderyn sighted along the blade and tested the edge lightly against her thumb, not pressing hard enough to draw blood. The hilt was wrapped in fine black leather, and the guard was thicker and longer than she expected from a knife this short and curved up at both ends, like the unknown blacksmith intended the wielder to catch an enemy's blade and take it from him. "I love it," she said. "How much?"

"For you, one gold and ten silver," the shopkeeper said.

Weston had opened his mouth to barter almost before the man stopped speaking, but instead of challenging him, he said, "That is an astonishing discount."

"You know the value of a good weapon, too, then," the shopkeeper said.

Aderyn, feeling uncomfortable, said, "I don't know that I deserve special treatment. What's the usual price?"

The shopkeeper gazed at her steadily. "Two things I'll give you for free," he said. "One, never reject a generous thought. You don't know when one of them will save your life. And two, my son was a Warmaster and he ended up traveling alone. You look like you have companions who care about you, and I wish he'd had that. I don't know, haven't seen him in years, so maybe he has now. But I have a soft spot for his class, so you pay what I tell you and don't argue."

Aderyn's mouth fell open. "I see," she said. "Thank you. I hope your son found the right partner. It's how the class works, you see. Paired skills."

"I've never heard of anything like that before. He said he had insights into fighting, but no one ever took the time to listen to him."

The shopkeeper's eyes shone with tears. "And is this young man your partner, then? This Swordsworn with the odd name?"

Aderyn's heart beat faster again. "He is," she said, and found she couldn't look Owen in the eye.

"Then I wish you luck in your class. Both of you. Well, all three of you, I suppose." The shopkeeper smiled and saluted them. Aderyn handed over the money, feeling she'd bought more than just a weapon.

CHAPTER TWENTY-SIX

Outside on the street, Weston said, "I hope you're not the only Warmaster who's learned how to make the class effective. That man's son... I hate to think what must have happened to him without a team, let alone without a partner."

Owen squeezed Aderyn's shoulder lightly. "Let's just be grateful it's not us, right? We should find that shop Livia mentioned, and you can explain what a Stalwart is while we walk. I'm guessing tank."

"Tank?" Aderyn smiled and shook her head. "Stalwarts are built for defense. They're strong and resilient so they can absorb damage and free up their teammates to attack without getting incapacitated. Is that what a tank is?"

"The way I meant it, yes." Owen's steps slowed. "People are staring at us."

"We look more like adventurers now," Weston said. He smiled and waved at a small child who gaped after them. "Just think how they'll feel about us when we're level ten, or level fifteen."

Aderyn had expected, when Livia mentioned the shop that sold odds and ends, that it would be one of those small, out-of-the-way shops, dimly lit and smelling of dust and disuse. Madoch's Emporium, though, was bigger than any of the other stores on the plaza, taking up enough space for three regular-sized shops. Large windows of glass panes in iron grids let in plenty of light, as did the skylights that ran in a row down the sides of the peaked roof. Shelves stood in ranks like city guards turned out for inspection, taller than Weston and stained a light amber brown that kept them from making the room oppressive.

The only thing that was as Aderyn had imagined was the shop's wares. There was no order to how things were laid out on the shelves, and cartons containing spools of colorful thread sat beside children's toys or engraved metal boxes lined with blue silk or a row of stone mortars with stained marble pestles. Aderyn didn't see anything in disrepair, though dust covered some of the items. She could easily imagine mysterious treasures lost in here forever.

"This is like the world's most disorganized Goodwill," Owen muttered. "I know Livia said there could be magic items here, but I don't know how anyone would ever find them."

"If you can perceive magic auras, finding those items is easy," Livia said from the next aisle over. "Though knowing something's magical doesn't mean I know what it does."

"That would be the job of a Herald," Isold said.

"How does your skill work?" Owen asked. "Is it like Aderyn's **[Improved Assess 1]**, where you see information written over a thing?"

"It's more a form of perfect recall," Isold said. "When I look at a magical item, the knowledge of its name and function comes to mind the way the name of a friend would when I see a familiar face. And if an item is too powerful, it feels like having the knowledge just out of reach—like it's something I knew once and can't bring to mind."

"What about this?" Livia said. She'd been digging through a bin full of belt pouches of all sizes and materials and now held one out to Isold. Aderyn moved a couple of wooden bowls aside so she could see through to the next aisle, where Livia stood. The pouch was of average size and made of quilted black satin rather than leather. It didn't look unusual to Aderyn except for the silver beads dangling from the ends of the cord cinching the bag shut; they were the size of Aderyn's pinky nail and shaped like blooming roses.

Isold took the pouch and ran his fingers over the smooth surface. "Interesting. This is a <**Purse of Great Capacity**>. No matter what you put into it, it appears empty, and it will hold five times as much as a normal purse of this size. Including accepting many objects that are apparently too big for it."

"Sounds useful," Owen said.

"I was just thinking I need a belt pouch, after all," Aderyn said. "Can I look at it?"

Isold handed it through the shelf to her, and she opened it and peered inside. "It's empty. No, let me check." She reached in, and her hands felt nothing, no soft sides of the purse, no mysterious contents. Then she realized her arm was in the purse up to her elbow. She yanked her arm free and tugged on the purse strings to close it. "That's very strange. I think I want it."

"We don't need a tent, do we?" Weston called out. He had his arms full of miscellaneous objects, some of which Aderyn didn't recognize. "The weather's nice enough, unless we get rained on."

"Too heavy," Owen said. "Especially if you're bringing that cookpot."

"Hey, there are five of us, and we all get hungry," Weston protested. "Rabbit soup, good for what ails you."

"Rabbit soup? But rabbits are too cute to eat!" Livia said.

"You'll change your mind when you smell it."

"It's like asking me to eat puppy chowder. I'll never budge on this."

"Cookpot, deep skillet, assorted spices," Isold said, ignoring the argument. "A new lantern—two new lanterns, in case Aderyn decides to crack skulls again."

"Ha ha, very funny," Aderyn said, scowling.

"I think that's everything, unless Livia sees any more magic items we might want," Owen said.

"There's not a lot here right now," Livia said, making a face at Weston. "Did we want to bring a camp spit along? They don't look heavy—just two forked iron rods and a heavier one to fit across over the fire." She shifted some metal bars standing propped against a waist-high bin filled with what looked to Aderyn like scrap metal.

"If we can make do with branches as we go, that would save room," Owen pointed out.

"There's not a lot of forest for the first three days," Aderyn said, having now memorized her father's map.

"Wait a minute," Livia said. "This one's magical." She held up a flattened iron rod about two feet long.

Isold hurried to her side. "Is there only one? Help me move these so she can look at the rest."

Owen and Aderyn shifted iron bars while Weston, his arms full, stood by offering advice. Finally, Livia said, "There aren't any others that are magic. And there aren't any others shaped like this one. They're all round bars, and this one is flat along two sides."

"Well, that's disappointing," Isold said. "This is a <**Skeleton Ladder**>. Half of one, at least. Hold it up, Livia. Horizontally."

Livia held the bar at eye level. Isold gripped one end of the rod and twisted. A previously invisible cap over the end rotated. "Let go," Isold said.

Livia released the bar, and it hung in midair, unsupported by anything.

"That's amazing," Owen said. "What a useful item."

"Even half is worth keeping. I think I'll buy this," Isold said.

Aderyn secretly hoped the store owner didn't know what he had, since the purse and the ladder rung had been mixed in among mundane items. But Madoch eyed the little purse, then reached inside to the shoulder. "Wouldn't want you walking out of here with something you didn't pay for," he said in a way that wasn't quite a joke. Aderyn just nodded and paid a gold and seventy-five silver for the magic purse.

While the others were paying for their gear, Aderyn searched her knapsack for the rest of her coin to put in the <**Purse of Great Capacity**>. She decided to add her <**Matchlighter**> and a few other small items to its contents. It couldn't hurt to have the <**Matchlighter**> closer to hand and not have to dig through the rest of her gear to find it.

Owen joined her where she waited near the door. "Was there anything else you wanted to do? Because I think we should leave as soon as we're finished here. It's not even eleven o'clock, and it's not as if we'd reach a town by nightfall even if we waited to leave early tomorrow morning."

"I'm ready to go," Aderyn said. "It feels like we've finally begun. I mean, not that what we've done so far isn't important—"

"But we've been in the newbie zone until now, and it's time to take the training wheels off," Owen said.

"I'm not going to ask what those words mean," Aderyn said, rolling her eyes. "I'm sure you said them just to see me wince."

"That's nothing," Owen said. "Wait until I tell you about the internal combustion engine."

THEY LEFT ASYLUM A LITTLE AFTER NOON. HIGH CLOUDS obscured the sun, and the air was cooler than it had been for several days. Aderyn walked beside Owen and considered whether it was worth trying Livia's trick of reading her Codex while walking. She was impatient to see how she'd advanced now that she was level five, but there hadn't been time that morning.

She squinched up her right eye and whispered, "Advancement."

The Codex filled her vision, and she immediately veered into

Owen, who caught her arm to keep her from tripping. "What happened?"

"I was stupid, that's all." She dismissed the Codex. "It will have to wait."

"I forgot to look at it, too," Owen said. "For level four and level five both. It's like a surprise present with every advancement."

"Were you serious about me gaining fighting skills when we talked to the armorer?"

"It's a guess, but—well, I think it's unlikely that a Warmaster doesn't do more than stand off to one side and shout encouragement. There's got to be an active component to the class. So I was wondering, if **[Improved Distraction]** is a thing, why not flanking?"

"I hadn't thought of that. You mean working together to keep a monster off balance."

"Right. Weston and I do it sometimes, but Weston's skills—"

"Why are you talking about me?" Weston asked from where he walked a little way ahead of them.

"Just discussing fighting styles. Weston, and I'm guessing Moonlighters in general, look to exploit weak spots in a monster's defense, but they do that without depending on another fighter. If we had another fighter class in our team, that person and I could coordinate attacks. My guess is that you and I will do that more efficiently than I and another Swordsworn would."

Aderyn scanned the horizon. "Now I want something to attack us so we can test that guess."

Owen laughed. "It doesn't look like you'll get your wish. The plains are empty of everything but us."

"Give it time," Isold said. "We're still very close to the sanctuary cities. Another day or two, and we could have all the monsters we want."

It didn't sound ominous, but despite her words Aderyn shivered.

CHAPTER TWENTY-SEVEN

They walked until just before sunset, heading north and east, and then set up camp for the night. There were no trees for shelter, no hills to give them a vantage point, just the endless grassy plains that turned into forest much farther west and north than they were, so they picked a spot at random and arranged their bedrolls around a fire Livia built. The fire was for comfort rather than warmth or cooking, since they hadn't caught any rabbits, something Livia loudly declared was a good thing. They sat around the fire and ate some of the rations they'd bought in Asylum, enjoying the peaceful evening.

Beside her, Owen murmured something Aderyn couldn't make out. She glanced at him and saw his eyes were focused on the middle distance, which reminded her of her desire to check her advancement. She set what was left of her dried meat aside and leaned forward, hugging her legs, to comfortably rest her chin on her knees. "Advancement," she whispered, squinching her right eye.

Name: Aderyn
Class: Warmaster
Level: 5

Skills: Bluff (3), Climb (1), Conversation (3), Intimidate (3), Sense Truth (5), Survival (1), Swim (1), Knowledge: Monsters (3)

Class Skills: Improved Assess 1 (6), Awareness (4), Knowledge: Geography (2), Spot (4), Discern Weakness (5), Dodge (4), Improvised Distraction (2), Outflank (0), Draw Fire (0)

"I have two new class skills!" she exclaimed. "But with no ranks. I guess that makes sense, since I haven't used them yet."

"I was right about flanking, if we both have this [Outflank] skill," Owen said.

"That's one of them. The other is [Draw Fire]." Aderyn scanned the list of skills. "And no weapon use skill. Maybe that's because I have to work with a weapon to get the skill, and the system won't provide me with a hint about which weapon it should be."

"I have some new sword fighting moves and an overall improvement to my weapon skill. Plus [Outflank]." Owen lay back on the grasses they'd stomped flat and flung his arms to both sides. "I don't like the sound of [Draw Fire], Aderyn. That might mean someone's shooting at you."

"It might be a kind of distraction," Weston said. "Like an advanced version of that thing where you throw stuff at the enemy so we can skewer them."

"It still sounds dangerous for someone who isn't a Stalwart."

"I guess we'll have to see how it works in combat," Aderyn said. "What about the rest of you?"

"As I said, I wasn't expecting a thrown weapons skill," Weston said, "but since I got a lot of other skills, I'm not complaining. I now have [Stealth] to enhance my already sneaky movements, and an improvement to my ability to find and exploit an enemy's weak spots, and—maybe I shouldn't be proud of the last ones."

"Why not?" Livia asked. "We already know you're a sneaky bastard."

"Thank you so much, half-pint spellslinger."

"Half-pint? What, because I'm not an over-muscled giant?"

"Better a giant than someone who needs a stepstool to reach the lowest shelf."

"At least I'm not brain-damaged from bashing my head against every door lintel in Asylum."

"Just tell us before Livia exhausts her supply of insults," Owen said with a grin.

Weston winked at Livia. "Well, actually, the skills are [Dirty Fighting] and [To the Heart]."

"What's [To the Heart]?" Livia asked.

"My mother said it's a refinement on finding weak spots. Literally striking to the heart, or the eye—hitting something a critical blow." Weston stopped smiling. "Sometimes with deadly effect."

"A kill shot," Owen said.

"That's a good way of putting it. I don't know why I find it disturbing. Taking a monster down before it can kill me or my friends is what I'm here for. But it feels—" He laughed. "It feels like cheating, which is stupid."

"I understand, though," Owen said. "Fights should be a challenge, or we won't grow."

"And if we fight and kill other humans, those deaths shouldn't be trivial," Isold said. "Even taking an evil life is serious business."

"I'm more pragmatic," Livia said. "I say use the skills you're given to keep your team alive, and don't worry about the details. I'd rather you kick an orc in the crotch and behead it as it's falling than that you face it in a fair fight and get injured."

"Definitely an Earthbreaker," Weston said, bowing as well as he could from a sitting position. "And you? New spells, new skills?"

"Spellslingers don't advance the way other classes do," Livia said. "Once we have a specialization, we get skills related to our element, but not every level. What we do get each level is a list of spells we can choose from to add to our knowledge. The higher my level, the more powerful the spells. So I now have..." She squinted the way Aderyn had shown all of them. "Eight simple spells, nine first-level spells, and four second-level spells, plus four class abilities."

"That seems like a lot," Aderyn said.

"It's a fraction of what is available to spellslingers," Isold said, startling Aderyn with his sudden entry into the conversation. He'd been so quiet she'd almost forgotten he was there. "I think nine is all the first-level spells you will ever get, Livia, am I right?"

"That's right." Livia's eyes focused on him. "And I get fewer than that of the higher-level spells, though I don't yet know the total. So I have to be careful in picking new spells. It's hard to exchange them once they're chosen. There's a ritual to undergo."

"That's still twenty-five spells, including the class abilities," Owen said.

"And the class abilities grow with me. That *elemental blast* of earth—spraying someone's eyes with dirt to blind them, remember? —is a *rain of stones* now." Livia held out her hand and summoned her *orb of light*. "This still needs to stay connected to me, though."

"What about you, Isold?" Aderyn asked.

"My class skills build on each other," Isold said, "and they do so gradually. In addition to my many knowledges and my ability to charm someone, I can create a magical distraction that leaves an enemy open to being attacked more easily. But of more interest to all of us is that I now have access to the system's maps."

All four sat up straight. "I thought that happened at level ten," Weston said.

"It's a Herald class skill, which makes sense given that it's a form of knowledge." Isold tilted his head forward and back swiftly, and his eyes glazed over like he was looking at the Codex. "It's a rudimentary map, not as detailed as Aderyn's father's, but as yet my skill ranking is only at one, so I hope that will change."

"That's a wonderful advantage," Owen said. "Maybe you should lead the way tomorrow, if that will build up your skill ranks."

"I've been experimenting already, and I can see a few ways to increase my ranks. But walking in the front for a while shouldn't hurt." Isold blinked and smiled at his companions. "Just think what we'll be capable of in two or three or ten levels!"

"I'm glad now that I don't know what skills I'll gain, because I'd be horribly impatient for each level to get here," Aderyn said.

"Yes, and you wouldn't enjoy the new level because you'd already be looking forward to the next one," Owen pointed out.

"I'll settle for being impatient for a fight," Aderyn replied.

They continued traveling through the plains all the next day and most of the third. Aderyn didn't get her wish. If there were monsters, they were smart enough to recognize the companions as too great a threat and stayed away. With the vast grassy expanse providing no cover, it would have taken a truly stupid monster to attack them, given how the team would see the monster coming from a mile away.

But in the afternoon of the third day, they reached the low hills where the forests began. Evergreens grew close together, overshadowing the road, which had narrowed gradually until the companions had to walk single file beneath the trees. The air smelled of pine, fresh and biting, and under the branches, no sunlight fell, so the air was cool as well as beautifully scented.

Aderyn didn't let the beauty of the place lower her guard. She stayed alert even though she generally walked near the middle of the group. Even so, the forest seemed empty of anything bigger than the squirrels that scampered across the path and up the tree trunks. Birds sang in the trees now and then, though they never came down where Aderyn could see them. This was just the time for an ambush.

Behind her, Owen slowed his steps. "Something's watching us. To the left," he whispered.

Weston, in the lead, nodded. Then he stopped. "Trap," he said. "Tripwire."

"Don't stop, they'll know—" Owen began.

A high-pitched warbling cry filled the air, echoing off the trees so it seemed to come from everywhere at once. Small shapes flung themselves at the companions from above. Aderyn caught a glimpse of fat, furry bodies with batlike wings before one of them hit her shoulder and clung, digging in sharp, tiny claws. She screamed and flung herself at the nearest tree, hoping to crush the creature. It scrambled from her shoulder to her back in time to avoid the worst of the blow.

Someone grabbed the creature and tore it from her body. Owen flung it away to impact against a tree trunk. "Get it off me!" he shouted. Aderyn realized one of the monsters had grabbed him around the shoulder and throat. She screamed again, this time in fury, and ripped it free. Owen let out a pained gasp as the thing's claws tore three fine scratches across his neck. Then he drew his sword. "We have to stop them digging in!"

Aderyn drew her sword as well and followed Owen. The little monsters were everywhere, bouncing from ground to tree to other tree like rodents the size of a small dog, spreading their membranous wings to glide between the bigger gaps. Owen aimed a blow at one of the creatures. It darted back—straight into Aderyn's blade. The monster let out a terrible shrill howl and sagged in death.

Congratulations! You have defeated [Bat-Kin]
You have earned [50 XP].

"What's a bat-kin?" Aderyn screamed as another one flew at her face.

Isold tore one of the vicious little creatures away from his chest and flung it toward Weston, who struck at the dazed monster and clipped its shoulder. "Carnivorous mammals related to both the bat and the monkey!" he shouted, backing away to give Livia a clear shot. "They glide rather than fly, they have claws and fangs, and they are known for attacking creatures much larger than they are."

Aderyn was too busy fighting to Assess the bat-kin, but it seemed **[Outflank]** worked. As long as she and Owen were on opposite sides of an enemy, the monster spun distractedly, exposing its back to one of them while trying to face the other. The monster defeat notices were coming so fast Aderyn barely saw them. She thrust, slashed, and ducked under another monster that flew screaming at her head. The screaming cut off abruptly as a shimmering bubble sprang up around the bat-kin, carrying it to the ground where it thrashed briefly for air and then lay still.

"There's not much I can do against flying creatures!" Livia called out. "Suffocation takes too long, and they move faster than my *mudball*."

"It's fine, they're leaving," Owen said. He lowered his sword and, breathing heavily, examined the many small corpses littering the ground. "That was crazy. Why would they attack us? Did we enter their territory or something?"

"I think we did," Isold said. He paced the edge of the path, scanning the tops of the trees. After a moment, he pointed. "Up there. That's a bat-kin nest. And—listen."

The five fell silent. At first, Aderyn only heard the sound of her breathing, gradually slowing to normal. Then Weston said, "Oh, listen to the cheeping. I think we killed their parents."

CHAPTER TWENTY-EIGHT

Straining, Aderyn could barely make out a high-pitched chirp like the sound of a distant baby bird. Then there were more of them. In the next moment, it was all she could hear—the faint *twit twit twit* of a baby creature crying out for its mother. "Oh, no," she said, feeling awful. She met Livia's eyes. The Earthbreaker was as devastated as she.

"Don't be soft," Owen warned. "Those were monsters. The babies will grow up to be... to be something horrible and deadly. And *they* attacked *us,* remember? I nearly got my throat slit!" He gingerly touched the scratches on his neck.

"We came into their territory and they defended their nests from us," Livia said. "Adventurers are supposed to make the world safer for everyone, not slaughter things indiscriminately."

"We didn't—" Owen threw his arms in the air. "If we're going to have second thoughts about all our battles, we're never going to make it to Guerdon Deep."

"There's no reason to burden ourselves with guilt," Isold said. "It's true, bat-kin attack without regard for sense or safety, and we did enter their territory and as far as they knew threatened their children. But we didn't know that's what we'd done, and I don't think any of us believe we should let ourselves be slaughtered rather than defend ourselves. And many of the bat-kin fled, so the little ones are not orphans."

"That makes me feel better," Aderyn said.

Owen scowled. "We need to find something definitely evil to kill. An owlbear. Do you have owlbears in this world?"

"I've never heard of that. Is it deadly?"

"Depends on which edition you play. How about goblins? Orcs?"

"Goblins and orcs, yes," Isold said, "but they roam farther north than we're going. We do have patchwork monsters, creatures bred from mingling monster types, though owlbear is not one of them. The cat-hawk, and werewolves, and I believe there's something called a tree weasel that's a cross between a caterpillar and a, well, a weasel. Those are more pitiful than terrifying."

"Cat-hawk? I'd like to see that."

"It might be the last thing you ever see," Weston said. "Those things are vicious. If you're picturing a cute little housecat with wings, forget about it. They're the size of a bear and their claws are about six inches long and razor-sharp all along the inner edge. My mother has a scar across one shoulder from a cat-hawk attack. Looks like someone carved her like a roast fowl."

"I bet they're worth a ton of experience, though," Owen persisted.

"Since when are you so bloodthirsty?" Weston asked.

"Since I found out half my team has qualms about killing monsters that aren't slavering, vicious brutes," Owen replied, with a smile to show he wasn't serious. "And I want us to gain at least two levels before reaching Guerdon Deep—or is that unlikely?"

"Advancement through level five is fast so youngling adventurers gain some skills to prevent them dying instantly at a real challenge," Isold said. "We might see that slow down after level five."

"'Might'?" Aderyn said.

"Traveling with a Fated One probably affects that. The system displays its interest in those... we can call them candidates, I suppose... by throwing greater challenges at them, or at least that's what my **[Knowledge: World Lore]** skill tells me now." Isold looked very serious. "I expect we'll fight a lot of battles in the next few days. And we might even pick up a quest."

"Out here? From who?" Weston said. "I doubt those bat-kin want us to collect food for their kits, or whatever their babies are called."

"We've already seen how many secret quests we unlocked," Isold said. "That's not normal. My theory is that the system puts those in our way, too, as part of the challenge."

"But Owen doesn't want to be the Fated One," Aderyn said. "Shouldn't we avoid those quests? I mean, if they're going to push him further down that path, we don't want them."

"They're still worth experience, Aderyn, and I don't want to analyze every opportunity we get, figuring out which is the right kind," Owen said. "We'll find someone to send me home before it becomes an issue."

Again the pang of sorrow Aderyn always felt when she thought of Owen going home struck her. "That's right, we will," she said, suppressing her hope that finding that person would take a much longer time than Owen expected.

They walked more cautiously now, scanning the treetops as well as the forest floor for signs of monstrous threats. No more bat-kin nests were visible, but since the trees grew increasingly close together, Aderyn feared they might only be obscured. Now that the threat was over, she felt stupid about her sentimental reaction. Isold was right; they shouldn't let themselves be attacked and injured or even killed just because the monsters attacking them had cute little families. She needed to take adventuring seriously, or she'd be no better than those gamers Owen had suggested would love being in her world.

The thought of Owen's world got her thinking again about him returning home. Contemplating it didn't make her feel any less unhappy even though she'd had time to get used to the idea. She liked him, she liked being around him, she liked fighting by his side, and if he left—she couldn't bring herself to consider it. She'd be alone and useless. Which was ridiculous. She had a sword, and she had other companions...though would they remain a team once the **[Return the Outlander]** quest was over?

Her thoughts circled around in this way, over and over, until she was in a truly foul mood. When Owen shouted, "We're under attack!" and an enormous gray pig-shaped horror ran right at them, Aderyn welcomed the distraction.

She took up a fighting stance opposite Owen and Assessed the oncoming monster.

Name: Blight Boar
Type: Magical Beast
Power Level: 5
This creature attacks with its tusks to knock an enemy down and then tears at the enemy's exposed vitals with its sharp hooves.

Aderyn was too focused on searching for a weak spot to be excited about this new development with **[Improved Assess 1]**. Blue lines of light swept over the blight boar and converged on a spot just below its breastbone and another, smaller one at the base of its throat. Its head and chest glowed red. "The belly, or the throat," Aderyn shouted. "Avoid the head and chest!"

The ground rumbled. A wave of earth rippled past, shaking Aderyn so she had to fling out her arms to stay upright. The wave shot toward the blight boar, striking it with its full force. The creature let out a guttural squeal and staggered, then fell, kicking all its legs in a futile attempt to right itself.

"Now!" Owen shouted, and he and Weston sprang toward the fallen monster, with Aderyn right behind. She sidestepped the slashing tusks and thrust for the center of the blue spot on its throat as Owen and Weston stabbed its belly. The blight boar squealed again and thrashed more wildly as hot purple-red blood gushed from its wounds. Owen signaled to the others to stand back. They watched it warily, in case it might somehow stand up, but its thrashing just grew weaker until it lay still.

**Congratulations! You have defeated [Blight Boar].
You have earned [500 XP].**

Aderyn breathed deeply to slow her racing heart. "That was easy," she said, "though maybe I shouldn't say that because it will jinx us."

"It was only easy because of the Warmaster advantage," Owen said. "And—what was that spell, Livia?"

"*Thunderstomp*," Livia said. "I need more practice with it. I saw it affect all of you, too. There's no point in a spell like that if it takes out my teammates."

"It was effective," Weston said.

"What are you doing, Isold?" Aderyn asked.

Isold knelt beside the steaming corpse with a short knife in one hand. "Blight boars have useful components," he said. He inserted the knife right between the blight boar's eyes and twisted. A purple-red lump popped free and bounced a short distance away. Isold picked it up and held it up to what little light made it through the trees. "Livia, if you wouldn't mind washing this?"

Livia summoned a mass of water that sluiced away the gore from the lump as well as from Isold's hands. Once clean, the lump looked like pale green glass, irregularly faceted and with a rough surface that didn't catch or reflect light. Livia gasped. "It's magic! Why didn't I notice that before?"

"The blight boar's physical body, including its fluids, conceals any magical aura." Isold put the glass away in his belt pouch. "This will be worth a lot to the right Spellcrafter."

"Nice," Owen said. "Have you always been able to harvest components?"

"Since level two. We just haven't encountered anything worth harvesting before." Isold stood. "I suggest we move on. Blight boars are good eating for most of what lives in these woods, and I don't know if we want to encounter those creatures."

They walked until the light faded, then left the road in search of a clearing to set up camp. They found one only a short distance to the east, a place where a fallen tree had prevented other trees from taking root. By this time, the companions had fallen into a pattern when it came to camping for the night. Livia built the fire. Isold gathered wood. Aderyn set up the spit—she was glad they'd chosen to buy one back in Asylum. Owen and Weston searched nearby for signs of animal or monster life. Then they all laid out their bedrolls while Livia summoned water into the pot to boil. Isold knew how to turn their rations into a delicious, hot soup, so welcome at the end of a long day of walking even when the weather was warm.

Aderyn sat on her bedroll and stared into the fire. She was tired, but it was the good kind of tired that happened after exertion. "Too bad that was a blight boar and not an ordinary pig," she mused. "There's good eating on a wild pig."

"I'd rather have experience," Owen said from his bedroll nearby.

"I'm greedy enough to wish for both," Weston said. "Seriously, though, everything tastes better when it's eaten outdoors after a day of healthy exercise."

"There you go with the exercise again," Livia said. "The way you talk, you'd think exercise was a high-level quest with a thousand gold for a reward."

"The reward is far better than that," Weston said in an affectedly prissy voice. "A sound mind in a strong body is the ultimate goal of every adventurer."

"I see no evidence that your mind is sound," Livia retorted. "Me, I'm in favor of a long soak in a large tub with a glass of wine at the end of the day."

"Oh, don't talk about that when there's no chance of it happening," Aderyn pleaded. She'd never had a large tub to soak in, just her family's round washtub that was barely big enough for her to sit in with her knees drawn up to her chest, but that was enough for her to imagine Livia's fantasy.

"Stop squabbling or I'll ask Isold to use **[Charm]** on you," Owen said without much force.

"You wouldn't do that, Isold?" Aderyn remembered thinking about Isold turning his power on them, and all her good cheer evaporated.

Isold looked up from where he was stirring the soup. "If it meant a peaceful night, maybe," he said with a smile.

"He wouldn't," Owen said. "I was just joking. It's not as if Weston and Livia's squabbling means anything."

"All joking aside, I won't use my skills on my friends. That would be a terrible betrayal." Isold was looking directly at Aderyn, an intent expression that made her suspect her fears were visible.

"Of course not," Owen said. "Is that soup ready?"

They ate soup and hard, dry rolls in peaceful silence, then banked the fire and settled in for the night. Aderyn lay on her bedroll and watched Isold, who had first watch, pass between her and the glowing embers. He wouldn't turn his skills on them, she was sure, at least not if he had a choice—but suppose something controlled him, and forced him to fight his companions? Aderyn wasn't sure why that was so much more horrifying than the idea of fighting Owen or Livia, since all of them had skills she'd have trouble defending against. It just was.

CHAPTER TWENTY-NINE

She drifted off finally and slept without dreaming until Owen shook her awake for her turn at watch. She put her boots back on and circled the camp, listening and gazing into the darkness. A lantern would make watching easier, but it would also draw the attention of nocturnal monsters, and with the moon just a day from full, the darkness wasn't as complete as it could be. She didn't hear or see anything out of the ordinary, though, just the high-pitched singing of insects and the occasional call of a hunting owl. The moon turned the tops of the trees blue-silver and cast patches of pale light on the ground where the light peeked through gaps in the branches.

Distantly, the undergrowth rustled. Aderyn put a hand on her sword hilt and stared into the darkness. The rustling came again. It sounded like someone pushing through the leafy plants and bushes that grew around the tree trunks. Aderyn silently walked to the side of their camp nearest the noise. Deeper darkness shrouded that side so all she could see were moving shadows. Shrubs, tall leafy plants— and something bigger. Something that walked on two legs.

Out of the darkness came the word, "Help."

Aderyn drew her sword. "Show yourself."

The figure drew nearer. It wasn't as big as Aderyn had first guessed, more the size of a human child than an adult. It had blond hair that gleamed in the moonlight and a pale face still too distant for Aderyn to make out an expression. "Help, please," the child said.

Aderyn stepped back. "Where did you come from?"

"From road. Bandits. Help." The child reached out its arms to Aderyn. Aderyn backed away further. Mysterious children appearing out of the dark couldn't be good. Instinctively, she Assessed it.

There was nothing there.

Aderyn drew in a breath and shouted, "Everyone up! We're under attack!"

A *thing* dropped out of the trees in front of her, indistinct in the low light. Aderyn saw giant eyes and rubbery, bloated skin and tentacles at least eight feet long before she tripped over someone's leg and fell sprawling beside the fire. The thing lunged for her, and she screamed and brought her sword up to block the attack.

Another sword appeared, swiping at the creature and forcing it back. Owen grabbed Aderyn's hand and hauled her to her feet. "What the hell is that?" he shouted.

This time, Assess was swift to respond.

Name: Cave Bladder

Type: Abomination

Power Level: 6

The cave bladder lives underground in caverns with many stalactites. When it comes aboveground it seeks out forests. It moves swiftly between stalactites or branches with its tentacles, but is awkward and slow on the ground. Its tentacles can only attack one enemy at a time.

Aderyn realized the cave bladder wasn't alone. At least three others attacked from the trees, clinging to the branches with some tentacles and lashing out at the companions with others. She let Owen step in front of her to give **[Discern Weakness]** time to work.

The blue lights gave the dull green skin of the cave bladders a sickly look as they converged—

"Go for the eyes!" she screamed. "And try to get them on the ground!"

Owen was already putting her advice into effect. The thick skin resisted the edge or point of his sword, but the cave bladder reacted abruptly every time his weapon came close to its enormous eyes. Tentacles lashed out, forcing Owen back until one grabbed his shoulder and dragged him toward its sharply pointed beak.

Aderyn struck at the tentacle holding Owen repeatedly. Nothing she did seemed to make a difference. Hitting the rubbery, rough skin felt like trying to cut an old tree stump in half. A second tentacle tried to pin Owen's sword arm to his side. Owen wrestled free and held his sword high, not striking. "What are you doing?" Aderyn screamed.

"Waiting for my moment," Owen shouted.

Aderyn circled, beating at the cave bladder with no effect as it dragged Owen closer. Then, in a flash, Owen thrust at one of the enormous eyes that looked far too human for Aderyn's comfort. Blood and sticky fluids gushed, and the cave bladder shuddered and relaxed its hold.

Congratulations! You have defeated [Cave Bladder].
You have earned [1000 XP].

Aderyn helped Owen wrench free and then cast about for her friends. Isold was struggling in the grip of several tentacles, but before Aderyn could react, Livia chanted something and Isold shot free as if greased. Weston was standing over a fallen cave bladder, unaware that another was clambering down the branches of a tree and would fall on his head in another second.

"Come on!" Owen shouted, and he and Aderyn raced toward Weston, screaming his name. Weston raised his head, then looked up and shouted in surprise. He flung himself to the side just as the cave bladder dropped. "We have to get it before it climbs away," Owen said to Aderyn. "Get behind it!"

Aderyn ran wide to the cave bladder's far side, stabbing at it randomly. She couldn't do any damage, but her blows annoyed the cave bladder, and it struggled to turn and face her. Its hard, sharp beak gnashed wildly, and Aderyn screamed and slashed its face, tearing across both its eyes. The cave bladder let out a shrill screech that froze Aderyn's blood, and Aderyn screamed again and thrust at its eye. She missed, striking the inside rim of its eye socket, but the glancing blow skidded off the tough, squishy hide and slid deep into the eyeball.

Congratulations! You have defeated [Cave Bladder].
You have earned [1000 XP].

Stunned, Aderyn at first just stood there staring at the dead monster. Then she heard more of the screeching cries and turned to see a terrible tentacled monster swinging through the trees, silhouetted against the full moon. A hail of stones struck it, making it lose its grip and fall to the ground near Isold. Terrifyingly aware that Isold had no weapon, Aderyn raced toward the two.

But the cave bladder didn't attack. It sprawled on the ground, swaying gently, as Isold sang. Aderyn heard the melody, which was nothing she recognized, before she came within earshot of the words.

"...lie still, we're all friends here, you don't want to attack," Isold was singing. In a more normal tone, he said, "Kill it quickly, Aderyn, and don't miss your blow because if you hit it without killing it, it will break the [Charm]." Before the cave bladder could do more than twitch its tentacles, Isold resumed singing: "You're not in danger, we're friends, stay calm..."

Aderyn shuffled to one side. The cave bladder's eyes were open—she didn't think they had lids to close—and the eerie pupils were shrunk to pinpoints. She used one as a guide and slowly brought her blade into position.

Before she could strike, Isold suddenly exclaimed, "It's breaking free!"

Aderyn nearly dropped her sword in her surprise, but she struck hard and fast, hitting the rapidly enlarging pupil at its center and thrusting the blade halfway to the hilt. The cave bladder spasmed, hitting Isold and Aderyn with its powerful tentacles and knocking them down but not grabbing them. Aderyn scrabbled away backwards out of range, but the thing was already dead.

**Congratulations! You have defeated [Cave Bladder].
You have earned [1000 XP].**

"That was close," Isold said as they both got to their feet.

Aderyn realized she no longer heard the screeching of cave bladders. "I think it's over," she said. She held her sword at the ready anyway.

They had strayed far from the site of the attack, and as they ran back through the forest Aderyn searched the trees for more of the hideous creatures. The memory of the one hanging silhouetted against the sky still terrified her.

When they reached the clearing, the sight of the other three companions relieved Aderyn's mind. Then she got closer, and that relief vanished. Owen's shoulder was bloody, and he held his left arm stiffly. Weston sat on the ground with his right leg extended in front of him like it hurt. "Is everyone all right?" Aderyn asked, though it was obvious they weren't.

"Twisted my ankle when I dove away from that thing," Weston said with a grimace. "I'll be fine. I don't think it's serious."

"Owen, what did it do to you?" Aderyn exclaimed.

"Those tentacles have barbs," Owen said, carefully removing his shirt and wincing when he rotated his shoulder. "I think we should make sure none of them broke off in the wounds."

Aderyn moved to his side and peered at the bloody mess, nearly black in the moonlight. "Livia, could I get a light?"

Livia joined her, holding her light orb high and out of the way. Owen's skin was pale gold in the dim, warm light, and his muscles shifted and tensed as he tried not to move his shoulder again. Aderyn gingerly prodded his shoulder and pulled back when he gasped in pain. "Sorry."

"It just surprised me, that's all," Owen said.

"There's nothing embedded here. It just looks like a lot of deep holes, and some of them are still bleeding." Aderyn stepped back to give Isold room to wield the healing wand. Green light dribbled from the wand's tip to cling to the many small wounds. When it vanished, Owen's shoulder didn't look any different for still being covered with blood, but he moved more easily. Livia dropped a mass of water on his shoulder, making him shout.

"Sorry, I forgot how cold that is," Livia exclaimed.

"It's fine," Owen said, scrubbing at the wound with his ruined shirt. "Though now I have no shirt."

"Oh, I can fix that," Livia said, taking the wad of cloth from him. She shook the shirt out, held it by the shoulders, and muttered a few syllables. In a flash of purple light, the tattered shirt was whole. A few faint stains were all that remained of the cave bladder's attack.

"Wow," Owen said. He put his shirt on and stretched his arm, examining the place where the shirt had been torn. "I didn't know you could do that."

"It only works on non-magical things that aren't missing a lot of their parts," Livia said. "But otherwise it's really useful."

Weston stood a few feet away, prodding one of the cave bladders with his toe. "These are disgusting. Why are they called cave bladders if they attacked us in the forest?"

"They live in caves, but venture aboveground for prey," Isold said. "They like human flesh—"

"Oh, gross," Livia said.

"And you already saw how comfortable they are in trees," Isold continued. "Their magic allows them to create minor illusions to lure their prey into a vulnerable position."

"I saw that," Aderyn said. "It didn't fool me. I had trouble believing a child would be alone in the woods, especially since we'd have heard the bandit attack she claimed had happened."

"They're not very clever, for all they have those huge brains," Isold said.

"We need to move camp," Owen said. "Isold, do these things have anything worth salvaging?"

"Nothing we want to carry," Isold said.

"Then let's pack up and get out of here." Owen gathered his bedroll. "I'm not sure some of them didn't escape. I don't want to stay where they might come back with friends."

CHAPTER THIRTY

They walked for about twenty minutes, putting plenty of distance between themselves and the gory battlefield. Finally, Owen said, "That looks good," and led them off the road to a clearing smaller than the one they'd used before, but still big enough to fit them comfortably. Aderyn settled herself near Owen and lay back, staring up at the sky. The moon now hid behind the branches, but there was still enough light for her to see the trees as more than black outlines.

On a whim, she opened the Codex and whispered, "Advancement."

Name: Aderyn

Class: Warmaster

Level: 5

<u>Skills</u>: **Bluff (3), Climb (1), Conversation (3), Intimidate (3), Sense Truth (5), Survival (1), Swim (1), Knowledge: Monsters (3)**

<u>Class Skills:</u> **Improved Assess 1 (7), Awareness (4), Knowledge: Geography (2), Spot (5), Discern Weakness (5), Dodge (4), Improvised Distraction (3), Outflank (2), Draw Fire (0)**

She sighed. She had hoped to see a weapons skill, given that she'd killed two of the cave bladders herself. But her parents had always said how much work it took to convince the system you deserved a particular skill, so she decided to be patient.

Owen rolled onto his side. "Aderyn, are you awake?"

Aderyn rolled to face him. "I'm still too tense from the fight to relax enough to sleep. You're sure you're all right?"

"Yeah. Just tense, like you said." He paused, then added, "That was terrifying. I don't think we've ever faced a more difficult challenge."

"I'd never even heard of cave bladders. They reminded me of octopuses, only in the air instead of the ocean."

Owen snorted. "Cave bladders. More like cave haggis."

"What's a haggis?"

"It's a sort of food made from sheep hearts and stuff. I had a girl-friend who was from Scotland and she convinced me to try it. It looked exactly like those cave bladders, except brown instead of green."

Aderyn wasn't sure why he had to specify that his friend was female, but she let it go. "Is Scotland a city in your world?"

"A country, actually. That's like a group of cities that are all ruled by the same government. It doesn't sound like you have those here."

"Not really. There are agreements between the sanctuary cities that they all follow the same laws, so if someone commits a crime in Asylum and flees to Market Warding, they can still be punished. But each city rules itself."

Owen nodded. "We used to have city-states like that in places in my world, but that was a long time ago."

The quiet darkness, and their conversation, calmed Aderyn more than simply staring at the stars would have. She was suddenly seized with a desire to know more about Owen's life. "What did you do before you were brought here?"

"What did I do? Nothing. I'd just graduated from college and I was taking some time off to see the country before I had to get a job." She could barely see him smile in the dimness. "College is a school where you study a specific thing in order to make it a career—a permanent job. Graduate means I finished those studies and can move on with my life. Did you have a job in Far Haven?"

Aderyn shook her head. "I helped around the house and I did odd jobs for my parents and our neighbors. Mostly I waited to get the Call. I didn't want to get tied down to work if I was going to go adventuring." She chuckled. "It sounds very dull now I come to say it."

"It makes sense, though. Look at how Isold got caught up in the apothecary business and then had all that jerked out from under him. Maybe it's better not to fall into thinking you know how your life is going to go. Though I guess—can you reject the Call?"

"You can, though I could never understand why anyone would. But there are plenty of people who prefer a quiet, orderly life. Like Ellias the farmer, or Mariet, the woman who made your clothes. There's nothing wrong with that, and my parents always say it takes all kinds to make the world spin round. But it's not what I wanted for myself."

"So if you knew you wanted to be an apothecary, you could apprentice yourself and then reject the Call." Owen propped himself on his elbow. "I wonder if Isold would have rejected it if he hadn't been so sure of what the system would make him."

"I'm glad he didn't. I like him."

"Yeah," Owen said. His voice had become distant, almost sleepy. "Yeah, he's all right." He lay back and added, "Good night, Aderyn."

"Good night," Aderyn said. She watched Livia pace the clearing, alert to any monster attacks, until she fell asleep.

AS IF THE SYSTEM KNEW THE TEAM HAD STRETCHED ITSELF to the limit, the following day was uneventful. Aderyn saw squirrels and chipmunks bound across the road in front of them, and around noon a fox darted from bush to bush off to one side and then disappeared. "There can't be any monsters around," she said, "or the animals would vanish."

"It's too bad. I feel like we're close to level six after that cave bladder fight," Owen said.

"Why does it matter, if you're going back to your world when we reach Guerdon Deep?" Livia asked.

"I—" Owen fell silent for a few seconds. "I don't know. I guess in part it's because I want to help you all level as much as I can, since you won't be finished adventuring when I'm gone. And in part it's the challenge—to see what I can accomplish in these few days. It's probably stupid."

"It's not stupid to want to achieve a high level," Aderyn said. "And we don't know for sure that we can find the right spellslinger in Guerdon Deep. Suppose we have to travel farther? We should be prepared for that." She didn't say that that was her wish. It was a selfish desire.

"You're right," Weston said. "I'd been thinking this quest was as simple as reaching the city, but the truth is it could take more than that."

"I hate that idea, but you're right," Owen said. He'd broken off a branch that hung low over the path, a length of wood taller than he was, and now dug it into the packed earth of the road with some ferocity. "Damn it, why can't things be simple?"

"You don't know they won't be, either," Livia said. "We just have to reach the city and figure things out from there. There's no sense planning too far ahead."

"Spoken like a true pragmatist," Weston said.

"Pragmatism gets you farther than pie-in-the-sky dreaming," Livia said, but not irritably.

"I can accept that life requires both approaches at different times," Weston replied.

"The world must be ending if the two of you agree on something," Isold joked.

They walked all day, camped without incident, and continued on the next morning. By midmorning, they reached the edge of the forest where it met the foothills of the distant mountains. Aderyn and Isold consulted the map and compared it to Isold's knowledge. "According to this, Guerdon Deep is backed into the slopes of that mountain range," Aderyn said, pointing to where the mountains rose, tiny and perfect, into the sky. They'd be enormous when the team drew nearer. "The far eastern end, where the valleys begin."

"Hence the 'deep' part of the name," Isold said. "We could reach Guerdon Deep by evening if we hurry. It's not that far, but the hills increase the distance we have to walk."

"Let's move, then," Owen said. "I'd love not to have to sleep on the ground again."

They hurried, jogging along at the fastest pace they could maintain without exhausting themselves. The hills grew steeper, though never steep enough to require climbing, and every time they crested another ridge, the mountains were larger. Aderyn surveyed the land in the distance and saw that eventually the hills smoothed into a vast plain, or a shallow bowl—something that looked like it funneled toward the mountains. After the third time she looked out from the top of a ridge, she realized she was looking at a city.

It was hard to tell its size, because it matched the mountains in color and angularity. It rose upward, clinging to the stone like a limpet, though every time Aderyn thought she'd identified a place where city and mountain met, her perspective changed and she realized she was wrong. The only thing she was sure of was that the plains sloped down to meet the base of the mountain, and the city was part of that base.

"We're almost there," Owen said, pointing. "Two more hills and then it's all downhill on that slope."

"Look at those birds," Weston said. "They're circling. Must see prey or something."

"It's nothing to do with us," Owen said. "Hurry now. Suppose Guerdon Deep shuts its gates after sunset? I do *not* want to camp just outside those walls."

They ran down the slopes now, slowing again to ascend and then running once more. Aderyn felt they were racing the sun. Owen's words about the gates being shut had taken hold of her imagination. It wasn't as if they couldn't camp easily, and there was no reason to think they'd lose their chance at returning Owen to his world if they entered the city tomorrow rather than tonight, but they were so close it felt wrong to have to sleep outdoors one more night.

She noticed the birds, still circling. They flew high in the sky, higher than made sense for carrion eaters who'd found a likely carcass. Unease crept over her, and she Assessed them as she ran.

Name: Cat-hawk

Type: Magical beast

Power Level: 8

Cat-hawks live in high places such as mountains and cliff-sides. They are top predators who make a game out of hunting prey. They prefer to chase a running target and will sometimes ignore a creature who remains still. Their vision is more acute at night, but their senses of smell and hearing are excellent at all times. Once a cat-hawk has identified its prey, it fights to the death.

Before she'd half finished reading, she tripped and rolled a short distance, where she lay panting. Owen returned to her side and helped her sit. "Are you all right?"

"We have a problem," Aderyn said. "Those are cat-hawks. And I think we're the prey."

The others returned to her side. "Cat-hawks?" Isold said, staring up at them.

"If we hold still, they won't come after us. Maybe," Aderyn said.

"We can't sit here motionless forever," Owen said. "We're close to the city. I say we make a run for it. The guards can help fight them off if they attack, right?"

Weston was staring in the direction of the city gate. "We're too far away. Those cat-hawks dive fast. It's part of their tactics, ram their prey to catch them off balance."

"That's right," Isold said. "But we're helpless in the open. And if they're circling like that, it means they've noticed us. We have to run, and hope we get close enough to Guerdon Deep before they attack that the city will send help."

"You don't sound certain," Livia said.

"Really? I hoped I projected an air of confidence to cover the fact that I'm pretty sure Guerdon Deep doesn't care about the fate of adventurers who can't defend themselves." Isold's smile was strained.

"Then we have to run even faster," Owen said. "Let's go!"

They took off running, Aderyn and Livia with their shorter legs pumping hard to keep up with the men. It didn't take long for it to be obvious that Livia was going to lag behind. With an oath, Weston swerved and picked Livia up, throwing her over his shoulder. Aderyn glanced up. The cat-hawks continued to circle. She went back to fixing her gaze on the distant city gate. Maybe this was all for nothing, and the cat-hawks weren't interested in them, after all.

Then Livia screamed, "They're diving! Put me down!"

Weston heaved Livia to the ground and steadied her with his hands on her shoulders. Aderyn swiveled and looked up. Sure enough, the cat-hawks, all five of them, were plummeting out of the sky in a terrible eerie silence.

Livia shouted a string of nonsense words, and a hail of stones blasted upward and outward, striking the lead cat-hawk in the chest and face. It checked in its dive, snarling, but when it resumed its attack, it wasn't moving as swiftly.

Aderyn drew her sword and brought up [Improved Assess 1]. The blue lines of [Discern Weakness] curved and slid rapidly across the lithe feline bodies and the banded hawk wings as if the system knew how fast she needed information.

"Their bellies are vulnerable," she shouted, "but don't let them get their claws into you, or they'll rake you with their back claws. If you can foul their wings, get them on the ground, and that will stop their primary attack."

"Damn it, why can't we fight something that *isn't* flying?" Livia exclaimed. An enormous ball of mud zoomed past, striking one of the cat-hawks and binding its wings so it fell the last fifteen feet and landed with a thump. Weston yelled a challenge and dove for the monster. That was all Aderyn had time to see before the next cat-hawk was upon her. She slashed at its stomach, but it darted back before swatting at her with a paw the size of a dinner plate edged with razors. She jumped out of the way, and Owen struck from the rear. The cat-hawk shrieked in pain as his sword cut deep into its rear flank. It turned to face this new threat, and Aderyn aimed another blow at that wound.

With [Outflank], she and Owen battered at the cat-hawk, but neither of them managed to land a killing blow. Aderyn was aware of more *mudballs* flying through the air, but Livia's stream of obscenities told her they weren't connecting.

Then a message flashed in her vision, distracting her.

**Congratulations! You have defeated [Cat-Hawk].
You have earned [3000 XP].**

"Weston?" Aderyn shouted.

"One down!" Weston replied.

Aderyn shrieked and brought her blade up to deflect a blow from a razor-tipped paw. It batted her weapon aside, and fire lanced through her chest as claws ripped into her shoulder and across her breastbone. Aderyn staggered back. The cat-hawk filled her vision, bearing down on her. Then it was falling, and another monster defeat message appeared. The letters were unexpectedly blurry around the edges, and she smelled blood.

A lot of blood.

All of it hers.

CHAPTER THIRTY-ONE

Owen was kneeling beside her—when had she fallen?—and had his arm around her shoulders, supporting her. "Aderyn, hold on," he said in a voice she could barely hear. "Isold, get over here now!"

Then he dropped her, and she cried out weakly because the movement hurt, but lying down was comfortable. She was sure she could fight lying down. Owen was back—no, it was Isold, gripping her hand and wielding a stick with his other hand. Green liquid light bubbled from the tip of the stick, foaming over and dribbling onto her chest. The light made the smell of blood vanish, though it didn't feel like anything, not even water. It filled the deep wounds on her chest—

Wounds. Yes. It was coming back to her now, the cat-hawk slashing her shoulder and chest. She'd been dying. She sat up, or tried to, but Isold gently pressed her down. "Not quite done," he said.

Aderyn nodded. Then she focused on the monster flying directly at them. "Isold, watch out!"

Isold had barely begun to turn when the cat-hawk grabbed the back of his shirt with its terrible fanged mouth and lifted him into the sky.

Aderyn leaped to her feet and pointed. "Somebody help!" She had no ranged weapons, nothing to keep Isold from being carried off.

Suddenly, the cat-hawk's wings glistened with an oily rainbow sheen. It flapped harder, but the thick layer of *grease* that now coated the wings made each movement a struggle. In the next moment, it was falling. Aderyn's relief vanished when she realized Isold would be beneath the monster when it hit the ground. She ran forward, though again she didn't know what she could do, and was there when the cat-hawk and Isold landed.

The cat-hawk was stunned from the fall, and Aderyn took advantage of its disorientation to slit its throat.

Congratulations! You have defeated [Cat-Hawk].
You have earned [3000 XP].

Welcome to Level Six

She shoved the bulk of the cat-hawk's corpse away and gradually revealed Isold, who lay unconscious beneath it. Swiftly Aderyn looked around for help. As she did, the monster defeat message flashed again, and past it she saw Weston and Owen circling a dead cat-hawk. The final cat-hawk staggered toward them, one wing hanging limply as if broken. It was the cat-hawk Livia had hit with her *elemental blast* of stones.

Aderyn almost raced to join them. Then she realized there was nothing she could do to help the other three. Isold, on the other hand, needed help immediately. She dragged him free of the corpse and searched all up and down his inert form for the healing wand. She didn't know how to use it, but she'd seen Isold activate it before, and how hard could it be?

Her hand fell on something narrow sticking out from beneath Isold. She pulled it out, and felt sick. The wand was snapped off about two-thirds of the way down its length. Pale green light trickled from the broken end. Next to it, the half of the <**Skeleton Ladder**> jabbed into Isold's side, drawing blood.

Someone crouched beside her. "What do we do?" Livia asked. Shifting plates of metal circled her, forming a constantly moving shield.

"I don't know. Isold, can you hear me?"

Isold's eyes fluttered open. "No use... the wand won't... internal injuries," he murmured. "Did we win?"

At that moment, Aderyn saw the monster defeat message. She counted. Five. "They're dead, and we reached level six," she said. "It's going to be all right. We just have to get you to the city—there are Bonemenders there—"

Isold coughed, and Aderyn flinched as spots of blood flecked her face. "Better hurry," he said, and closed his eyes. Aderyn nearly screamed his name before she realized he was still breathing steadily.

"Where's the healing wand?" Owen said, dropping to his knees beside them.

"It's broken. We have to get him to a Bonemender," Aderyn said. She removed the <**Skeleton Ladder**>, reasoning it couldn't hurt to have it no longer injuring him. She didn't want to carry it, and it was too big for her knapsack. On a whim, she inserted it into the <**Purse of Great Capacity**> and was mildly heartened when it fit.

Weston carefully lifted Isold in his massive arms. "It's not good to move someone with internal injuries," he said. "We have to be careful not to hurt him further."

"It's that or let him die out here," Owen said. "Let's go."

They walked, so slowly compared to their earlier mad run, but everyone was conscious of how even Weston's steady gait and strong arms jogged Isold. Aderyn kept having to slow herself, she was so eager to reach the city. They'd come farther than she'd realized before the attack, but it was still a good quarter-mile's distance still to Guerdon Deep.

To distract herself from her worries, she observed the city. **[Improved Assess 1]** told her nothing except *Exceeds authority limit*, which was reassuring because it meant someday she'd be able to Assess a city. Guerdon Deep's walls were at least forty feet high and made of the same stone as the mountain, which explained why the city looked so much like the mountain. It backed into a great crevasse or valley, she wasn't sure which, but in either case the walls of the mountain reared high above the city, protecting it from a rear attack.

The gates were half the height of the walls, blackened oak banded with iron, and Aderyn couldn't imagine the army that could break them down. Watchtowers loomed over each side of the gates, and dimly-visible figures strode back and forth within them, sometimes leaving the towers for the wall-walk, where they were easier to see. Seeing them clearly didn't reassure Aderyn, because they held crossbows, the heavy kind that took a major effort to load and could send a steel bolt through most of that oak gate and through all of a person. Those guards didn't have the look of people who cared that others might need medical help.

Finally, she couldn't take it any longer, and she ran ahead, shouting, "We're adventurers from Asylum, and one of us is hurt. Will you let us in?"

Someone Aderyn couldn't see who stood in the left-hand watchtower said, "You took out five cat-hawks at your level? Impressive." Her voice was unexpectedly high-pitched, though Aderyn didn't know why she thought all guards needed to have deep, commanding voices.

"Thank you. We need a Bonemender—will you help us find one? Maybe just tell us where to go?" It hadn't escaped Aderyn's notice that this admiring guard hadn't given the order to open the gate.

"Five gold each entrance fee," the woman replied.

"*Five gold each?*" That was all of the reward they'd gotten from the magistrate of Asylum.

"You heard me. Five gold." The woman didn't sound as if she cared much whether they entered or not.

"But—we might not have enough for a Bonemender!" Aderyn exclaimed.

"Not my problem. Do you want in or not?"

Aderyn ground her teeth together and ran back to her companions. She'd outpaced them by more than she'd realized. "It's five gold each to enter," she said.

"Well, crap," Owen said. "Do we have that much?"

"We do. I don't know if we'll have enough for a Bonemender afterward."

"It's fine," Owen said. "Everyone give Aderyn your money. We'll figure out the rest later."

Aderyn collected the twenty-five gold and hurried back to the gate. The light was fading as sunset approached, but she could see now the outline of a smaller door set into the right side of the gate. A shutter above a shallow dish-shaped niche slid open at her arrival. "How many?" the same woman asked.

"There are five of us. Here's twenty-five gold," Aderyn said, controlling her desire to spit at the woman. She put the coins in the niche and waited for the woman to scoop them up. The shutter stayed open. "Could you hurry, please? Our companion is badly hurt."

"Five cat-hawks. That's daring," the woman said.

"It was that or die at their claws and fangs," Aderyn said, again controlling her impulses. Shouting at this woman would do no good, even if it made Aderyn feel better.

"Even so." Five gold coins rattled into the niche. "Call it recognition of the underdog's valor."

Aderyn blessed her self-control and picked up the coins. "Thanks."

"Welcome to Guerdon Deep," the woman said, and the great gates swung silently inward.

Within the walls, Guerdon Deep was as gray and forbidding as it had looked from the outside. A broad street lined with tall, narrow stone buildings led away from the gate, as if the city wanted to make sure people entering were absorbed into it as quickly as possible. It was also eerily quiet, with the few people still on the street at this hour making so little noise they might have been illusions. Lanterns burned all along the left-hand side of the street, but a Flamecrafter strode away from them, pausing at each dark lantern on the right-hand side to kindle it into life. The lights burned brightly without illuminating much.

The encounter at the gate had sapped Aderyn's remaining energy, and she stared dully at the passersby, none of whom looked as if they noticed the companions at all. Owen hurried forward to stop someone who was about to enter one of the buildings. "We need a Bonemender. Do you know where we can find one?"

"I've only been here three days. Ask someone else," the man said irritably, and slammed the door behind him.

Owen muttered something under his breath and strode to accost the next nearest person. "We need a—"

"I heard you," the woman said. "Down that way three streets."

Silver flashed in the low light as Owen held up a couple of coins. "Take us there, and I'll give you twice this much again."

The woman eyed him curiously, then snatched the coins out of his hand. "This way."

They walked at a regular pace, with Weston moving more cautiously than the rest. Aderyn's heart was torn between the need to hurry and her awareness that Isold was in really bad shape. He'd stopped moving some time ago, and Aderyn reminded herself that he was just unconscious, because Weston would have said if he were—

she cut off that line of thought. They'd come all this way, and losing any one of them would be terrible.

Their guide took them off the main road into narrow streets barely wide enough for two people to pass one another. By the light of more lanterns, Aderyn saw balconies of wrought iron extending out from the second and third stories, taking advantage of the space between the buildings. It had been dark before with the sun setting, but the looming buildings of unrelieved gray stone and the rickety balconies overhead made the street feel like a tunnel deep beneath the mountains despite the lanterns.

It didn't take long for Aderyn to be grateful for their guide. The route to the Bonemender's home, or shop, was considerably more complicated than "three streets down," and without the woman, they would likely have gotten lost. Her spirits lifted as she heard voices and music coming from some of the upper windows, reminding her that Guerdon Deep couldn't be completely bleak and lifeless.

After what felt like forever, the woman stopped before a door bearing the two crossed sticks that symbolized a Bonemender. Owen handed over more coins and said, "Thank you."

"Good luck to you," the woman said. "You're going to need it." She eyed the motionless Isold and then walked back the way they'd come.

There were no windows at ground level—Aderyn hadn't seen any windows at ground level the whole way there—but lights illuminated the sign, and the windows of the second and third stories were also lit. Owen banged on the door. "I hope," he said, then didn't finish that sentence.

Soon, the door opened, and a man with flyaway white hair and a gaunt face and limbs peered out at them. "Yes?"

"Our friend was badly hurt. We need healing," Owen said. "We can pay."

Aderyn considered how little money they had, even with the gatekeeper's generosity, and hoped they had enough.

The old man opened the door wider. "Let me get Soline. Come in, all of you."

Aderyn followed Weston inside and stopped, stunned. She'd expected bleak gray walls, cold floors, tiny rooms like cells, the smell of damp stone. Instead, she found herself in a chamber big enough to comfortably fit twelve, the stone walls plastered and painted a creamy white, a dozen lanterns illuminating the many brightly colored cushions softening the chairs. Thick rugs as colorful as the cushions softened the floor and swallowed up any dismal echoes.

The old man stiffly crossed the room to a door covered with a beaded curtain that swished like rainfall when he pushed it aside. He opened the door and stepped inside, and they heard a low-voiced conversation. Then the old man emerged, followed by a middle-aged woman as plump as he was thin. Instinctively, Aderyn Assessed them.

Name: Soline
Class: Bonemender (retired)
Level: Exceeds authority limit
Name: Cavan
Class: Staffsworn (retired)
Level: Exceeds authority limit

Aderyn suppressed a gasp of astonishment. She immediately felt ashamed of herself for having assumed the old man was nothing more than a servant. Old adventurers were to be honored for their achievements... but he was so thin, and he moved so stiffly, it was hard to imagine him as he would have been in his prime.

The Bonemender, Soline, surveyed their little group swiftly, then focused her gaze on Isold. Aderyn had a feeling Soline was Assessing him with her skill the way Aderyn would Assess a monster. "Carry him through here," she said. "You know you shouldn't have moved him."

"We didn't have a choice," Owen said.

"That's how it goes sometimes," Soline said. "Well, he's not dead, and where there's life, there's hope."

Aderyn, looking at Isold's pale, still face, didn't feel much hope at all.

CHAPTER THIRTY-TWO

S oline opened a second door next to the first and did
something that made a brilliant white light, cooler than lamp
light, spill out into the sitting room. Aderyn had ended up
near the back of the group, and when she crowded close to Livia to
see inside, she couldn't make out anything past Weston's bulk except
several magic-lit lanterns and a bare table.

"Lay him down, and then leave me to work," Soline said. "Make
yourselves comfortable. Father will bring you something to drink."

Caught off-guard by the woman's hospitality, Aderyn let herself
be swept backward into the sitting room, where she took a seat next
to Owen and stared at her clenched hands. Owen murmured, "He'll
be all right."

"She's powerful, at least level twelve," Aderyn whispered back.
"I'm more worried that we won't have enough to pay."

"Worry about that when the time comes," Owen replied.
"There's always work for adventurers in towns like this, right?"

Aderyn nodded. She didn't think she could stop worrying.

The Staffsworn, Cavan, had left the room while they were
finding seats, and now he returned with a tray on which rested a

metal pitcher sweating droplets in the warmth of the room and a handful of tin mugs. He poured water into each of the mugs and handed them round, startling Aderyn when the mug turned out to be icy cold. The cold water refreshed her, renewing her hope for Isold. Surely everything would be all right.

"So. What happened to your companion?" Cavan took a seat more gracefully than he walked and helped himself to a mug of water.

"He was carried off by a cat-hawk, and when it fell, it landed on him," Owen said.

"A cat-hawk?" Cavan's eyebrows raised. "That's quite a challenge for level six adventurers, even five of you."

"There were five of them," Weston said, for once not full of good cheer to say anything amusing like "so it was an equal fight."

"Holy shit." Cavan leaned forward. "It's amazing you survived. Good luck, or good strategy?"

"Our Warmaster saw their weaknesses, and we exploited them." Owen didn't sound any more cheerful than Weston had.

Cavan whistled. "No offense, but I didn't know Warmasters were good for anything."

"Not on my own," Aderyn explained. "Warmasters need a partner to be effective. Owen and I work together, and my skills help the rest of my team too." She refused to be offended by his blunt statement. It wasn't anything her own parents hadn't believed.

"Interesting," Cavan said. "I guess even at my age I can learn things. Are you hungry? We're going to eat in about half an hour."

"We don't want to keep you from your dinner," Owen said.

"It's no trouble. Young adventurers remind me of my own adventuring days, about a million years ago." Cavan winked, an expression that made him look twenty years younger. He heaved himself to his feet. "Excuse me, I'll go check on the roast. And—relax. Soline is level twenty and she's brought more than one person back from the brink of death." He nodded and left the room.

The companions exchanged glances. "What a piece of luck," Livia said. "I think the system must be looking out for us."

"Or looking out for Owen," Weston said. "If he's a potential Fated One..."

"But it's Isold who was injured," Aderyn said. "Not Owen. Why would the system care about Isold?"

"A Fated One can't succeed alone. He or she needs support. Maybe Isold is part of that." Livia shrugged. "It's a theory."

The door to the Bonemender's room opened, and Soline emerged. Behind her, looking completely well, stood Isold.

"Isold!" Livia exclaimed.

"I feel very awkward, so please stop staring," Isold said with a rueful grin. "Like I did something remarkable in not dying."

"That's mostly true," Soline said. "You had extensive internal injuries and three broken bones. Another half hour, and you would have been beyond my ability to help. So, let's all be grateful you found your way here in time, shall we?"

Owen rose and extended a hand to shake Soline's. "Thank you," he said. "What do we owe you?"

Soline looked him over, then glanced quickly at each of the others. Aderyn had to work at not wincing when it was her turn; the woman wasn't Assessing them, just looking closely, but it felt as if Soline could see through her skin to her heart even without a Bonemender's skill. "Call it four gold," she said.

"That can't be enough," Aderyn said without thinking.

"I choose my rates according to what I think someone can afford, young Warmaster," Soline said. "Ultimately, I don't believe anyone can put a value on a human life—it would either be priceless, or worthless, if you take my meaning. But if I charged nothing, no one would appreciate the value of my time. So, it's four gold."

Owen was already digging into his pocket. "Thank you. I was afraid this might leave us unable to rent rooms."

"I'm glad of that, because anyone too poor to rent a room is kicked out of Guerdon Deep overnight." Soline nodded at Cavan, who'd returned followed by the smell of hot pork roast. "Did Father invite you to dinner? Eat with us, and tell us stories of your adventures. No, don't say it's too much. Learn to accept hospitality when it's offered."

The room all the good smells came from was almost entirely filled by a table made from a slab of oak that could have served as Guerdon Deep's gate. The companions sat, and Cavan served everyone roast pork in honey and fresh steamed green beans and slices of thick, nutty bread. Aderyn drank the ale Soline poured and felt relaxed for the first time in days.

She hadn't meant to tell all the details of their adventures—certainly nothing about the Fated One business—but somehow things just slipped out. It seemed her friends felt the same, because they soon were talking over one another, filling in details someone else forgot. Nobody mentioned Owen being from another world, or Fated Ones, or their true reason for coming to Guerdon Deep, but aside from that, they shared everything. Soline and Cavan listened avidly, occasionally asking questions or exclaiming their astonishment.

When the last of the pork roast was gone, and the stories had wound down, Soline brought out a bottle of fine wine and said, "That calls for a toast. And maybe then you'll tell us what you have in mind next."

Aderyn toasted with the rest of them, then sipped her wine as Weston said, "We're here looking for work—"

"Actually, that's not the whole truth," Owen said. He spoke as if he'd been thinking things over for a while. "We're looking for someone who knows about other worlds."

"Other worlds? Like the demon void?" Cavan said.

"No. Other worlds similar to this one. Worlds where humans live."

Aderyn choked on her wine and made a sputtering noise. "Owen," she warned.

"We have to tell someone eventually, and I feel it's time," Owen said. "I'm not from your world. I came from a different one. One without a system or levels or magic."

Soline's eyes widened. "You're not serious."

"Serious as a heart attack. I'm telling you because I trust you and Cavan, and we have to find someone who can send me home. I'd rather not ask random people in the street, and I bet you know all the spellslingers in Guerdon Deep and might be able to direct us."

"Amazing," Cavan said. He set his wine glass down as precisely as if it was the key to a lock. "You look entirely human."

"Because I am human," Owen said. "Human enough to be able to perceive the Codex, and for the system to have made me a Swordsworn."

"How many other worlds are there?" Soline asked. "Their inhabitants can't have come to our world often, or we would have heard about it."

"We don't know," Isold said. "And we don't know whether it matters. That is, if there are lots of other worlds, finding Owen's might be difficult. That's why we need someone who might be able to answer that question."

Soline and Cavan exchanged glances. Aderyn, watching them, thought they were the kind of glances that said they knew what each other were thinking and didn't like it. "You do know someone," she said impulsively.

"We do," Cavan said. "But I don't know how much we trust him. You see, he's a reformed Diabolist."

Aderyn sucked in a horrified gasp as all her companions except Owen reacted similarly. "A Diabolist?"

"*Reformed*," Soline said. "It's possible."

"I'm not sure I believe that, begging your pardon," Weston said.

"What's a Diabolist? Someone who does things with demons, it sounds like?" Owen said.

"I forgot you wouldn't know," Cavan said. "Diabolists summon and control demons, usually to manipulate or terrorize people. Some of them claim only to want to understand the system better by studying demons, but even they are considered an evil class for nego-tiating with demons instead of killing them. The man we're talking about, Jedrek, he started life as a Spellcrafter."

"He and I were on the same team for a while," Soline said. "He was always interested in why Spellcrafting worked. What it was about the world, or the system, or something else that allowed items to be imbued with magic. That's what got him interested in demons. He believed the place they came from was the source of the magic he used to imbue things, because demons are beings of pure magic."

"I didn't know that," Isold said. "But I don't seem to have much knowledge about demons, though I have a skill for it."

"You have to have direct contact with demons, one way or another, to improve that knowledge skill," Cavan said. "Have you seen a demon?"

"Once," Isold replied, frowning. "It's not a memory I cherish."

"That's why you know anything about them." Cavan looked as grim as Isold. "I won't ask for the details. It's bad luck to talk too much about them—makes you vulnerable to their influence."

"Anyway, Jedrek got more and more involved in studying demons," Soline went on. "Then he learned to summon them—purely for research, he claimed—but it wasn't long before his class changed. That was when our team expelled him. He never used demons to hurt people, so we didn't kill him, but we warned him if he continued on that path, we'd be the first to hunt him down and destroy him."

"But you said he was reformed. When did that happen?" Livia asked.

Soline refilled her wine glass and took a long drink. "About five years ago, he returned to Guerdon Deep. I'd been retired from adventuring for years, and I never thought to see Jedrek again. Honestly, I thought he'd been killed long ago. But he showed up on my doorstep, and he was a Spellcrafter again. He said he'd seen how foolish he was to mess around with demons and had battled long and hard to recover his original class."

"But couldn't he have concealed his class? Pretended not to be a Diabolist?" Weston said.

"You Moonlighters think in sideways paths, don't you?" Cavan smiled and saluted Weston with his glass. "Soline and I thought that, too. But Jedrek passed every test we could think of."

"You said you weren't sure you trust him," Owen said.

"We're sure he's no longer a Diabolist," Soline said. "But Jedrek is still Jedrek, and I'm sure his inquisitive nature and disregard for basic morality are still there. He might see you as a test subject rather than a person, Owen."

"If he can get me home, I'll be his guinea pig for however long it takes." Owen drained his glass and set it down as precisely as Cavan had. "I'm guessing it's too late to pay him a visit tonight."

"We can take you to meet him tomorrow morning," Soline said. "He's an early riser."

"Then he can't be all bad," Weston joked.

"Can you recommend a good inn?" Owen said. "Something not terribly expensive. Our resources are a bit thin."

"Sure. Try the Horse and Hound," Cavan said. "Clerra, the owner, never saw a horse or a hound in her life, not living in Guerdon Deep, but she's sentimental about animals. Tell her my name and she'll give you a good rate. No, actually, I'll take you there."

"We don't want you to put yourself out," Aderyn said. It was foolish, but she didn't want this apparently frail old man going out alone at night. Then she reminded herself that a former adventurer and level twenty Staffsworn wasn't weak no matter how he appeared.

"It's no trouble. Just let me get Old Hickory." Cavan pushed back from the table and left the room.

"His staff," Soline said when she saw their confusion. "Father's a sentimentalist, too."

They all rose from the table and gathered in the sitting room, where Cavan soon joined them carrying a length of age-polished hickory. It was gnarled rather than perfectly straight, with a knob at one end that looked big enough to brain someone with, and Cavan held it lightly, as if it was an extension of himself. "Don't wait up, daughter," he said, and led the way out of the house.

CHAPTER THIRTY-THREE

Full dark had fallen, but the streets of Guerdon Deep were livelier than they'd been an hour before. Men and women strolled in pairs or groups, talking loudly to one another and laughing at jokes Aderyn was too far away to hear. Cavan led them through the streets to an even noisier and more active neighborhood. The streets were as narrow as ever, but lights blazed at every window and beside every door, and the sounds of music competed with each other, making a discordant melody that somehow suited the place. Every third door seemed to be a tavern or inn, and all of them teemed with activity.

Cavan led them to a door beneath a sign with a crudely painted horse head facing an equally awkward picture of a dog's face. The door was open wide, and as the companions entered, a burst of music startled them as a fiddler began playing with more energy than accuracy. The patrons shouted approval anyway, stomping their feet and banging mugs on tables.

Behind the bar, two men rapidly served drinks that were carried away by several sweaty, overworked young women. Cavan waved at the third person behind the bar, a heavyset lady with a cheerful face who was currently hauling a new keg of ale into its braces. "Clerra!"

Clerra tapped the barrel with a mighty whack of the mallet she held. "Cavan, what are you doing out at this hour? Don't you usually go to bed with the sun?"

"An exaggeration," Cavan said. "I'd like you to meet some young adventurers Soline and I met today. They're in need of rooms, and I told them you'd give them a good rate."

"A good rate?" Clerra squinted at each of them, and Aderyn realized she was extremely nearsighted. "Sure, if they're willing to double up. Don't got a lot of rooms left."

"We only need two," Owen said. "We appreciate anything you can give us."

Clerra focused on Owen, and her lips curved in a lascivious smile. "Good looking young man like you, I wouldn't mind giving you just about anything."

Owen blushed. Aderyn, irritated, said, "We just need rooms, thanks."

"Ah, young love," Clerra said, and it was Aderyn's turn to blush. Really, why did old people feel entitled to tease about romances that didn't exist? She couldn't bring herself to look at Owen, and that was stupid, because the teasing didn't mean anything. Even if he was handsome.

"All right, rooms five and six upstairs," Clerra said, laughing. "Second floor, to the right of the stairs. Twenty silver each per night, payment in advance."

Aderyn groped in her purse, pushed aside the <**Skeleton Ladder**> rod, and found a handful of coins in the capacious storage space. All around her, her friends were patting themselves down, looking for money. She collected coin from everyone and handed it over. "Just the one night for now," she said.

"Oh, and aren't you the proud one? You didn't like me teasing you about your young man." Clerra smiled again.

"He's my partner, he's not my young man," Aderyn said, then wondered why she was making such a fuss. "Let's go."

She hurried ahead of the others and had to slow when she reached the stairs or look stupid for running beyond her companions. Cavan said goodbye to them at the base of the stairs. "Come back in the morning, and we'll introduce you to Jedrek. Good night."

When he was gone, the five continued up the stairs more slowly. Aderyn found herself beside Owen. She felt unexpectedly tired, enough that talking was an effort, and Owen seemed to feel the same. So she was surprised when Owen said, "You were awfully quick to say we weren't together. You know that woman didn't mean anything by it. She's just the type who likes to make people blush."

That made Aderyn blush again. "I know. I was stupid. It didn't mean anything."

"I ought to be insulted, like you think I'm a fate worse than death," Owen said with a smile.

Aderyn managed a weak laugh. "Of course not. You're not bad for an otherworlder."

"Right. And really, is it so strange? You and me, I mean?"

She dared to glance his way. He wasn't looking at her, and his cheeks were unexpectedly red. An unfamiliar pulse of energy, warm and thrilling, shot through her. For a moment, she considered it, and her heart swelled. Then she remembered what had brought them to Guerdon Deep, and it was as if a gallon of Livia's coldest summoned water drenched her, killing that beautiful warm feeling.

"I guess it's not," she said, sounding offhanded. "But you're going home soon. It's not like it matters."

Owen nodded. "That's true."

They reached the second floor and found two doors with the numbers 5 and 6 painted neatly on them. Owen put a hand on Aderyn's wrist when she would have followed Livia into room six. "Aderyn," he said, "whatever happens—I mean, I hope this means

I'm going home, and I want you to know how much I appreciate what you've done for me. You've been the best friend I could hope for."

Aderyn's heart constricted. Again, she felt the selfish, grasping impulse that wanted this to be a failure, that wanted Owen to stay in her world. But he was right—they were close friends, and friends wanted the best for each other no matter how it hurt. "I'll miss you, but this is for the best," she said.

"Yeah," Owen said. He looked as if he was searching for more words, but ultimately he just repeated, "Yeah. Good night, Aderyn."

Aderyn's last sight of him, before she shut the door, was of his blond head, bowed as if under a tremendous weight. He needed to return home, and she needed to let him go.

Long after Livia had begun snoring, Aderyn lay awake, staring into the darkness. Occasionally, she called up the Codex and checked her advancement, though it wasn't any different the other five times than the first.

Name: Aderyn

Class: Warmaster

Level: 6

<u>Skills</u>: **Bluff (4), Climb (1), Conversation (4), Intimidate (3), Sense Truth (6), Survival (2), Swim (1), Knowledge: Monsters (4)**

<u>Class Skills:</u> **Improved Assess 1 (8), Awareness (4), Knowledge: Geography (3), Spot (6), Discern Weakness (7), Dodge (6), Improvised Distraction (4), Outflank (3), Draw Fire (0), Keep Pace (1)**

She didn't know what **[Keep Pace]** was, or how she'd managed to gain a rank in it without knowing about it, but she suspected it was another paired skill like **[Discern Weakness]** and **[Outflank]**. She'd have to ask Owen about it in the morning—but did it matter, if he wasn't going to be around for the two of them to discover it?

The silver lines of the Codex blurred, and she wiped tears away.

She was being stupid. People went through several teams in their adventuring careers, sometimes because of deaths, sometimes because of teammates advancing to level twenty or retiring early. Sometimes it happened because of personality conflicts, even. So being mopey over losing a teammate, even one as close to her as Owen, was ridiculous. He'd probably be embarrassed if he knew she was crying over him.

But there in the darkness, it was hard to forget the single most important detail related to Owen returning to his world: a Warmaster without a partner was useless. She didn't know if a Warmaster's partner had to be a Swordsworn, or even if they had to be a fighting class of some sort, but she felt certain none of her other companions could fill the spot. It was true Weston had benefited from her Warmaster knowledge, but he didn't have any of the paired skills, and Livia and Isold... no. She was on her own again, only it was worse because she had friends who would do their best to make her feel needed, and she did not want pity, not from them, not from anyone.

She wiped more tears away. She needed to be honest with herself: it wasn't just losing her partner, it was losing *Owen* that hurt. They'd known each other barely two weeks, and already he was her closest friend. Closest friend, and... well, he was right, it wouldn't be terrible if they were more to each other than friends. What *was* terrible was that with him going home, that was a bad line of thought to pursue, one that would only make things hurt more.

But she fell asleep wishing they'd kissed even once.

SHE SLEPT POORLY AND WOKE IN A FOUL MOOD SHE struggled not to take out on her friends. Since Livia was her usual grouchy self, nobody paid Aderyn any attention except to tease her that sharing a room with Livia meant Livia's attitudes rubbed off on Aderyn. Aderyn smiled and pretended that was funny.

She didn't exchange more than a few words with Owen, who was quieter than usual, but she thought he looked unhappy. That made *her* unhappy. He was close to finding a way home—at least, she hoped they were close—and he ought to be excited about that. So she exerted herself to be as cheerful as Weston, who was packing away food like he wasn't going to see another meal in his lifetime.

"I wonder what a reformed Diabolist looks like," she mused aloud. "Gaunt and pale-skinned with hollow eyes. You know, because he's seen things no mortal man should."

"That's as reasonable as anything," Isold said. "Demons are terrible creatures."

"You've never said how you came to see a demon," Weston said between bites of ham.

"Because I'd rather not inflict that knowledge on my friends," Isold replied with a shudder. "I was out collecting herbs with some other apprentices when we encountered it. It had already eaten, I think, and that's why it didn't kill any of us. It enjoyed threatening us with the worst torments imaginable, though. Playing with us like we were baby animals it intended to torture."

"That's awful," Aderyn said. "Are demons as ugly as everyone says?"

"Ugly is the wrong word. The one I met was actually quite beautiful. But it was... not right. Looking at it felt like seeing the world through fractured glass. I felt as if I was being pulled toward it and the void it came from, like a fish on a line." Isold took a long drink of his ale. "I can't describe it better than that. I hope none of you ever get that close. We only escaped because it found us boring."

"So, if demons are that terrible, why do Diabolists summon them?" Owen asked.

"Demons have great knowledge about our world, since they observe it closely, looking for ways in," Isold said. "They can locate treasures, identify lost dungeons, tell secrets... there are great benefits to being able to summon and control a demon."

"And great disadvantages," Livia said. "Losing control of a demon usually means the death of the summoner."

"That's what I thought," Owen said. "So, this Jedrek stopped being a Diabolist because he realized how he was risking his life. Makes sense."

"You don't sound convinced," Aderyn said.

Owen glanced her way. "I'm not sure how easy it is to change your behavior. I believe Soline and Cavan, of course, but I'll be more comfortable once I've met Jedrek and know what he's like."

"I feel uncertain, too," Aderyn said. "But more because I'm used to keeping the secret of your identity."

"A former Diabolist, if nothing else, will not need to be convinced of the existence of other worlds," Isold pointed out. "I think it's as safe as we're likely to get."

Owen shoved back from the table. "Then let's get going."

"You barely ate," Aderyn protested, eyeing his mostly-full plate.

"Would you be able to eat if you were me?" Owen still looked unhappy. Aderyn wished she knew what to say to ease his mind.

She took a few last bites of sausage and washed them down with ale. "You're right. We shouldn't delay."

Guerdon Deep by day was even busier than it had been the previous night. People thronged the streets, calling out to one another or bartering with merchants at barrows that hadn't been there before. It would have been cheerful if the stone walls hadn't still felt oppressive.

"Do you suppose all the houses are like Soline's?" Aderyn asked Owen, who walked beside her in a silence nearly as oppressive as the walls.

Owen shrugged. "You mean, beautiful and comfortable inside? Maybe. In my world, at least, there are places like this, forbidding and bleak outside. But I've never seen pictures of the insides of those houses." His voice was dull, like he was responding by rote.

Aderyn let out an exasperated breath. "Would you stop acting like we're going to your funeral? We've been working toward this for weeks. You get to go back to your world. Why is that suddenly so awful?"

Owen shook his head. "It's not awful. I'm just not as thrilled as I would have been two weeks ago. I've made good friends I'm never going to see again, Aderyn. So what I'm saying is this isn't an unmixed pleasure."

"I understand," Aderyn said. "I'll miss you, too. But you said you have a family who doesn't know what happened to you. You did the graduated thing so you can do a job—you can't use that knowledge here." She hesitated. "Or maybe you can. I don't actually know what you studied at school."

"History. I was going to be a history teacher. My world's history, obviously. So you're right, I can't exactly use what I studied here. There aren't even many parallels to my world in yours, like how you have the printing press but not newspapers." Owen sighed. "I'm sorry. I'm probably making things worse by not being cheerful."

"I don't know. What's the point in pretending to be happier than you are?"

"My mother would say you become the thing you choose to be. Like, putting on a happy attitude eventually makes it real. I'm not sure I believe her."

"Well," Aderyn said, "I'd rather feel happy than miserable, so I'll give it a try." She smiled hugely and pointed at the sky. "Look, birds! They're probably looking forward to a long day of eating people's fallen food."

Owen raised his eyebrows. "You think scavenging bits of old bread is a happy thing?"

"Sure. I'm not the one eating the bits of old bread, for one."

Owen stared at her in disbelief. Then he laughed. "You have the strangest ideas of what makes someone cheerful. All right. If you can do it, so can I. Look, that man is wearing a cap that doesn't match his coat. I'm happy not to have his poor fashion sense."

"And that stall owner doesn't see that little kid who just stole an apple and ran away. He looks like the kind of man people do that to often. You know, that sort of pinched, irritated look. It makes me want to steal an apple myself."

"Steal one for both of us," Owen said.

CHAPTER THIRTY-FOUR

They bantered all the way to Soline's house, where Cavan let them in. "Bright and early, that's what I like to see," he said.

Livia muttered something incoherent. "Sorry?" Cavan said.

"She's just regretting her life choices again," Weston said. "She'll be awake in half an hour."

Cavan looked at Livia as if he didn't understand how she could be asleep on her feet. "Soline is finishing up a few things, and then she'll take you to meet Jedrek."

"Not you?" Owen asked.

"Jedrek and I don't like each other much," Cavan said with a wink. "He put Soline in danger a few times—not typical adventuring danger, but the sort that results from carelessness—and he knows I haven't forgiven him. You're better off with Soline introducing you."

On those words, Soline emerged from her treatment room. She was dressed plainly, with nothing on her clothes to indicate her class, but she carried a satchel over her shoulder marked with the crossed sticks of the Bonemender. "Oh, good, you're early," she said.

"We should have asked how early this Jedrek is willing to see strangers," Owen said.

"Jedrek barely sleeps," Soline said. "He says he's one of those people who needs no more than three or four hours to be fresh and alert. He'll have been awake since five. Oh, and be prepared to leave your weapons outside Jedrek's quarters. He's paranoid about being attacked."

"That doesn't sound promising. Why would we attack him? That sounds more like he wants to be able to attack us without us fighting back."

Soline shrugged. "He's just like that. It's a harmless whim, since most adventurers have the skill to fight him without weaponry, particularly spellslingers. I, for one, could take him apart in seconds. Between us, I think weapons scare him, like they might leap up and attack him independent of their owners. Is this going to be a problem?"

Owen shook his head. "I guess not."

"Good. So, let's see about getting you home, Owen."

Soline led them through the narrow streets Aderyn still felt lost in, even with the sky clear of clouds and the bright sun illuminating Guerdon Deep as best it could. She observed the houses as they went, curious about what kind of people lived there. Were they all as friendly and helpful as Soline and Cavan, or did the city's dour surface make them cranky? The windows were too high for her to see inside, so she didn't know if it was true that Guerdon Deep's residents put all their creative energies into decorating their homes' interiors. Maybe nobody saw the point of trying to make the city more pleasing to the eye.

Soline stopped in front of a door that looked like all the other doors on the street, weathered wood that had once been painted black and was now peeling and depressing. Above the door hung a plaque with the barred circle, symbolic of a ring and a wand, indicating a Spellcrafter lived there. Soline knocked, then opened the door without waiting for an invitation. "Jedrek? I've brought some people who need your services." To the companions, she said, "You can put your weapons over here. Including belt knives." Her eyes rolled, showing how stupid she thought Jedrek's prohibition was.

The room just inside the door was lit by magical lights and was bright and welcoming, proving at least part of Aderyn's theory. One open doorway led deeper into the house, though curtains kept Aderyn from seeing further. The plastered walls were painted a light eggshell blue, and paintings hung on three of the four walls. Aderyn had never seen paintings so detailed before. She felt she might be able to reach through the frames to the landscapes beyond: a field of sun-touched grass covered with wildflowers, a stark mountain standing alone that wasn't like the ones surrounding Guerdon Deep, and a broad, sandy-pale beach with waves crashing down on it.

Beneath the paintings, glass-topped cabinets of golden maple lined the walls. They were filled with rings, slim wands, fatter and longer rods, and a few miscellaneous items like a pair of gloves and a length of iron Aderyn recognized. "That's half a **<Skeleton Ladder>**," she exclaimed. She still had Isold's half-ladder stowed in her **<Purse of Great Capacity>**.

Livia's eyes, which were still half-shut, narrowed further as if someone had shone a bright light in her face. "They're all magical. Representative of what Jedrek can do, maybe."

"You are absolutely right," said a man from the doorway. He was middle aged, short and plump, with longish dark hair and round, rosy cheeks. Owen wouldn't be able to criticize his fashion sense; he was impeccably garbed in a silk shirt and billowing silk trousers that coordinated exactly, as well as a fringed sash for a belt and black boots that shouldn't have matched the trousers, but did. "I keep these for demonstration purposes, though of course my business is imbuing objects my clients bring me, not selling already-imbued wares. Soline, who are these fine people?"

"Jedrek, these adventurers have a problem I think you can help with," Soline said. "Can we come in? It's not a short story."

Jedrek's eyebrows rose. "You intrigue me. Of course, come in, make yourselves comfortable."

Beyond the curtain lay a sitting room similar in size and contents to Soline's. The décor, however, was dramatically different. More landscape paintings hung on the walls so everywhere Aderyn looked, she saw something beautiful. Instead of rugs, the floor was of planed lumber, something Aderyn had never seen before. She liked it better than the stone of her family home.

"Take a seat, just anywhere. Yes, drag those chairs closer. I'm always rearranging." Jedrek sat in a chair overflowing with cushions and lightly gripped the armrests. "So, can we have introductions? I'm Jedrek, but I'm sure Soline has told you that."

As Soline introduced each of the companions, Aderyn took the opportunity to Assess Jedrek.

Name: Jedrek

Class: Spellcrafter (retired)

Level: Exceeds authority limit

He didn't look at all like a formerly evil person. Aderyn suppressed her suspicions. If he wasn't what he appeared to be, **[Improved Assess 1]** would have showed her those weird corrupted symbols in the Codex display. Still, she found herself agreeing with Owen: how likely was it that anyone could reverse their behavior, come back from having an evil class? All right, Jedrek was sitting right there, living proof that it was possible, and Aderyn needed to stop being paranoid.

"Owen, why don't you explain the situation to Jedrek," Soline suggested when introductions were over.

Owen nodded. "Sir," he said, "Soline tells me I can be open with you. I'm not from your world. I came here from another world, not the demon void, that has humans just like everyone here."

Jedrek's eyes widened. "I can't believe it," he said. "I—well, I think I know now why Soline brought you here. She must have told you about my past."

"She said you were a Diabolist once."

"I was, to my shame," Jedrek said. "But I can't deny the knowledge I gained during the years of that foul pursuit. I'm not at all surprised at your declaration. My studies indicated the possibility of other worlds—other human worlds—but that was all it was, possibility. Now you tell me it's actually true..." His eyes gleamed with excitement. "How astonishing."

"We're here because I hope you might know how to send me back," Owen said. "If your research said places like my world exist, that seems likely."

Jedrek steepled his fingers in front of him and frowned. "That's mostly true. At least, we know there's a place for you to go as opposed to simply opening a gate to the void. Whether that's possible is another issue."

"What does that mean?" Aderyn asked.

Jedrek switched his gaze to her. "When a Diabolist summons a demon, he does so by making a door—a connection between our world and the void. Diabolists have done this for centuries, and opening the door is as simple as thought. But because this is true, it means the connection between the world and the void is... you might think of it as having worn a groove in reality. It's automatic. Opening that door to another human world instead means fighting the inertia of centuries that makes the door want to open on the void. It will be difficult, if not impossible. I feel I shouldn't give you false hope."

"I appreciate your honesty." Owen leaned forward. "I'd still like to try."

"Of course you would." Jedrek smiled brilliantly, making his cheeks even rounder. "And, honestly, I'd love an opportunity to do good with those ill-gotten skills. Everyone push back your chairs."

"What, you mean you'll try right now?" Owen sounded taken aback.

"I did say it's a matter of thought, right?" Jedrek stood and shoved his own chair into a corner.

"Wait a minute." Owen embraced each of his companions, ending with Aderyn. He held her a little longer than the others and whispered in her ear, "I won't forget you."

Aderyn squeezed her eyes shut so she wouldn't cry. "I'm not going to find another partner like you," she murmured.

Owen released her and smiled, a wobbly sort of smile, but his blue eyes were direct and unshadowed by sadness. "All right. I'm ready. Let's clear a space."

They all moved chairs, even Soline, who said, "I'm not going to miss this." When the wooden floor was empty, Jedrek directed all of them to stand in an uneven circle centered on him. "This is going to be tricky, and it may take a few tries, so be patient. There's no danger."

Aderyn, who'd been about to ask if there was any chance a door to the demon void might open and a demon appear, closed her mouth.

Jedrek breathed rhythmically in and out through his nose, his breath slightly whistling as he exhaled. It was a soothing sound, and Aderyn felt more relaxed listening to it. Sure, this had been abrupt, but maybe it was better they not draw out their goodbyes. She was calm enough her heart no longer ached as badly.

Wait. That made no sense. Aderyn opened eyes she hadn't realized were closed and watched her companions. They all looked as peaceful as she felt, even Owen, who ought to have been tenser than anyone. "I don't—" she began.

"Hush, now," Jedrek said, and Aderyn's peaceful feeling returned. Deep within her, something screamed this was wrong. She struggled to open her mouth, but she felt so calm it was too difficult to move.

With a snap, a black spot popped into existence between Jedrek and Owen. It roiled and bubbled as it spread outward like an ink spill that ran up against an invisible barrier until a black oval hung in the air. Its matte surface made it look like it had been painted there, but then Aderyn saw it was slowly rotating, and as it turned, the surface became liquid and then matte again. It felt so wrong she cringed.

Her friends began to move, tiny fidgets like they'd run into the same problem she had. Aderyn looked to Soline, who looked drugged, her head lolling, her eyes half-lidded.

Aderyn's attention was drawn to the oval again. Something was coming through.

It looked like a dog that stood on its hind legs, with a pointed muzzle and erect, triangular ears, but something was wrong with it. The legs were jointed backward so it stood more upright than a real dog could, and its coat glistened with what in one moment was rainbow oil and in the next was a rime of frost like frozen dew. It caught Aderyn's eye, and she wanted to be sick at how intelligent, how horribly and maliciously intelligent, it was.

Then the demon was fully present, and Jedrek snapped, "Do it, minion."

In a flash, the demon dove at Soline and in the next breath ripped her throat out with its vicious jaws. Blood sprayed across the polished wood floor. Soline made no sound, just sagged in death.

"What..." Aderyn managed.

"You're not reformed," Owen said, sounding remarkably alert. "You're a Diabolist."

"You're very good at spotting the obvious, aren't you?" Jedrek said, as jovially as ever. "Yes, I'm a Diabolist. And you're going to unlock the way to your world for me."

Chapter Thirty-Five

"You can't be a Diabolist," Aderyn managed. "I would have known."

"Please," Jedrek said scornfully. "I've spent years concealing my true class from people much higher level than you. I think I can deceive one Warmaster who's just starting out."

He walked around the circle until he came to Soline's crumpled, bloody body. "And you made me kill Soline," he said, absently prodding her with a black-booted toe. "Pity. She was always good to me, and I appreciated that even though she was a fool not to know my real nature. But she would have interfered, and she was a powerful spellslinger who could have stopped me if she knew my plan."

"And what plan is that?" Owen's voice was as strong as ever, but he stood rigidly, like he was tied to a post. "I don't believe you've been waiting all this time for an otherworlder to show up on your doorstep, and I doubt you decided to betray us in the few minutes between learning my identity and now."

"You're mostly right," Jedrek said. He circled their group again, but Aderyn's attention was all on the demon. It was watching Jedrek, not her, but its presence sucked at her body like a current, and if Jedrek's magic hadn't been holding her as tightly as it was Owen, she would have staggered toward the demon until they collided.

"I discovered the existence of other worlds years ago, when I was just starting out as a Diabolist," Jedrek went on. "Other worlds that are shadows of this one, the prime world. In those worlds, elements of our culture exist in warped fragments or memories, fantasy stories they tell their children. They were oddities, but nothing more—at least, that's what I believed. It was a while before I realized their potential. All those worlds in which humans can survive, none of them with magic in a fully-formed state, most of them with no magic at all... a high-level adventurer of any class could rule those worlds."

"Why are you telling us this?" Livia asked. "Gloating?" Her voice was slurred, and her head lolled the way Soline's had.

Jedrek appeared taken aback. "I thought you'd be interested. You've got a companion from one of those worlds; don't you care at all about what they're like?"

"Let us go," Owen said. He twitched as if straining against his invisible bonds.

"All right, I will," Jedrek said with a sneer. "Why would I let you go before I have what I need?"

"Which is... what?" Owen asked. His twitching movements increased.

"Stop struggling, you're embarrassing yourself," Jedrek said. He gestured, and Owen fell still. Aderyn nearly cried out in fear for him until she realized he was still conscious and alert. "I need a key to attune the door to a different world. Your world, obviously."

"You don't need to do this," Isold said, his voice low and melodic. "We don't have what you want. Let us go. We're all friends here."

"Don't waste your voice on me, Herald," Jedrek said. He waved a hand, and Isold's head sagged in sleep, though his body stayed upright.

"Leave him alone! We don't have any keys," Weston shouted.

"A figure of speech. It's actually a piece of knowledge, something that makes a unique connection to your world. I don't suppose you know what that is?"

"Like I'd tell you even if I did," Owen snarled.

"Don't worry, I'll get it out of you eventually." Jedrek lazily scanned the five of them. His gaze settled on Aderyn. "Let's start by torturing this one. You adventurers are all the same, so devoted to your teammates. It gives anyone like me a powerful hold on your obedience."

Aderyn glared at him. "That's what you think," she said. "They don't care about me at all."

"Aderyn!" Owen shouted.

She ignored him. "They talk a good line about all of us being companions, but they only brought me along as a guide, because I have a map and a compass. *He*—" She jerked her head in Owen's direction— "tried to seduce me so I'd stay ignorant of their intentions. I stuck around for the money, but now I just want to be free."

Jedrek gazed at her, his eyes narrowed. "I think you're bluffing," he said.

"You *bitch*," Weston shouted. "We treated you like an equal, and this is how you repay us?"

Aderyn concealed her relief that one of her companions was quick on the uptake. Now, if only the others would play along... "You said it yourself," she told Jedrek. "I'm a low-level Warmaster. I'm useless. I'd be useless no matter what my level. I'm sick of being looked down on by these so-called friends. Let me go, and I'll tell you what your key is."

"Aderyn, don't you dare," Owen shouted. "Look, I was serious, I really do care about you—"

Aderyn laughed, putting as much bitterness into the sound as she could. "Of course you do," she sneered. "I already know you're sleeping with Livia. Did she approve of you cheating on her, or was it her idea to manipulate me?"

"You don't deserve our companionship," Livia said. Her voice was still slurred, like she couldn't focus. Aderyn hadn't thought to wonder why Livia hadn't cast any spells, but now she suspected Jedrek's magic kept a level six Earthbreaker under control where it couldn't stop a level twenty Bonemender. The idea filled her with gratitude that Jedrek hadn't thought Livia worth killing.

"Like I care," Aderyn shot back.

She became aware of the demon's attention on her, how its malevolent red eyes surveyed her body, not in a lascivious way, but the way a butcher assesses a carcass, deciding which cut to make first. She pretended not to notice, though she felt like throwing up.

Jedrek approached Aderyn, one slow step at a time, and took her chin in his hand, raising her head so their eyes met. "If they don't care about you, why should I believe you know that otherworlder's secret?"

"He was careless," Aderyn said. "He talks about his world all the time, all the ways it's superior, like that matters to us. They don't even have magic. But that's what the key is—it's a thing they have that works by something called technology instead of magic. I'm sure of it."

Weston and Owen began shouting, words made incomprehensible by how they tangled with each other. Jedrek ignored them. "And what if it's not?"

Aderyn tossed her head, the closest she could come to a shrug. "Then torture him until he reveals the right one. But I know I'm right. And my terms are that you let me go. Do what you like with the others. Give them to your demon pet."

The demon shifted, and despite herself Aderyn glanced its way. The fur along its massive shoulders stood on end, and it stood as if it meant to attack. It had not liked being referred to as a pet.

"You're not in a position to bargain," Jedrek said.

"Of course I am. You want what I know. Oh, shut up," she shouted at Owen, who was still yelling. "You've lost. Maybe you should have considered what would happen if you treated me like dirt."

"I'm going to get free, and I swear I'll kill you myself," Owen said.

Aderyn fixed her gaze on Jedrek. "Let me go, and I'll give you your key."

Jedrek watched her for another long moment, during which a dozen possibilities whirled through Aderyn's head. If he knew she was bluffing, he might sic the demon on her. Or he might let her free so he could taunt her before killing her. Or maybe he didn't know she was bluffing, and he was so paranoid he still didn't believe her.

Finally, Jedrek snapped his fingers, and the feeling came back into Aderyn's muscles, just as if she'd never been paralyzed. She rotated her neck anyway and flexed her fingers. "What should I do?"

"Tell me what the key is," Jedrek said.

"I understand, but is it enough for me to tell you the name of it, or do I need to describe it?" Aderyn desperately stalled for time. She hadn't planned past getting free. She needed to incapacitate Jedrek, since his restraining spell wouldn't persist while he was unconscious, but how?

Jedrek hesitated. "That's a good question. I'm not sure how much information the door needs as a focus. Let's start with a name —no, give me a moment to prepare."

Aderyn didn't dare look to Owen for help. If Jedrek saw them trying to communicate, it would all be over. Maybe Jedrek's preparations would distract him. But instead, he walked around the door the demon had come through, staring at the floor and muttering. Aderyn couldn't overpower him physically, she didn't have a weapon skill, she didn't even have a weapon—

Memory struck. Aderyn held her breath, hoping Jedrek hadn't

seen her expression of hope just now. She had a weapon, if she could get to it.

Jedrek stopped midway between Owen and Livia. "I'll start to open a door," he said, "and you say the name of the thing when I signal. If it doesn't work, we'll try the description, and if that doesn't work..." He smiled nastily. "You'll find out how long it takes to die at the claws of a demon."

Aderyn pretended she wasn't scared by this threat. She didn't think she was successful. Maybe that was a good thing, if it made Jedrek believe she was too cowed to fight back. She walked wide around the door and the demon to stand near Jedrek, close to Owen and a little behind the Diabolist.

Jedrek didn't do anything, but another black spot appeared, closer to them than to the first door. Jedrek waved a hand. Aderyn said, "It's 'toilet.'"

The black spot grew, roiling painfully, but Jedrek gestured again and it collapsed and disappeared before it could fully form. "Toilet?" Jedrek said. "What's that?"

"Shouldn't I describe it while you open the door?" Owen and Weston had fallen silent, and Aderyn hoped they were prepared to attack as soon as they were free.

"True. I hope for your sake you're not lying to me." Jedrek smiled again. "Oh, what am I saying? I don't care about your sake. I hope not to have to make a mess getting the truth out of the others if you're lying."

Aderyn nodded. Her hands were trembling with the urge to retrieve the weapon right now, but she had to choose her moment.

Again, the black spot formed, and Aderyn took a step back as if alarmed, putting herself where Jedrek would have to turn around to see her. "A toilet is a magic chamber pot," she said, and slipped her hand inside the <**Purse of Great Capacity**>. Her fingers immediately fell on the smooth, cold surface of the <**Skeleton Ladder**>. "It disposes of waste with the press of a button." She gripped the iron bar and slid it noiselessly out of the purse. "It's part of something called 'indoor plumbing.'"

With one smooth move, she cracked Jedrek across the back of his head with a blow that rang through the iron all down her arm. Jedrek jerked, then folded at the knees. The door he'd begun to open vanished, leaving only the first terrible black oval pulsing in the center of the room.

Aderyn became aware of Owen's arm around her shoulders. She could barely hear him asking if she was all right over the ringing in her ears. "I think I killed him," she said.

"You didn't, because we didn't get the defeat notice," Owen said. "That was amazing."

Weston was kneeling, supporting Livia, who still looked disoriented and had fallen when Jedrek's spell ended. Now he let out a hiss of dismay and hauled Livia backwards. The demon was approaching Jedrek's fallen form, which meant it was nearing Owen and Aderyn. Its bloody eyes fixed on the Diabolist, but again its presence dragged at Aderyn, filling her with a terrible desire to walk toward it.

The demon stopped. Its too-familiar head lifted, and in that moment, it looked for the first time like a real dog, scenting prey. It took another step, this one in Owen's direction. Owen removed the **<Skeleton Ladder>** from Aderyn's loose grasp and raised it to shoulder height, holding it at one end with both hands. He moved so he stood protectively in front of Aderyn.

"You have your prey," he said. "Take him and go. If you try to come after us, we'll give you a fight you won't forget."

The demon cocked its head to one side, again exactly like an inquisitive hound. Its mouth stretched in an impossible smile. Then it swept Owen a mocking bow and picked Jedrek up by the back of his neck like he was a kitten. It dragged the fallen Diabolist through the black door, glancing once over its shoulder at Owen as if to suggest it was leaving because it wanted to and not because Owen or his metal stick were a threat. With a snap, the door vanished.

**Congratulations! You have defeated [Jedrek the Diabolist].
You have earned [5000 XP].**

**Congratulations! You have completed the secret quest [Danger
Hidden in Plain Sight].
You have earned [3000 XP].**

CHAPTER THIRTY-SIX

Aderyn let out a deep breath and threw her arms around Owen, who let the ladder rung fall with a chiming thud to make a dent in the polished floorboards. "I can't believe that worked. I can't believe we're alive."

"*I* can't believe you took such a risk," Owen said, hugging her back. "That was daring. Is everyone all right?"

"Isold's waking up," Weston said. "Isold, you need to stop getting yourself injured or unconscious. We're going to think you're not committed to this team."

"I should have known better than to try *charm* on an adventurer of that level, but I figured the situation was desperate," Isold said, sitting up. He didn't sound woozy or confused, which relieved Aderyn's mind. "What happened?"

"Aderyn bluffed like a Moonlighter and then knocked Jedrek out with the ladder rung," Weston said. "I had no idea she had it in her. Too bad no one can have more than one class, because I'd nominate you to join mine."

Aderyn blushed. "I just thought, if he knew Warmasters are useless, he might believe you all felt the same."

"Definitely not," Owen said, releasing her. "What should we do now? Somebody needs to know the truth, if only because Jedrek killed Soline. And Cavan needs to know as well."

"We report to the magistrates," Weston said, "and get one of them to verify that we defeated Jedrek in fair combat. Also that we didn't kill Soline, though it's obvious a demon did it. And then we collect our reward."

"Reward? I thought that was the experience," Owen said. "What more is there?"

Weston smiled. "Jedrek might not have been a real Spellcrafter," he said, "but there's nothing fake about what's in those cabinets."

THE HALF OF THE <SKELETON LADDER> WAS AN OBVIOUS choice. Aderyn handed her half to Isold and watched him stow both iron bars in his knapsack, which was bigger than hers. She felt better having it out of her hands; Jedrek might have been a Diabolist, and evil, and would probably have killed her and her friends, but she couldn't forget the meaty thunk of the blow that had incapacitated him. She didn't regret it, but it was an uncomfortable memory.

The magistrate, a slim Deadeye named Obadus, had looked shocked and then devastated when he arrived and saw Soline's body. "She was a friend of mine," he'd said, his voice hollow. "A friend to half the city. I can't believe..." He'd stopped speaking and wiped his eyes, then cleared his throat. "You're lucky this was obviously a demon attack, because you'd be executed for her murder. And if you weren't so low level, I'd make a case for your negligence in letting the demon get away with Jedrek."

"I know you're grieving," Owen had said. "We did what we could. You know where the blame lies."

Obadus had sighed, nodded once, and then turned his back on the team to give a series of orders to the guards who'd followed him.

Aderyn, relieved, had wanted to suggest they leave then, but Owen had said, "Just wait. He's not angry with us. He's angry with himself."

Sure enough, Obadus had returned to supervise their selection of their reward: one item each from Jedrek's stash. "Most of it probably came from before he changed his class," Obadus had said, "so I'm not sure how powerful the items are. But you've earned it." He still looked furious, almost as angry as he'd been when he arrived and learned what had happened to Soline.

Now Aderyn wandered between the cabinets, not really seeing their contents. Having survived her encounter with Jedrek and the demon, she didn't really feel any other reward mattered. Weston was fiddling with a ring shaped like a serpent biting its tail. "Isold says it's a <**Ring of Dismantling**>," he told her. "It improves my [**Assess**] skill when I'm dealing with traps, and it works on both mundane and magical traps. I like it. What did you choose?"

"I'm still thinking," Aderyn said.

"Well, think faster, because I don't want to hang around here and give that magistrate time to change his mind," Owen said. He wore an unexpectedly dainty gold chain necklace from which hung four tiny gold spheres the size of his pinky nail.

"That's... an interesting look for you," she said, not hiding her skepticism.

Owen gave her a look of pretended scorn. "Each of these little balls becomes a fireball when I throw it at something. It's practically the only magical item I recognize from—" He cast a guilty glance at the magistrate, who wasn't paying attention and looked like he was ready for them to finish, too. "Anyway, I wanted a ranged attack, and this one will be useful."

"I like the idea, so long as you don't throw it at anything fire-proof," Aderyn said. "Or maybe I mean something horribly flamma-ble. We've already nearly set one town on fire accidentally."

Owen lowered his hand. "Is something wrong?"

"I don't know. I just feel a little off. Like I can't forget that demon staring me down." Aderyn waved a hand at the cabinets. "None of this appeals to me."

"Then I'll choose for you," Owen declared.

Aderyn shrugged and nodded her permission. Owen closed his eyes and groped dramatically across the objects, drawing an unexpected laugh from her that made her feel a little better. After a few seconds, he stopped, and his hand closed on something metal and square Aderyn couldn't see clearly past his body. Owen turned and offered it to her. He frowned. "That's sort of plain. I think I may have cheated you."

The cube was about four inches on a side, a tin box with holes punched in its lid and sides in a decorative pattern. Aderyn opened it and found it was empty. She turned it upside down and silently read the words *Fire, Fight, Riot, Slaughter,* and *Time.* "Huh," she said. "Isold, what's this?"

Isold came to their side and took the box from Aderyn, turning it over as she had. "How unusual," he said. "This is a **<Ruckus Box>**. It produces a loud noise for a short period of time, usually no more than five minutes. The words control what sort of noise it makes and how long a pause before it begins making that noise. I don't know how useful it is, but—"

"Distraction," Aderyn said promptly. "Diversion. Deception. I like it." She smiled at Owen. "Thank you. This is perfect."

"I guess if anyone could find a use for a **<Ruckus Box>**, it's you," Owen said with a matching smile. "And Livia has that wand that puts people to sleep, so I think we're good."

The door opened, and Cavan entered. He had the hard look of someone controlling a strong emotion, and Aderyn immediately felt inappropriate guilt. Soline and Cavan had been so welcoming, and it had resulted in Soline's death. "Cavan, I'm so sorry," she said.

Cavan nodded. "I don't blame you. This is all Jedrek's fault. I should have killed Jedrek the first time he endangered her."

"But you didn't know he was secretly still a Diabolist," Livia said.

"No, but I knew he was a rat bastard, and that should have been enough." Cavan drew in a deep breath. "Where is she?"

"Maybe you shouldn't—" Owen began.

"Don't tell me what I can't endure, young man," Cavan said. "I sat by her mother's bedside as she wasted away into death, and I've buried two sons and seven teammates. Loss is part of life." Tears slipped down his cheeks. "I need to see Soline."

Owen stepped aside and let Cavan pass him into the blood-smeared sitting room, and they all waited, awkwardly not meeting each other's eyes, until Cavan emerged. His eyes were reddened, but dry. He joined Obadus on the far side of the room, and they had a low-voiced conversation. Then Cavan returned to where the team stood. "I've arranged to have her body taken to where it can be prepared for burial. I want you all to come back to the house with me. I want to know what happened, and I don't want to hear it in this evil place."

Their journey back to Cavan's house felt strange to Aderyn. It had only been about an hour since they'd made the trip going the other way, but so much had happened it felt like it had been a year. And yet everything looked the same. Aderyn ran her fingers over her sword hilt. That bastard Jedrek, killing people and threatening to kill people for his selfish desires. And Soline was dead. It still felt so wrong, even though Aderyn knew none of what had happened was their fault.

Cavan opened the door and led them inside with no trace of good humor. He waved them to take seats before dropping heavily into the chair Soline had sat in the night before. "Tell me every-thing," he said. "I can't believe she's gone. I wish—but there's no sense dwelling on what's done. Just... I need to know."

Owen told the story, with the others filling in details he left out. Cavan listened in silence, though his gaze fixed on Aderyn when Owen explained about how she'd bluffed for all their lives. When

Owen finished, at the point where they'd fetched the magistrate, Cavan didn't say anything for a few seconds. Finally, he said, "They read your Codex, right?"

"I didn't know that was possible," Owen said, "but magistrates have magic that lets them see, like, your achievement history. What in my world would be your game record. And it shows all your quests and all the monsters you've killed."

"Sometimes adventurers fight each other," Cavan said, "and while most of the time that happens out in the Forsaken Lands, sometimes it's in cities, and there's need to prove who was at fault and whether punishment is justified. I was wondering, though, if they saw anything that revealed you're an otherworlder."

"Nothing," Owen said. "Or, if Magistrate Obadus did see something, he kept it to himself."

"That's what makes me wonder." Cavan didn't elaborate.

Aderyn fidgeted for a minute, until nerves overcame her, and she said, "We should be going. We don't want to impose on you in your time of grief."

"You're not imposing. And I've had an idea." Cavan leaned forward, his long, bony fingers intertwined on his knee. "There's a magic item I've heard of that might be relevant to your search. I didn't think of it yesterday, because it's not a gate or a portal, but it can scry into other places. Including the demon void. That tells me it might be able to see into your world, Owen."

"That's great, but you're right, if it doesn't open a gate—" Owen began.

"But there are spellslingers who know how to link two places long enough for someone to step through," Isold said. He sounded excited. "The spell is most efficient if the spellslinger knows both locations, but in some cases, they use that magical item, the <**Eye of Space and Time**>, to show them the destination. There's no reason it shouldn't work to connect this world to another."

Owen said nothing.

"This is good!" Aderyn said, trying to sound enthusiastic.

"I'm just thinking how Soline would be alive now if I hadn't been so damned eager to take the first solution that presented itself," Owen said bitterly.

"Don't think like that," Aderyn said. "If we went around blaming ourselves for all the things we don't know, we'd never accomplish anything. Grieve, yes, but keep moving forward."

"Always the sensible one, huh?" Owen smiled, and while it still looked bitter, it was a real smile. "Fine. Sure. Let's try it. It's a powerful object, so is it in some distant city? Somewhere bigger than Guerdon Deep?"

"There are several of them," Cavan said. "One is here, in the possession of a Tidecaller named Noetta. She's curious about everything and very generous with her talents, and I'm sure she won't be thrown by the explanation of your origins, Owen."

Owen rose to face Cavan. "Then, if you'll introduce us, I'd like to go now."

CHAPTER THIRTY-SEVEN

This time, the path they took led them deep into the city, toward the mountain. The cliffs towered over them, blocking the sun even more thoroughly than the tall buildings did. It felt uncomfortably like being enfolded in the embrace of a stony, terrible giant, and Aderyn instinctively drew closer to Owen. He didn't seem to notice. Aderyn suspected he was caught up in his own inner turmoil. Wanting to go home, wanting not to leave friends behind... it made sense that he wouldn't notice anything else going on around him.

The deeper they got, the less the buildings looked like buildings and the more they looked like rough-hewn stone, with holes cut out of the mountain for windows and doors. The doors were stone slabs, not oak, and when they were closed their outlines were nearly imperceptible. They encountered few people on the streets, and the ones they met wouldn't look them in the eye and scuttled along like rodents.

"A Tidecaller lives here?" Livia asked, sounding astonished. "I could understand an Earthbreaker, because this place feels comfortable to me, but not a Tidecaller."

"Noetta hates open spaces," Cavan said. "She's only comfortable with piles of stone weighing her roof down. It's why she quit adventuring when she was level thirteen—she couldn't bear the out-of-doors life anymore. And why we have to go to her instead of the other way round."

He stopped at one of the nearly invisible doors and lifted the stone mallet hanging by a loop of string from the doorpost. "Knocking the traditional way is pointless as well as painful," he said, and rapped sharply on the stone. The mallet made a loud, high-pitched cracking sound that echoed down the street and made a couple of passersby look up briefly.

Shortly, the door opened, and a tall, willowy woman with dark brown hair and deep-set brown eyes looked out at them. "Cavan," she said. "I wasn't expecting you."

"I know, and I'm sorry, Noetta, but there wasn't time," Cavan said. "Can we come in? I have some terrible news, and a puzzle."

Noetta's finely arched eyebrows drew down in a frown. She nodded and backed away from the door, giving them room to enter. To Aderyn, it looked like the motion of a fox retreating into its own safe den.

Unlike the other homes they'd seen in Guerdon Deep, Noetta's walls remained rough stone, not plastered or painted. A long hallway extended from the door, with wooden doors lining both sides and lamps dimly illuminating the stone. Noetta pushed open the second door on the right and said, "Please, come in. Sit down. I think there's seating for all of us if I bring a chair from the kitchen."

The group shuffled inside, where Aderyn had another surprise: the walls were still stone, but it was smooth and highly polished to the point she could see her dim reflection. The surfaces reflected the many lamps so the room was much brighter than the hall. A couch and four armchairs were grouped at the center of the room, around a small glass-topped table that shone like a mirror in the bright light.

Aderyn sat on the couch beside Owen and waited for Noetta to return with another chair. When she did, Cavan offered to sit on it, but Noetta waved him off and positioned it where she subtly became the focus of the room. "Tell me, what brings you here unannounced?"

"It's Jedrek," Cavan said bluntly. "He concealed his true class. He was a Diabolist, and he killed Soline."

Noetta's eyes widened, but she made no other movement and remained silent. Cavan went on, "Soline went to Jedrek to help this young man. He's not from our world. He's from another human world, not the demon void, and he needs to return there."

"And so you asked Jedrek," Noetta said in a toneless voice. "That bastard. I'm so sorry, Cavan."

"Thank you," Cavan said. "But now I need your help more than your sympathy. We were thinking, if the <**Eye of Space and Time**> can scry out Owen's world, we might be able to find a spellslinger who can create a portal between this place and that."

"Of course," Noetta said. She bit her lip nervously. "But—"

"I've already beaten myself up for not thinking of this before Soline approached Jedrek," Cavan said. He wiped a bony hand across his eyes. "But no sense dwelling on the past. Can you do it?"

"I can't cast the *world door* spell," Noetta said.

"We just want to establish that scrying my world is possible," Owen said. "We'll worry about the rest later."

Noetta nodded. She stood and moved her chair closer to the glass-topped table. "Otherworlder, put your left hand flat on the glass until I say."

Owen did as he was told. Immediately, the glass glowed with a pale pink light like the first light of dawn. Noetta gripped the rim of the table and bowed her head. "Now, tell me about your world," she said. "Some place familiar to you. Just talk."

"Oh, well, um, I guess that would be my parents' house," Owen said. "We moved there when I was five and I don't remember any other home. It's two story, with a two-car garage. The roof is dark gray, and the siding is slate blue—they redid the siding six years ago, and all I can remember is my mom talking about whether it should be slate blue or country blue, which to me look exactly the same..."

As Owen spoke, Aderyn peered over his shoulder at the glass— the <Eye of Space and Time>. Colored mists, all shades of pink and peach, ambled lazily across the glass, soothing to Aderyn's troubled heart. They weren't in a hurry to get wherever they were going, which was entirely different from how Aderyn's life had been the last two weeks, and she envied them. Then she felt stupid for envying colored mists that probably didn't have any real existence.

She turned her attention on Noetta, who had her eyes closed and her jaw clenched like she was exerting herself to lift the table, though it didn't look all that heavy and wasn't shifting the way it would if she really were lifting up on it. Beads of sweat glimmered along the willowy woman's hairline. Aderyn resisted the urge to ask if she was all right. Interrupting spells was never a good idea.

Noetta let out a pained gasp and released the table. The mists disappeared. "Something's wrong," she said.

"Wrong? Wrong how?" Owen exclaimed, jerking his hand away.

"Tell me how you came to this world," Noetta demanded.

"I—I was traveling cross-country by bus—never mind, you don't know what that is. Anyway, I was jumped by three guys who beat me up and took all my stuff. They knocked me unconscious, and when I woke up, I was in the woods outside Far Haven." Owen looked like he wanted to demand why this mattered.

"I see," Noetta said, her voice distant. "How badly injured were you when you woke?"

"I... wasn't," Owen said in surprise. "I didn't hurt at all."

"Hmm." Noetta regarded him closely. "How do you feel about needles?"

"Are you planning to draw my blood?" Owen asked.

"Just a little prick of the finger. I need a drop of your blood. Maybe three drops."

Owen immediately extended his left hand with the forefinger outstretched. Noetta dug in a soft tapestry bag sitting on the floor next to the couch and extracted a bundle of sewing, from which she removed a long, sharp needle. Gripping Owen's hand firmly, she jabbed his finger with the needle, making him wince. She squeezed his finger, and two drops fell on the eye's surface, followed a second later by a third.

The surface of the eye immediately frothed with waves of peach and pink, roiling like storm clouds under the last light of the setting sun. Owen wiped his finger on his trousers and leaned forward to watch. Noetta once more gripped the sides of the table, though she didn't look as harried as she had before.

"That is it," she said. All the companions leaned forward now. The clouds were gone, replaced by something bright green and indistinct and fuzzy that filled the round eye.

"What is it?" Weston asked.

"It shows a location of importance to the otherworlder," Noetta said. "Give it a moment."

Gradually, the scene came into focus. "Grass," Owen said, puzzled. "Why grass? I guess it could be my parents' lawn."

"I've never seen grass look like that," Aderyn said. "All short and perfect."

"My father is a little obsessed with lawn care."

"Hmm," Noetta said under her breath. She bowed her head, and her knuckles paled to pure white as her grip tightened.

Slowly, as if the eye were an actual eye looking at the world, the view shifted. It looked like someone walking across the grass with his head bowed so that was all he could see. Then, in the upper right corner of the circle, gray stone came into focus. The view slid across it until it was clearly a stone slab, deeply engraved with lines and curves.

Owen drew in a breath. "Make it back away," he demanded. "Show it from farther back."

The view changed, and the stone grew more distant. Now the lines and curves showed letters and numbers. JACOB OWEN LINDBERG, it read, and below that ran a line of numbers.

"But that's—" Owen's voice shook. "That's a gravestone."

"It is," Noetta said. "In your world, you are dead."

CHAPTER THIRTY-EIGHT

Owen rose explosively, accidentally kicking the table. The eye's image shivered and vanished, leaving only cool, shining glass. "It's not true," he shouted. "You're lying. This is a trick!"

"Owen, what is she saying?" Aderyn asked.

Owen ignored her. "You think this is funny? You get off on playing tricks on ignorant low-level adventurers? Don't you dare think—"

"I suspected," Noetta said. She released the table and wrung feeling back into her hands. "The **<Eye of Space and Time>** connects to what part of you is still present in that other place. It does not work on the dead."

"But Owen's not dead!" Aderyn exclaimed.

"Right?" Owen waved a hand in Noetta's face. "Corpses don't bleed."

"You were attacked by three men in your world," Noetta said, not reacting. "They killed you. Whatever part of you remains, your spirit, your awareness, was brought here and placed in a new body."

"Now, that's just ridiculous," Weston said. "Why would his new body be identical to his original body? Since I assume Owen would have noticed if he was now blond instead of a redhead."

"And there's never been anything to indicate that people exist after they die," Livia said. "They get absorbed into the system. That's all."

"I did not say I had all the answers," Noetta replied. "But my scenario is the only one that accounts for all the details. The eye's inability to see where this otherworlder exists in his world. The vision of the grave marker. The lack of wounds after his beating. I am certain of this conclusion."

Owen was breathing heavily. "No," he whispered. "It's not true."

"I'm sorry," Noetta said, sounding dispassionate and not at all sorry.

Owen shoved past Isold and ran out of the room. Aderyn leaped to her feet and ran after him, ignoring her companions' protests.

She was right behind him, calling his name, when he burst through the door and took off running. She ran after him, distantly aware that he could outpace her and then they'd both be lost separately in Guerdon Deep. To her surprise, instead she gained on him until they were running side by side through the narrow streets.

Out of breath, she gasped, "Owen, stop, my heart's going to explode."

Owen slowed, then came to a stop and bent over with his hands on his knees, sucking in air. Eventually, he said, "How did you do that?"

"I think it's [Keep Pace]," Aderyn wheezed. "Makes us run at the same speed. That's good, since otherwise we might outrace each other, make things like [Outflank] useless."

For a while, they waited, not speaking, until the sound of their breathing no longer echoed off the walls. Finally, Owen said, "I'm not dead."

"Not here, you're not," Aderyn said. "But... I'm sorry, Owen, but she made some good points. I think she's right. How else could you have survived that beating—something vicious enough it left you unconscious—without having a single mark after it?"

Owen's mouth thinned into a hard, white line. He gazed into the distance. Aderyn waited, not wanting to draw attention to his emotional pain. Finally, he drew in a deep breath and released it slowly. "I don't know what to think," he said. "I'm dead. My parents think I'm dead. I can never go back to where I belong."

Again, Aderyn waited. That had sounded like the beginning of something more.

"But I'm not sure that's where I belong, really," Owen went on. "I never did anything that mattered, nothing big. I didn't stand out academically. I had friends, but not close ones. I was going into a profession a million other guys could do. Aside from my family, no one will miss me."

He put a hand on Aderyn's shoulder. "I have value here. I have friends, real friends. I even have a destiny, or at least the possibility of a destiny. And... the thing is, Aderyn, the first emotion that hit me when I saw that gravestone was relief. Relief that I don't have to leave you and the others behind. Relief that the decision was taken out of my hands. Is that awful? I mean, I should at least worry about how my family will feel."

"Owen, I've spent the last five days hating myself for wishing it was impossible for you to return to your world," Aderyn said. "I'm the wrong person to ask about awful wishes."

Owen laughed. "It's still hard," he said. "I'm a stranger here, and there's a lot I don't understand. And—I guess there's a part of me that's grieving my own death, because I know how devastated my parents will be. But mostly, I love the idea that you and I are going to go on finding out what a Swordsworn and a Warmaster can do."

A system message appeared, startling Aderyn. By the way Owen jumped, she guessed he saw the same thing.

Warning: The quest [Return the Otherworlder] has become invalid. It will be removed from your quest list. Select a new primary quest? Y / N

Without hesitating, she selected N. The message vanished. There'd be plenty of time for a new quest later.

"That's pretty definitive," Owen said. His hand on her shoulder was warm and comforting, and Aderyn briefly considered hugging him. But it was the wrong time, and for the wrong reasons.

So she only smiled and said, "Right now, we're going to find out if a Swordsworn and a Warmaster can manage to find their way back to their friends without getting even more permanently lost in this awful city."

He laughed again. "I don't think it's so awful. It's sort of interesting, the contrast between the stone exteriors and the comfortable interiors."

"It's nice to visit, but I don't want to live here."

Owen clapped her on the shoulder again. "We're not settling down any time soon."

She understood his meaning, but it was fun to imagine something more intimate.

BACK AT THE HORSE AND HOUND, OWEN SEEMED perfectly recovered from his disappointment by dinnertime, and laughed and joked as readily as ever. But he was serious when he said, after the plates were cleared, "We need to consider this Fated One thing."

"What about it?" Weston said, waving down the serving maid for more ale.

"Whether we want to pursue it," Owen said.

That sobered them all. Isold said, "It might not matter, not if the system believes you need to be tested. We might not have a choice."

"The system might send tests, true," Owen said. "That's not the same as actively seeking them out."

"I thought you didn't want that," Livia said.

"I'm not sure anymore. Now that I'm not focused on finding a way home, I've been thinking—what, exactly, does the Fated One do? I know you said it has something to do with removing the level cap so people can progress past level twenty, but how does that happen? Fight a dragon, solve a puzzle, what?"

"I have no idea," Isold said. "No one really knows. There are stories, of course, and theories, but mostly those who believe they are the Fated One expect the system to reveal the truth when they achieve their destiny."

"That's what I thought." Owen drained his mug. "So what if we set out to discover the truth? Not wander around killing strange monsters and uncover secret quests, but learn what it is the Fated One has to do. Go after it deliberately."

Aderyn frowned. "I'm not sure what the difference is, Owen."

"I'm having trouble articulating, I guess." Owen chewed his lip in thought. "Look. All these Fated One candidates, they sort of do generic adventuring things, right? They depend on the system to give them appropriate challenges. But they don't know what it takes to achieve the ultimate goal. The end of the level cap, I mean. Whereas *we* would be searching for that ultimate goal. Trying to find out what it is, and then deciding if it's really something we want to tackle. Because the truth is that we could short-circuit the Fated One thing by adventuring for a while and then retiring. There aren't any retired adventurers who are Fated One candidates, right?"

"What does 'short-circuit' mean?" asked Livia.

Owen waved that away. "Does that make more sense?" he asked Aderyn. "Or am I still babbling?"

"No, I get it now." Excitement bubbled up inside her. "I like it. It's like telling the system where to get off."

"You're speaking my language," Owen said. "So, are we agreed?"

"It's a good idea," Isold said. "I'm sure no one's ever thought of it before."

"I'd rather take charge of my destiny than wait for the system to foist it on me," Weston said. "I'm in."

"And somebody has to keep Weston from getting you all into trouble," Livia said, winking at Weston.

A system message appeared in front of Aderyn's eyes.

**A new quest is available: [The Fated One's Destiny].
Accept? Y / N**

Once Aderyn accepted it, a new message took its place.

You have accepted the quest [The Fated One's Destiny]. This quest is first in a quest chain. Set as primary quest?

"It's our primary quest, right?" she said.

"I've never seen a quest chain before," Isold said. "This should be interesting."

"I suppose it is our primary quest," Owen said.

Aderyn watched the words shrink into a point at the upper right of her vision that glowed gold. "Accepted."

"Then we start tomorrow," Owen said. "And I say that with great confidence despite not having any idea where to start."

That drew a laugh from his companions. "I have some thoughts," Isold said. "I'll want to talk to a few people who live here in Guerdon Deep before we head out. Call it another week here in the city, and then we'll have a starting point."

Owen poked Aderyn in the side. "Think you can endure this hostile city for a week?"

"I'll survive," Aderyn said with a grin.

That night, she lay in her bed while Livia snored and stared at the silver letters of the Codex.

Name: Aderyn

Class: Warmaster

Level: 7

<u>Skills</u>: **Bluff (5), Climb (1), Conversation (4), Intimidate (3), Sense Truth (7), Survival (2), Swim (1), Knowledge: Monsters (4), Knowledge: Demons (1)**

<u>Class Skills</u>: **Improved Assess 1 (9), Awareness (5), Knowledge: Geography (4), Spot (6), Discern Weakness (7), Dodge (6) Improvised Distraction (4), Outflank (3), Draw Fire (0), Keep Pace (2), Amplify Voice (0)**

So many skills to practice. She smiled at the thought that she'd have plenty of time to develop them. Time with her partner. She still wasn't sure what she wanted from Owen, whether friendship was enough, or if romance might happen between them, but what she did know was that she now had the time to find out. Her heart ached again, this time with happiness.

She rolled onto her side and stretched. In the other bed, Livia let out a tortured snort and a long, drawn-out buzz of a snore. Did Owen snore? It might be worth starting a romance just to get a quieter roommate.

Aderyn muffled a laugh at the idea. No, romance was nice, but what mattered was that she wasn't a useless, partnerless Warmaster. And she and Owen would prove to the world that a Swordsworn and a Warmaster together could conquer anything.

APPENDIX A: CHARACTER SHEETS

NOTE: These character sheets represent the status of the companions at the end of the book, which means it reveals everything the companions learn about their skills throughout the book. If you haven't finished the book, don't read this unless you don't mind spoilers!

Name: Aderyn

    Class: Warmaster

    Level: 7

    <u>Skills</u>: Bluff (5), Climb (1), Conversation (4), Intimidate (3), Sense Truth (7), Survival (2), Swim (1), Knowledge: Monsters (4), Knowledge: Demons (1)

    <u>Class Skills:</u> Improved Assess 1 (9), Awareness (5), Knowledge: Geography (4), Spot (6), *Discern Weakness* (7), Dodge (6), Improvised Distraction (4), *Outflank* (3), Draw Fire (0), *Keep Pace* (2), Amplify Voice (0)

    *italics are paired skills with partner

Name: Jacob Owen Lindberg

Class: Swordsworn

Level: 7

Skills: Assess (5), Awareness (7), Climb (4), Conversation (5), Intimidate (5), Sense Truth (7), Spot (4), Survival (2), Swim (10), Knowledge: Demons (1)

Class Skills: Improved Weapon Proficiency (9), Improved Armor Proficiency (6), Knowledge: Monsters (5), *Exploit Weakness* (7), Dodge (7), Parry (6), Improved Bluff (6), *Outflank* (3), Trip (1), *Keep Pace* (2), Disarm (0)

*italics are paired skills with Warmaster

Name: Weston

Class: Moonlighter

Level: 7

Skills: Assess (6), Climb (4), Conversation (5), Intimidate (3), Sense Truth (7), Survival (3), Swim (2), Knowledge: Social (4), Knowledge: Demons (1)

Class Skills: Pick Locks (6), Improved Sneak Attack (9), Improved Weapons Proficiency (7), Basic Armor Proficiency (4), Detect Traps (6), Disable Traps (4), Spot (9), Awareness (6), Dodge (5), Stealth (6), Improved Bluff (7), Dirty Fighting (2), To the Heart (3), Hide (1), Basic Thrown Weapons Proficiency (0)

Name: Isold

Class: Herald

Level: 7

Skills: Assess (7), Awareness (7), Climb (2), Conversation (8), Intimidate (2), Sense Truth (7), Spot (6), Survival (2), Swim (1), Knowledge: Demons (2)

Class Skills: Perform (singing) (10); Knowledge: Magic (7); Knowledge: Monsters (7); Knowledge: History (2); Knowledge: Social (3); Knowledge: World Lore (5); Identify Magic

Items (8); Charm (7); Distraction (4); Map Access (3); Inspire Courage (1); Fascination (1); Persuasion (0)

Name: Livia
  Class: Earthbreaker
  Level: 7
  Skills: Assess (4), Awareness (4), Bluff (2), Climb (1), Conversation (4), Intimidate (6), Sense Truth (5), Spot (4), Survival (1), Swim (1), Knowledge: Demons (1)
  Class Skills: Knowledge: Magic (7), Perceive Magic (7), Elemental Blast (earth spray, shower of small stones) (9), Earth to Mud/Mud to Earth (2), Mage Armor (shifting plates of metal) (3), Excavate (0)

Spell List

0-level spells
Daze; Drench; Light; Telekinesis, minor; Mending; Freezing Ray, minor; Root, Spark

1st Level spells
Air Bubble; Break; Force Shield; Grease; Heat Metal (slow); Freedom; Mudball; Sunder Weapon; Thunder Punch

2nd Level spells
Create Pit; Thunderstomp; Mirror Image; Mud Minion; Improved Mending; Protection from Fire, Mass (big earth dome)

3rd Level spells
Iron Spike Attack; Thunderstomp, Greater (directed); Clairvoyance; Dispel Magic

Appendix B: Owen's List of Classes

Owen knows fantasy roleplaying games well enough that as he learns the names and definitions of the classes the system assigns, he mentally translates them at first into terms he is familiar with. This is the list of classes adventurers might be given, along with his translations and notes in parentheses.

Deadeye (archer): specialist with bows

Herald (bard): master of manipulation, knowledges

Lightfingers (rogue): pickpocket

Lone Wolf (fighter/rogue): vigilante (*Owen: I think. We haven't met one of these yet*)

Moonlighter (rogue): infiltrator, sneak thief

Pathseer (ranger): tracker or hunter of monsters

Spellcrafter (enchanter): imbues items with magic or creates magic items

Spellslinger (wizard): wields raw elemental magic. Spellslinger is not a class, but a category, just as Swordsworn and Staffsworn are both in the fighter category.

Earth—Earthbreaker

Air—Windwarden

Fire—Flamecrafter

Water—Tidecaller

Life—Bonemender

Death (evil)—Lightsnuffer *(Owen: Nobody ever talks about these guys, and I can't tell if they're just that scary or if they're a myth)*

Spider (rogue): second-story man, acrobat

Spiritsmith (alchemist): creator of potions and/or scrolls

Staffsworn (fighter): bludgeoning weapons

Stalwart (fighter): hand-to-hand combat. Tank *(Owen: Weston really does look like he ought to be a Stalwart, so I guess that shows how the system doesn't think like people)*

Swifthands (monk): martial artist

Swordsworn (fighter): bladed weapons

Warmaster (no equivalent class): tactician, support

(Owen: There are evil classes, too, but they don't get talked about much, so I only know a few)

Evil Classes:

Brigand (fighter): uses his fighting skills to hurt innocents

Diabolist: summons and controls demons *(Owen: I hope we never meet one of these guys again)*

Lightsnuffer: death magic

AND NOW FOR A SPECIAL MESSAGE...

Did you enjoy this book? Want more LitRPG adventure goodness? Then the LitRPG Books Facebook group is for you! Find new recommendations, connect with fellow readers, and more!

About the Author

In addition to the Warmaster series, Melissa McShane is the author of many fantasy novels, including the novels of Tremontane, the first of which is *Servant of the Crown;* The Extraordinaries series, beginning with *Burning Bright;* and *The Book of Secrets,* first book in The Last Oracle series.

While her home remains in the mountains out West with her family and two very needy cats, she currently lives in Kerala, India. She wrote reviews and critical essays for many years before turning to fiction, which is much more fun than anyone ought to be allowed to have.

You can visit her at her website
   www.melissamcshanewrites.com
   for more information on other books and upcoming releases.

To subscribe to her newsletter, which is published monthly, visit **www.melissamcshanewrites.com/contact-me-2/join-my-mailing-list**

Also by Melissa McShane

WARMASTER

Warmaster 1: Dungeon Spiteful

Warmaster 2: Winter's Peril (forthcoming 2024)

Warmaster 3: Gamboling Coil (forthcoming 2024)

THE BOOKS OF THE DARK GODDESS

Silver and Shadow

Missing by Moonlight

Shades of the Past

Path of the Paladin

Bright Moon Deception (forthcoming 2024)

THE LAST ORACLE

The Book of Secrets

The Book of Peril

The Book of Mayhem

The Book of Lies

The Book of Betrayal

The Book of Havoc

The Book of Harmony

The Book of War

The Book of Destiny

THE LIVING ORACLE

Company of Strangers

Stone of Inheritance

Mortal Rites

Shifting Loyalties

Sands of Memory

Call of Wizardry

THE DRAGONS OF MOTHER STONE

Spark the Fire

Faith in Flames

Ember in Shadow

Skies Will Burn

THE CONVERGENCE TRILOGY

The Summoned Mage

The Wandering Mage

The Unconquered Mage

THE BOOKS OF DALANINE

The Smoke-Scented Girl

The God-Touched Man

Emissary

Warts and All: The Deluxe Expanded Edition (forthcoming)

The View from Castle Always

Winter Across Worlds: A Holiday Collection